The Terrace

C R
Gilfillan

The
Terrace

Book 1 of the Rags Whistledown
North Norfolk series

Cowslip

First published in Great Britain in 2018 by Cowslip Press.

Cataloguing in Publication Data for this book is available from the British Library.

ISBN 978 1 9996097 0 2 *[paperback]*

ISBN 978 1 9996097 1 9 *[ebook]*

Cowslip Press
9 Casson Street
Ulverston
LA12 7JQ

To Heather de Lyon and my other Norfolk friends.
You know who you are.

1

Rags

You couldn't miss him – the man at the bar of the Rampaging Bull.

Tall, slender, in a charcoal suit and black Kurt Geiger loafers, he was sitting with an easy, casual grace on a bar stool. As I watched, he turned his head and caught my gaze, his eyes lingering for a second, tugging at me with an invisible thread. Then he looked away, running a hand through glossy, dark-brown hair cut to perfection above a sun-tanned neck.

I sipped my Sauvignon and wondered what he was doing here. In his well-cut threads he looked way too smart, too classy for this no-nonsense Norfolk pub. Most of the clientele consisted of lush women in short skirts out on the razz on a Friday night and big guys clutching pints of lager to generous bellies. But this man was something different. He was talking in a low voice to a weedy bloke who had his back to me, and whose wispy hair was held in place with plenty of hair product. As I watched, the weedy bloke held up his finger and ordered drinks for them both.

With a sigh I looked into my disappearing glass of wine, wishing I could scrape up the cash for another.

Early that morning I'd been sitting in my flat in Stoke Newington, sipping an espresso, admiring a clutch of purple tulips clustered in a white jug. The next thing I knew, a bailiff was hammering on the front door, yelling up at my window while I cowered behind the blinds.

'Get down here! I've got an order for vacant possession.'

Yes, I'd received a letter from my money-grabbing landlord when I'd fallen behind with the rent, but I'd assumed I had a few weeks to get out – not a few days. When the bailiff stomped off, presumably to get reinforcements, I started packing. Fast. Now the jug, my furniture, clothes, and books were stored in my best friend Carola's basement, and I'd exiled myself to Middleham, aka Back of Beyond, with just my battered Burberry suitcase and Epiphone guitar for company.

I'd fallen asleep on the train from King's Cross and woken as it was bumbling through fens lit up by a huge, cloud-filled sky towards Cambridge. Soon after that the black soil gave way to reed beds, glistening ditches and flowered gardens as we rocked into Norfolk, with the train emptying at each small station, until we drew to a halt at King's Lynn. After that I picked up a bus which swished through the gentle slopes of North Norfolk to the market town of Middleham. The landscape was so familiar: I'd been born and raised in King's Lynn until the age of nine, when my mother left Dad and whisked me off to Devon. I'd not visited much since then – it was steeped in a sadness I wanted to leave behind. That solemn, small person living in a house where her parents were unhappy: that wasn't me! I was Rags Whistledown, successful journalist at the heart of the action in London town.

Except that wasn't me either. Not anymore. I was Rags Whistledown, out of work, out of funds and out of luck.

My phone's ring-tone started up – *Respect*, by Aretha Franklin. My pulse did a huge thump. I fumbled the phone out of my bag. Let out a breath of relief. No, it wasn't my landlord hassling me for money yet again, but Carola, my oldest and closest friend. Though we're both the same age (43), she's everything I'm not: sensible, solvent and married.

'How's it going, babes?'

'Great! I'm here and in the local pub,' I said, brightening up my voice because I was plucky Rags who never let anything get her down for long.

'Easy journey?'

'Yup. And the sun's come out.'

Her voice softened. 'It'll be all right, you know. Promise.'

As she spoke I could visualise her calm, brown eyes, and wished they were here in front of me. We'd met as students, and had cheered each other on through thick and thin. She'd dried my tears and shared my plonk. She was also a mean bridge player, and once a month for the past two decades we'd met up at her house with two gay friends to play cards, drink wine and put the world to rights.

'I'll be fine,' I said. 'And it won't be for long.'

'Are you sure you don't want to borrow any more money?'

'No!'

'Think of it as a prolonged holiday. Your stuff can stay in my basement as long as you want. You can rest while you're there. Relax. Save some money. Bee Cool will be bringing in some dosh, won't she?'

'I suppose so.'

'You may be fed up with writing her stuff, but she's popular,' said Carola, reading my mind as usual.

'I know,' I said, telling myself to be grateful. Bee Cool, my alter ego who churned out articles like *Finding that Elusive Orgasm* for glossy magazines, had just about kept me afloat for the past couple of years. Until my landlord doubled the rent.

Carola's voice became brisk and encouraging. 'Come on. At least the bailiffs won't find you. You've had a crap time, but you're a clever, resourceful woman. Things will look up.'

'Will they?' I said, sounding forlorn even to myself.

'Yes. Take some walks by the sea. Go to Holkham. Play the slot machines at Wells. My kids always loved going there.'

'I don't like slot machines.'

'Then buy yourself some fish and chips.' Even saintly Carola was sounding exasperated with me now.

The weedy bloke had moved off to sit at a nearby table. Mr Handsome was on his own. He looked over and held my gaze again, with a smile lifting the corners of his mouth.

'What about debt counselling?' said Carola in my ear. 'It really can help.'

'I'll think about it.'

'And you're entitled to benefits.'

I drained the last drops of my wine. We'd been round this one before. I couldn't face putting myself through the ordeal of the Job Centre. Now I'd got the crippling burden of renting a London flat off my back I planned to hide out in Norfolk, make some money and pay off my debts.

Mr Handsome lifted his glass of red wine and mouthed, 'Drink?'

'Rags?' said Carola, her voice a tad irritated. 'Are you listening?'

'Sorry, babes. I'm losing my signal. Got to go!'

And I cut her off.

Turned out Mr Handsome was Michael Cleverly, an estate agent. We exchanged names. I told him mine was Ragnell, 'but everyone calls me Rags,' adding that I was named after Gawain's wife. He gave me a blank look then moved on.

After he'd presented me with a chilled glass of Sauvignon, he asked me what I did. I told him I was a writer.

'Have you written a bestseller?'

Sigh. The question all writers get. 'I write features for magazines.'

'What about?'

'Contemporary issues, mainly.' I wasn't going to tell him I penned pieces that helped women up their orgasm count.

We chatted. I listened with half an ear, happy to be distracted from my woes, for Michael Cleverly was seriously well put together. Slim but not gangly, he fitted his clothes to perfection. He had charm, too: his grey-blue eyes watched me with keen attention as he listened to whatever came out of my mouth. Yet a couple of things made him more interesting than your usual run-of-the mill chancer. A scar ran through one of his eyebrows, and his voice had a thread of Norfolk backwater running under his estate agency accent that suggested he hadn't come from money.

He soon steered the conversation towards the topic he really wanted to talk about: Cleverly-Made, his fledgling property development company. Turned out he was setting up a deal for an apartment block in the South of France ('immaculate new build') and looking for investors.

'It's a one-off opportunity to get an excellent return for your money. I can email the literature to you right now, if you're interested,' he said, pulling out a sparkling new iPhone.

I spluttered into my glass of wine. 'Who says I've got spare cash lying around?'

He laughed, showing snowy teeth. 'Or perhaps you've got friends who'd like to take advantage of my offer. A woman like you must be well connected. And I can guarantee that any investment will double within three years.'

Bollocks, I wanted to say, but didn't, because being conned

by him was much more fun than sitting on my lonesome. I knew why he'd targeted me – my Whistles dress and natty Hobbs ankle boots, a legacy from my days of earning a fat salary – but I wasn't going to tell him that I'd fled London to escape the bailiffs over the little matter of £4,200 owed in back rent.

His mouth moved closer to my ear – close enough for me to feel the warmth of his breath. 'Have I told you you're the most interesting woman I've met in a long while?'

I laughed. 'No, but please do,' thinking that flattery is always welcome, particularly when you've had the day from hell. As he waxed lyrical about Cleverly-Made I tried to guess his age. Early thirties? He'd stopped talking now, and was smiling, his mouth half-open, as if he were about to say something of great importance, when suddenly he swayed to one side, almost losing his balance. I grabbed his arm, so he wouldn't fall off the stool and make a complete arse of himself.

'I think I'd better visit the facilities,' he said, getting carefully to his feet. A burst of laughter erupted from behind us. I turned to see the weedy bloke and a couple of his pals doubled up with stifled giggles.

Daft, but I felt protective towards this bullshit-spouting show-off. Yes, he was a hustler, but I liked him more than the idiots laughing at him. 'I'll give you a hand,' I said, then found myself blushing. 'Not like that!'

'I should hope not.' His eyes, fringed in thick lashes, held mine. 'I'm spoken for.'

'I know.' I'd seen his wedding ring, and he'd told me his 'lovely wife' would have dinner waiting for him when he got in, but we were only chatting, weren't we?

I steered him towards the loos, but as we turned into the corridor, he stumbled and the pair of us ended up leaning against the cold wall. My mouth was inches away from his, and the scent of his woody cologne hummed through my tired body. I found myself hungry for a kiss that would blot out the crap day I'd had. Our mouths moved closer and ...

... and his phone beeped. With a jerk, he pulled back. 'Sorry,' he breathed. 'Sorry about that.' As he read the text a slow smile spread over his face, softening its sharp planes. Slipping the phone back into his pocket, he turned and headed for the Gents. I dashed into the Ladies and splashed cold water on my face. Dilated pupils looked back at me from the mirror. Just the thought of kissing him had made me dizzy, light-headed. I dithered in the loo for a bit, composing myself before heading back out to the bar, which was getting noisier as more booze was consumed. Be sensible, I told myself. Be sensible, and leave him alone. He's married and you're up shit creek. Nonetheless, the not-sensible me looked over to the bar stool he'd occupied all evening.

It was empty. He was gone.

2

Iona Goodchild

Iona had half an hour to kill before she met her friend Debbie for a sleepover, and was killing it in the park opposite The Terrace. She'd blown the seed heads off a few dandelions, contriving to make two of them finish on *He loves me*. She'd read a bit of *Animal Farm*, one of her set books for GCSE, but got bored after five pages. She'd eaten a packet of plain crisps – the only flavour she liked – and posted a few pictures of herself posing on the outdoor gym equipment.

Now she was perched on a swing in the park playground, ignoring the smouldering looks coming from Darren Wortley, who'd turned up a few minutes ago and was sitting on a bench smoking a cigarette in swift, furtive bursts. She started to twizzle the swing in one direction then the other, long legs stretched out in front of her, admiring her new lime-green trainers. She'd spent hours here as a little girl, when Mum was more chilled, and the swings seemed twice as big.

Iona let the swing come to a halt and looked at her phone. Five likes for the photograph of her on the shoulder press. There were still twenty-two minutes until she was due to meet Debbie in the Asda car park. Yawning, she was slipping her phone back in her bag when she heard a shout and a squeal of bicycle brakes. She jumped off the swing and ran to the park gate to peer up the street. Outside the pub someone wearing a black beany cap was straddling a bicycle, and Michael was on the floor! The man in the cap was saying something she couldn't quite hear, though it sounded like he was royally pissed off. As Michael scrambled to his feet, the cyclist rode away.

'What you looking at?' said Darren Wortley shoving his spots into her face. 'It's that flash git from down your street, isn't it? You fancy him, don't you?'

The proximity of Darren's mouth and bright blue eyes gave her a jolt. 'Piss off,' she said, shoving him away. She broke into a run, dragging her overnight bag behind her, until she caught up with Michael, who'd dusted off his clothes and started to walk into town.

'Hello,' she puffed.

Michael winked. 'Hello, gorgeous.'

Iona's pulse skipped: he'd never called her that before. 'Are you all right?' she breathed.

'Me? Never better.'

'Didn't that cyclist knock you over?'

'Nah. I just tripped.'

'Where you going?'

'None of your business,' said Michael, but with a quick smile that took the sting out of the words. 'I'm just taking a little stroll. Need some fresh air.'

'Can I come with you?'

'No.'

'I won't tell my mum. I never tell her anything.'

'No can do.'

'Please.'

Michael came to a halt, steadying himself against the window of the health food shop. He smiled at her – a slow, lazy smile that sent a burning sensation through her whole body. 'Go on, sweetheart. Go home.'

'But I want to go for a walk with you, like we did before. Just for a bit. Please.'

Michael's smile disappeared behind a screen, and became the face he showed people most of the time – the face that was cold as an ice bucket. 'I said no. Now piss off and leave me alone.'

A pot of fury boiled over in Iona's head as she watched him walk away, up the High Street. He was just like everyone else, wasn't he? And she'd thought he was different. Why did everyone treat her like a child?

She hesitated for a moment, then followed him.

* * *

Patsy Cleverly

In a kitchen full of hefty oak units too large for the room, (Daddy had insisted on them when he'd paid to have the kitchen done) Patsy Cleverly, married to the most handsome man in The Terrace (and possibly in the whole of Middleham) reached into an Asda carrier bag and extracted a bottle of vodka. She unscrewed the cap and took a big slug. Ah! That was better. As the alcohol swam through her blood, she started to rehearse what she'd say to Michael when he came in.

'Michael? About Animal Rescue: I want to go for the job there. I know it's part-time but we can manage on a bit less money, can't we? Working with animals is something

I've always wanted to do. It's my passion. And you believe in people following their passion, don't you?'

That sounded good, didn't it? She jumped up and went over to the mirror to repeat the words to her own reflection, as her *Improve your Self Confidence* book had recommended. Plain brown eyes and a snub nose looked back at her. Oh, crap. Was that a spot coming up on her chin? She leant closer. Yes! With a cross exclamation she worried away at it with the nails of her two index fingers, but it refused to be squeezed. By the time she'd given up, her positive mood had drained away.

She sloshed some vodka into a tumbler and added ice, a wedge of lemon, and a splash of tonic. Took a few crisp mouthfuls. And as the vodka slipped down, she started to simmer. Michael had gone to the Rampaging Bull, hadn't he? He went to the pub every Friday evening, even though he'd told her they were all losers in there.

'Why?' she'd shouted that morning, head throbbing, as he tweaked his tie into a perfect knot. 'Why do you do it?'

His gaze had been steady, unapologetic. 'It helps me unwind. I work my arse off, and I deserve a bit of down time.' Then, after a pause: 'Anyway, you stink of booze by the time I get in.'

With a moan, Patsy ripped open a large bag of Kettle chips and started to work her way through them. Then she pulled a slab of cheddar from the fridge and buttered some expensive crackers. Sod it: Michael was forever bleating about not spending too much, but she deserved some treats, didn't she? I mean, she worked too, in *Norfolk Treasure* and she hated it. Hated the naff knick-knacks and over-priced mugs. Hated the long hours standing beside the till or dusting the mini anchors and shell houses. Hated her boss, Melinda, who treated her as if she was a moron, not letting her cash up, or do the ordering, or make suggestions. She'd got her Business Studies GCSE last year – had stuck it for a whole year at evening classes – but Melinda had refused to give her a pay rise or any more responsibility.

As she hacked at the lump of cheese the knife slipped and nicked the end of her finger. Ouch! Something exploded in her brain and before she could stop herself she'd picked up her plate and hurled it at the wall. It shattered with a satisfying smash. In a daze, she watched the shards spin into the air and across the floor, then, with a gulp, dropped her head in her hands and wept.

She'd met Michael down the Thieves Kitchen in Fairham Market, where she was downing a large glass of wine after work before enduring another mind-numbing evening with Daddy watching reruns of *Midsomer Murders*. Michael had been so charming, so interested in her. She'd found herself telling him about how Daddy was a control freak who insisted she pay £50 a week towards the bills. 'And he's loaded. Absolutely loaded.' They'd talked until closing time, then Michael had walked her home, though she hadn't asked him in because she knew Daddy wouldn't approve. His accent wasn't quite right. It was common. *He* was common. She could see that, despite his smart suit. But he was so bloody fit he made her go weak at the knees. They'd kissed for ages under the shadow of the neighbour's huge oak tree Daddy was always saying should be chopped down. A few days later he'd turned up at the shop and asked her out.

'Me?' she'd gasped, feeling her mouth fall open.

'Yes, you,' said Michael, with that smile that turned your legs to water.

They'd got married within six months – a big wedding with a marquee on the green, though she'd had to tell Daddy a little white lie about being pregnant to get things moving (and then of course she'd had to tell him that she'd made a mistake, and wasn't expecting after all.) To begin with she and Michael had such plans! He was going to make a fortune, and she was going to persuade Daddy to invest in his company. But Michael didn't understand how stubborn Daddy could be. It had taken weeks of wheedling to get him to stump up the money for the deposit on this house.

She loved Michael – loved him so much it hurt. When she woke in the night, she propped herself up on one elbow and watched his sleeping face – the thick eyelashes and the lock of hair that fell over his forehead. The regular rise and fall of his breath. She knew she wasn't in his league. She was terrified he was going to leave her one day, for someone prettier and smarter.

Oh, shit. She blew her nose on a square of kitchen roll and swept up the broken plate, then pulled out her phone and scrolled through to the job description of the admin assistant at Animal Rescue. She'd visited the centre several times, and had been allowed to stroke the donkeys and horses. The yelping of the rescued dogs had plucked at her heartstrings, and made her determined to change her life and do something useful.

She matched every point required in the person specification, and was sure she'd get an interview. If she got the job, she'd be able to spend loads of time with the animals. She knew she'd be good with them: she'd had a hamster and a rabbit when she was little, before Mummy died, and she'd loved feeding them, cuddling them, cleaning out their cages. She'd been devastated when she came back from her first term at that horrible boarding school and Daddy told her they'd died.

She *had* to persuade Michael. The last time she'd brought it up he'd given her a long, cool look and said they needed her full-time wage to help pay the mortgage. 'And you'd have to lay off the booze. You can't be drunk in charge of a rescued donkey.'

As she fiddled with her phone, scrolling through the pics of the horses, the cats, the pot-bellied pigs, it slipped through her fingers, skittered across the table and fell onto the quarry tiles. Its light went out. 'Oh, shit!' She picked it up, pressed it, shook it. No joy: it was broken. And her laptop was in the repair shop, too.

Now what was she going to do?

She poured herself another vodka and tonic.

Should she go to the pub? Give Michael a piece of her mind? No. In some oily corner of her brain she knew she'd make an idiot of herself. Then Michael would be angry and they'd end up yelling at each other, and he'd sleep in the spare room.

She sniffed: something was burning. The lasagne! She dashed to the oven, flung the door open. Black smoke billowed out. No! Not again. She slammed the oven door shut and took the bottle of vodka and the remainder of the crisps into the front room. After a bit of fumbling with the remote, she found a programme about mountain gorillas. She must have drifted off to sleep, because the next thing she knew she was jerked awake by shouts and yells. Unsteady, she climbed out of the comfortable armchair and peeped out of the curtains into the street, wondering if some of the town's louts were on their way home. But the street was empty, with just the graceful leaves of the willow opposite swaying in the breeze. It was not yet dark, she realised: nowhere near chucking-out time. Through a fog she realised that the noises had come from out the back: threatening voices and something that sounded like a loud thump. Her heart began to race. Was someone trying to break in? Daddy was forever telling her that Middleham was rough, but she'd taken no notice, thinking he was just being a snob.

Mouth dry, heart filling her eardrums, she crept towards the back door, grabbing a heavy iron frying pan as she went. Just in case.

3

Rags

I should have left the pub after Michael disappeared, but didn't. You see, I was heading for my dad's house that night, and I hadn't asked him if I could stay. I hadn't dared: I couldn't risk him saying no. Things hadn't gone well the last time we'd met, in London. In fact they couldn't have gone worse. I'd just lost my job. He'd told me it was all my fault. I'd exploded. He'd stormed out. That had been two years before, and we'd hardly spoken since. Both too proud and pig-headed, I suppose.

Jason, one of the amiable blokes propping up the bar, came to my rescue by insisting on buying me another glass of wine, 'Because I don't like to see a gorgeous girl sitting all on her own.' Turned out he was a guitarist in a band called Mangle Strangle who blitzed the Norfolk pubs on Saturday nights. His absolute heroes were The Quo, and I must have pulled a face when he said they were like gods to him, because he went into a passionate spiel about how Francis Rossi and Rick Parfitt were total geniuses. Oh well: it takes all sorts. I let his hymns of praise to the Quo wash over me as the divine grape danced along my veins. One glass of wine led to another, and it was nearly eleven before I knew it. I said goodbye to Jason, and dragged my case into the dark street. Here I paused, and took a few deep breaths to settle my nerves.

I hadn't been to Dad's house before: he'd moved here just before our catastrophic row. Since then he hadn't issued an invitation to visit, and I hadn't asked. I didn't know what sort of reception I'd get.

I took out my phone to check the way. His street, The Terrace, was less than a quarter of a mile away. I set off with my guitar on my back and suitcase trundling along behind me. A few yards beyond the nearest street light I came to a halt. Wow. Now the clouds had cleared, a velvet sky embroidered with the Milky Way arched above me. The air was scented with the thin honey of cow parsley in bloom. The pub hummed and thrummed behind me, but otherwise the night was quiet except for the shrill cry of an owl, and the distant burr of a car pootling along the bypass. Perhaps a few weeks here wouldn't be so bad, if I could keep my mouth shut and not get into too many arguments with Dad.

I plodded on, tugging my case past the sombre yews of a graveyard and the empty swings and roundabout of a park playground. Three minutes later I turned into the street – and nearly went flat on my face, tripping over a stone sticking up from the unmade road. 'Shit!' I turned on the torch on my phone so I could see where I was going.

Holding it up, I saw that Dad's street was a short cul-de-sac with a row of houses on my right with flat fronts and doors that opened onto a narrow pavement. I made my way round the back of the houses to a tiled path that divided the backyards of the houses from their leaf-heavy gardens. Seconds later the number two tacked neatly to a white wooden gate told me I'd arrived at the right place. My fingers grasped the cool metal of the key Dad had given me before we had our catastrophic row. I slipped through the gate into the backyard, and up to a freshly painted door, relieved to see that no lights were on. Good: I could postpone our difficult conversation until the morning. Releasing a grapey breath I slipped the key in the lock.

The kitchen, lit by moonlight, had nothing out of place. It smelled faintly of a pot of red geraniums placed precisely in the centre of the shelf under the kitchen window. Spotting a bread bin, I slid it open and found two granary rolls. As quietly as I could I opened drawers until I found a knife, and spread one of the rolls with butter from the fridge, stuffing it in my mouth, with a little moan of satisfaction. I hadn't eaten a thing since I wolfed down a slice of toast at Carola's house that afternoon, and never had a granary roll tasted so good. I found a blue and white striped mug in one of the kitchen cupboards, and filled it with water. Then I lugged my suitcase and guitar into the front room, shut the door, and changed into a pair of cotton pyjamas. I bedded down under a white throw and a couple of jumpers pulled out of my case.

Within seconds I was out for the count.

I was woken up by something warm, wet and salty working its way round my face. 'Ugh!' Two black-button eyes were staring into mine. A pink tongue delivered another long lick. I shoved at a warm body. 'Go away.' A small, piebald mutt jumped off the sofa, wagging its tail, and sat down to watch the show.

My dad's face loomed over me. 'Rags? What the heck are you doing here?'

With a groan, I reached for my mug of water and took a big gulp.

'Well?'

'Sorry,' I croaked. 'I meant to call.'

'You gave me the fright of my life! I don't hear a dicky bird from you for months, and then you let yourself in, without so much as a by-your-leave, and park yourself in my front room. I thought you never wanted to see me again!'

'I – er …' In the Sauvignon swamp that was my brain I remembered that I might have said something like that last time we met, but I hadn't *meant* it. Not literally.

'What the hell do you think you're playing at? I almost had a heart attack when I came in here. I thought someone had broken in.'

'Sorry, Dad. It was a spur of the moment decision.' I levered myself up onto my elbows and glanced at my phone. 6.24 am.

'Anyway,' he said, his voice losing some of its gruffness. 'What are you doing here?' Then, after a pause, 'Are you all right?'

'Yes!' I said, in a feeble voice – and burst into tears.

'Oh, for goodness' sake!' Dad dug a large cotton handkerchief out of his jeans pocket. 'There. Blow your nose on that, and tell me what's happened.'

I dabbed my eyes, swallowing tears. 'I've had to leave my flat, because I couldn't keep up with the rent. And I've got … I've got a huge favour to ask.' I took a deep breath and ploughed on. 'I need somewhere to stay, while I get back on my feet. It wouldn't be for long – a few weeks maybe. I'll pay my way. I've got some freelance work, and I can always get a job in a bar, or something.'

'And why are you so keen to come here, all of a sudden? Can't you find somewhere in London?'

The hurt in his voice put me on the defensive. 'Are you kidding? Have you seen how much it costs to rent in London?'

'Then why can't you stay with one of your fancy friends?'

'None of them have room.' And this was true. All my pals had produced children in the last two decades. Their wildly expensive flats were full of nappies, school shoes, toys, tantrums and sulky teens. Plus, there was the little problem of having the bailiffs on my tail. I was nervous – perhaps paranoid – that they'd track me down if I stayed in London. I thought of telling Dad about them, but decided against it for now. It would add another blot to my copybook. 'Please, Dad. I'm desperate,' I said, with a tremble in my voice, because if he didn't take me in, I didn't know what I'd do.

Dad looked down at me, immaculate in his striped tee-shirt and faded jeans. He shook his head, his expression softening. 'Of course you can stay, you daft thing.'

I let out the breath I'd been holding, struggled up from the sofa and threw my arms round him. He smelled of lemony soap and clean laundry. 'Thanks, Dad.'

After a few moments he gave me some awkward pats on the back, as if he was trying to get me to cough up a piece of carrot that had gone down the wrong way. He extricated himself and held me at arm's length. 'Now, I don't want you telling me what's what or giving me political lectures,' he said, stern.

'I promise,' I said, blushing to think how I'd rounded on him the last time we met. I'd been belligerent, pompous, pissed. I may have shouted that he didn't know his arse from his elbow.

'And you're to be nice to Napoleon.' The little dog wagged its tail. 'And, before you ask, I was studying that period of history at the time I got him.'

'I didn't think you liked dogs.'

'I like this one,' said Dad, looking down at the dog with pride. 'He's smart as paint.'

Jealousy stabbed its knife into my aching head. How long was it since he'd given *me* a word of praise? Then I told myself to get a grip. Being jealous of a dog? Oh p-lease. 'He's lovely,' I said, because he really was rather cute – something like a Jack Russell, but with longer legs and a softer face.

'He's just a cross-breed,' said Dad, bending down to stroke Napoleon's silky ears. 'But he's a good little soul, and you're not to spoil him.' He gave me a sharp look. 'Don't give him scraps from the table. I don't want him getting into bad habits.'

'I promise. And thanks for letting me stay. You're a diamond.'

Painted white, with a single bed, Dad's spare room was a third of the size of the bedroom in my old flat, but it had everything I needed: a small table, a wardrobe and chest of drawers. After I'd unpacked I peered through the window. I had a good view of the shared path that divided the backyards from long gardens. All the gardens were over-flowing with flowers, but the garden of number three, to the right of Dad's house, was particularly beautiful, dancing with colourful shrubs and flowerbeds laid out in sinuous curves. Fuchsias spilled out of hanging baskets and a glade of bluebells lingered under mature fruit trees at the back. I nodded my head in appreciation: I'd had a garden something like that (though less tidy) when I lived in Halifax in my mid-twenties, and was earning my stripes as a cub reporter. I knew how much work went into creating it.

A woman with a severe haircut was working her way along the white-washed garden wall overshadowed by a lilac in full bloom, removing every trace of dirt. I pulled on a pair of skinny jeans, a white vest and a loose, pink shirt, and bowled down stairs and out of the house: time to bond with one of Dad's neighbours.

'Lovely morning!' I called, coming out of Dad's backyard

and onto the shared path. 'Your lilac's gorgeous. Like the rest of your garden.'

The woman's stern face softened a fraction. 'That's Doll. She does the garden.'

I held out my hand. 'Pleased to meet you. I'm Ragnell.'

After a small hesitation the woman dried her hands on an old cloth and came over. 'Susan. Susan Fredericks,' she said, giving my hand a firm shake. Freckles were dusted over her nose and cheeks, and her face would have been handsome but for the knot of a frown tied between her brown eyes. 'But people usually call me Freddy.'

'And everyone calls me Rags,' I said, waiting for her to smile or ask a question about my name. When her stony expression didn't change, I went on, 'I'm going to be staying with my dad for the next few weeks.' I pointed at her bucket. 'You're a dab hand with that brush. Your walls will be spotless by the time you've finished.'

Her face closed up even further. 'Look,' she said. 'I can't stand here chatting all day. I've got to get on.' And, with that, she turned and went back into her house, shutting the door firmly behind her.

And a good morning to you, too. So much for friendly, rural neighbours; I'd had more pleasant conversations with the Hackney dustbin men.

Then, as I turned to go back to Dad's house, a young woman smelling strongly of alcohol appeared out of nowhere on the shared path, and slammed into me, almost knocking me for six.

'Hey! Watch out!'

'Sorry. I'm really, really sorry,' she slurred, propping herself up on the wall of Dad's yard, 'Only I'm looking for my husband, because he's not in the spare room and I can't find him anywhere and he's never stayed out ... and I'm afraid ...' Her words dissolved into incoherent moans.

I looked more closely at her. She was in her early twenties, shortish, with shoulder-length sandy hair and a turned-up nose. Her earnest face was blotched with weeping.

'Are you all right?'

She shook her head, unable to get any sensible words out.

'Here. Come and sit down for a moment.' I took her arm and steered her gently into Dad's garden and onto his pristine wooden bench.

'Thank you. Thank you.' She gasped and hiccupped and I thought for a moment she was going to throw up on Dad's lawn, but she managed to swallow and focus on me with swollen eyes. 'Have you seen him? He's tall, with dark hair, and really really good looking. And I thought I heard him but ... Oh, I can't quite remember ... it's all a blur, but I'm afraid I ...'

With this, she broke into sobs. After a moment, I took her hand. Her clothes were good quality but crumpled – a pair of black jeans and a white Hollister tee-shirt. Top-notch blue and white Nikes with the laces half undone.

'Shall I get you some water? Or a cup of coffee?'

The girl shook her head vehemently and continued, between gasps and sobs, squeezing my hand with every panicky breath. 'I love him so much, but he's ... and I'm ... I'm ...' She stared at me with a stricken face. 'He's left me, hasn't he? Left me for someone ...' she gasped and collapsed into pitiful weeping again.

'Shhhh.' I extricated my hand from her desperate grip, and stroked her back until her sobs died down. 'He's probably just gone out to buy some stuff for breakfast.'

She made a bitter sound at the back of her throat. 'He never does things like that. Not any more.'

'Or maybe he's gone round to see a friend.'

'Michael doesn't have friends. He just goes on and on

23

about his bloody property company, and I've *tried* to talk Daddy round, really I have, but …'

'Patricia!' The girl's head snapped up. 'Patricia!' The bark was louder this time, coming from a thin-faced man in a tweed jacket and ironed jeans marching up the footpath. 'Come here this instant.'

With a whimper the girl struggled to her feet, mumbling, 'That's Daddy. I rang him because I didn't know what else to do, and …'

But I missed the rest of her rambling explanation because I had a chill in my stomach. An attractive man called Michael intent on building a property empire? Oh, shit. It had to be the same man. Had to be. A stab of guilt pierced my ribs, though nothing had happened, had it? Nothing at all.

The girl's father marched into Dad's garden, grabbed her arm and pulled her back to the shared path, lecturing as he went in a voice like a ruler cracking down on knuckles. 'Will you stop making an exhibition of yourself? The whole street is watching.'

'Sorry, Daddy, sorry, I …'

He shoved her inside the back door of number four and slammed the door.

I rushed back into the house to find Dad sitting at the dining room table in front of a laptop. 'Did you hear that?'

'Hear what?'

'I nearly got knocked for six by a drunken girl.'

'Oh, that'll be Patsy. She's a bloody nuisance. She managed to smash two of Gerry's champagne glasses last Christmas, yet if you meet her when she's not on the sauce, she's nice as pie.'

'And she's married to a man called Michael?'

Dad turned towards me and pulled a face. 'Yes.'

'I ran into him in the pub last night, and he was trying to get me to invest in some dodgy deal.'

Dad made a scoffing sound. 'That's him, all right. Always on the make.'

'She's really upset. Says he didn't come home last night.'

'Oh, they're forever arguing, and then she goes round with a face on her like a wet weekend.'

'Her father's just turned up. He seems to be ...' I searched for the right words.

'A little Hitler,' said Dad, decisively. 'Marches around like he's still in the army. He's convinced Michael only married Patsy for her money.'

'Is she rich, then?'

'She will be one day, when he pegs it.'

For a moment I let myself remember Michael's sexy mouth moving towards mine, the delicious smell of his woody cologne. Be honest: at the back of my mind I'd been hoping to run into him again, if only for a bit of light flirting to alleviate the boredom.

As if Dad could read my thoughts, he said sharply, 'Michael's a nasty piece of work. You take my word for it.' And returned to tapping carefully at his keyboard.

I realised that Dad was working on a state of the art MacBook. Well, well. For years he'd been moaning about everyone being glued to screens and declared that he didn't go in for Facebook or Twitter or any of that rubbish.

'How long have you had that?' I asked, trying to keep the envy from my voice as I thought of my laptop, a clapped out Dell Carola had given me when my old Mac died on me.

With a decisive click he closed the MacBook's silvery lid. 'If you must know, I bought it after Christmas, when a little savings plan matured. And I don't see why you're so surprised; I'm not a dimwit, you know.'

I bit back what I wanted to say – that he'd been a card-carrying Luddite for the past decade. 'I'm just jealous. Mine goes so slowly you practically have to wind it up by hand.'

'Well you can keep your hands off this. I've got it set up just as I want, and I don't want you messing around with it.'

I bristled. 'Don't worry. I won't touch your precious computer. But can I have your broadband password? I need to check my emails, and send off an attachment.'

'What sort of attachment?'

'A pitch for an article I'm writing.' I wasn't going to tell him that it was a Bee Cool special, *Sex Toys: Play Dates for Grownups*, waxing lyrical about vibrators and vagina pleasure balls.

'What sort of article?'

'Something for a women's magazine.'

Dad groaned, half joking. 'You're not still writing that celebrity rubbish, are you?'

'No. I've left all that behind,' I said, through gritted teeth, determined not to let his digs get to me. 'I'm writing self-help pieces now.'

With a theatrical sigh he pulled open a drawer and handed me the card with the admin password for his broadband. 'Here you are, then.'

I scooted upstairs and fired up my computer. Checked my emails: nothing urgent, though the commissioning editor at *All Woman* had reminded me that she was waiting for my next Bee Cool pitch. '*Finding that Elusive Orgasm* has attracted shedloads of positive comments!!!' I pulled a face. Yawn.

Then I saw something interesting out of the window: Patsy was stumbling along the shared path behind her father, pulling a large, wheeled suitcase. A question lit up in my head. Last night Michael had told me his wife was cooking dinner for him.

Why hadn't he gone home?

4

Rags

I spent the next few days researching pieces for the industrious Bee Cool and learning songs on my guitar. My Epiphone was one of the few things I hadn't sold, mainly because it was only worth a few quid. A boyfriend at university had passed it onto me when he upgraded to a Martin, and I'd tinkered with it on and off for the past couple of decades. Since I'd been freelancing I'd played it a lot more, not least because I didn't have the dosh to go out and hang around for hours in cafes and bars. I was working through Joni Mitchell's back catalogue and had got to *Blue* – an album of such genius it brought tears to my eyes whenever I listened to it. My current favourite was *A Case of You*. I could just about get round the chords, though I must admit my vocal performance was not a patch on Joni's.

Dad and I skirted round each other. In the evenings we watched the history and nature documentaries that were his choice. I thought I'd miss binge watching box sets, but it was restful to give up on all that for a while.

Thursday – nearly a week since I landed in Dad's house – was Middleham market day. Some money from a Bee Cool feature had landed in my bank account, so I nipped into town to suss out the stalls. Dad had gone to a lecture on moths at a nearby bird reserve with some old pals in King's Lynn, and wouldn't be back until late in the evening. I was looking forward to a leisurely day on my own.

The footpath into town was shadowed by trees full of birds. I stopped for a few moments to listen to the songs of sparrows and blackbirds, with a bitter-sweet feeling of melancholy running through me, because they reminded me of my mother, Gwendolyn. (Not Gwen, and certainly not Mum – I was never allowed to call her that.) Obsessed with Arthurian legends, she'd cast off the name her parents had given her (Janine) and rechristened herself as Gwendolyn, after Merlin's wife, saying she had 'a mystical connection' with the wizard. I was named after Ragnell, wife of Gawain – the chivalrous one who fought the Green Knight. As a child I hated my name, but I've come to love its quirkiness, particularly its shortened version, which is used by everyone who knows me well.

I'm not close to Gwendolyn. Women are supposed to be soppy about their mothers, aren't they? They're supposed to say things like, 'She's my best friend.' Well she's not my best friend: I haven't seen her for a decade, and we speak on the phone and swap emails a couple of times a year at most. Dad, for all his grumpiness, is the one who's stuck around.

I adored her when I was small. Longed for her love and attention (though I seldom got it). At the time we lived in King's Lynn, in a scruffy house off Gayton Road. Dad worked in a big commercial printing works near the docks. Gwendolyn stayed at home. Now and then, on days of dazzling sunshine, she'd take me to the local park. I loved the feeling of my hand in hers, the musky scent of patchouli as she bent down to show me particular flowers, the music of their names – dandelion, violet, daisy, vetch – which I can still reel off. And once in a blue moon she and I would take the bus from King's Lynn to the coast, swishing past verges splashed with purple foxgloves and red campion. At the beach she'd identify the birds running to and fro as the waves broke on a broad stretch of sand. At night I'd roll the names she'd taught me round my mouth before drifting off to sleep: oystercatcher, sanderling, redshank. They beckoned me into the world of words that has been my life ever since. I treasured those outings, fuelled by crisp sandwiches munched on the beach at Hunstanton, because they were so rare.

But most of the time she lolled around on the sofa, painting her nails purple and reading books about fortune-telling. Dad worked long hours, then came in and cooked us tea – usually something like beans on toast or spaghetti hoops. It wasn't quite as bad as it sounds, as I had school dinners, and he had lunch at the works canteen. In the school holidays we ate lots of fish and chips. Gwendolyn was forever, 'coming down with something' so Dad got lumbered with most of the housework. I helped him with the chores. My favourite was doing the Saturday wash at the twin-tub, plunging the long wooden grabbers into the water to scoop the soapy clothes out of the washing tub and drop them into the spinning compartment.

Dad was short tempered and boring, while Gwendolyn was bewitching, elusive. Now, of course, I can see that she was totally Me, Me, Me, forever looking in the mirror, drinking in her own reflection – the long blonde hair snaking to below her waist, her soulful eyes, the hollows of her face below high cheekbones. The house was a place of scratchy silences which I grew to resent as I got older. Yes, crap things had happened to her – her parents had died in a car crash just before she met Dad – but boy, was she hard work. Everything was about *her*. I couldn't tell her about the girl who was pulling my hair at school because it might bring on a headache. She couldn't come to parents' evening because people stared at her. She couldn't take me shopping to buy a new school uniform because her nerves were bad. She called Dad a peasant and an ignoramus, though her background was not exactly la-di-da: her father had had a milk round before he drove his car into a tree.

Then, one day, when I was nine going on ten, Gwendolyn met me at the door as I got back from school, and announced that we were taking a holiday. She ushered me to a sleek, red car driven by a man with a clipped beard. This turned out to be Nigel, a hedge fund manager Gwendolyn had met on one of her infrequent trips to London to stock up on espresso coffee and palmistry magazines. Nigel was a nice-enough sort of man, besotted with Gwendolyn, who transported us to his large bungalow in Devon. The holiday turned out to be permanent. Gwendolyn and Nigel got married two years later, as soon as she'd got a divorce from Dad. She set herself up as a palmist and tarot reader, holding consultations in the conservatory. I was roped in as her assistant, answering the door and leading people to the chairs in the hall if they had to wait to see her. Though still a lazy mare, (Nigel paid for a cleaner as soon as he realised Gwendolyn wasn't going to lift a finger round the house) she soon had a long list of clients who hung on her every word. And, though I wouldn't admit it at the time, she was happier.

My half-brother Tarquin was born when I was twelve, and after that all Gwendolyn's attention was lavished on him. His every squawk and burp was rewarded with showers of praise. Gwendolyn announced when he was six weeks old that he was *quite exceptional*. I smouldered with jealousy and considered killing him by holding a pillow over his face. Now he and I are the best of friends. A hat designer, he lives in New York and is camp as a row of tents. Gwendolyn and

Nigel have moved to Florida, where they bought a condominium in a gated community for 'seniors' where children and pets are not allowed.

The town centre was crammed with a jumble of stalls. I stood for a moment, drinking it all in: not bad, not bad at all. Barrows stacked with fresh vegetables and fruit stood next to a flower stall wreathed in the sultry perfume of lilies crowded into green plastic buckets beside sunflowers, tulips, chrysanthemums and gerberas. The white roses were cheap as chips, so I bought a bunch. Then I couldn't resist buying a camembert and a jar of juicy black olives from a grocery stall flogging stuff that looked like repackaged leftovers from Waitrose and M and S. Round the corner the bric-a-brac stalls filling what was usually a dismal car park made me rub my hands in glee. Some were run by traders who clearly did the rounds of street markets. Their crockery, vases, cutlery and knick-knacks were set out in tidy rows. Other stalls featured stuff laid out higgledy-piggledy on decorators' folding wallpaper tables, and muddled in cardboard boxes on the ground. I made a beeline for the disorderly stalls and set to sorting through the dusty piles of odd plates, single wine glasses, seventies casserole dishes and foxed prints of rural scenes. I was familiar with this sort of bric-a-brac from London's meandering street markets – Brick Lane had long been a favourite – but in the gritty old capital the stallholders had eyes of ice and the prices were three times what they were here.

I knew I shouldn't be buying things, not with my debts, but couldn't resist a green pottery vase, pure nineteen-thirties, for the flowers I'd just bought. It was only a quid.

I fancied sitting in the sun watching the pulse of the market, so went into the Market View Cafe and bought myself a coffee. The bitter espresso scorched my tongue with its intense flavour. Closing my eyes, I savoured the warmth of the sun kissing my face.

Coffee craving satisfied, I strolled back home along the footpath that ran from the parish church to Dad's street, and was almost at Dad's back gate, when a voice called, 'Hey!' I turned to see a willowy woman wearing skin-tight jeans and lime-green Louboutin pumps hurrying down the path towards me. My mouth fell open: she was at least six feet tall, with milky-brown skin and black hair falling in loose waves halfway down her back. Her cleavage peeped out from the undone top button of a cream silk shirt that probably cost more than I spent on groceries for a month. Over her shoulder hung an aquamarine Prada bag, swinging on its gilt chain against slender hips. Whoever she was, she didn't belong in Middleham.

Seeing she'd caught my attention she broke into a jog trot, calling, 'Can I please have a word with you?'

'Me?' I did that thing of pointing at my own chest.

'Yes, you.' She blinked long lashes. 'It's Rags, isn't it? Rags Whistledown. I never forget a name.'

A cold current ran through my stomach: oh dear God let her not be from a debt recovery agency. 'Who's asking?'

'Shell. Shell Dupont. We met a few years ago.'

I peered at her more closely, but didn't recognise this woman with a flood of ebony hair and immaculate make-up. 'Sorry, but I can't place you.'

She released an impatient breath. 'You were doing a feature on young, female entrepreneurs living in Tottenham.'

I rummaged in the memory drawer. Yes, I had a faint recollection of a mouthy woman wearing purple Doc Martens, though back then her hair had been clipped close to her skull. 'Didn't you set up some sort of hot-desking rental business? And weren't you called SayShell back them?'

Shell swatted my questions away with a manicured hand. 'I *knew* it was you. I saw you in the market sitting at the cafe. Please. I must talk to you.'

I hesitated for a nanosecond then invited her into the house. This was the most interesting thing that had happened since I nearly got flattened by Patsy Cleverly. She followed me in as I hastily put the roses in my new vase and the cheese in the fridge.

'Can I get you something to drink?'

'Just water, please.' Her voice was lower, huskier than I remembered. She'd ditched the Tottenham glottal stops and upped the French accent. If I remembered rightly, she'd come over to Britain as a child from an island in the French Caribbean and ended up in a sink council estate with her mum and Jamaican dad. When we met, her parents had already returned to the Caribbean, and she was making her own way in the world.

She perched on one of the sixties kitchen chairs that Dad had brought from our old house in King's Lynn, looking too leggy for the room, downed the glass of water in three long swallows then looked me in the eye. 'You live here, don't you?'

'Yes,' then added, 'for the time being,' since I didn't intend being stuck in the Back of Beyond for long.

'Good. Then you can help me. I'm looking for Michael. Michael Cleverly.'

'Oh.' As I looked at Shell, one piece of the puzzle fell into place: the way Michael had said he was 'spoken for' even though he'd left his wife at home with only the bottle for company.

'No one is at his house. And I have tried other houses in the street, but no one will speak to me. In the first house a woman with a screaming baby has looked at me through the window, but she will not come when I ring the bell.' She sat up a little straighter. 'And then I didn't know what to do so I walked into town and there I saw *you*. At first I couldn't believe it, but when I came a little closer I was sure you were the *journaliste* who interviewed me all those years ago. And so I have followed you here and find you live in his street.' Her hand gripped my arm so hard I yelped. 'Have you seen him? Do you know what's happened to him? Please. Do you know anything?'

'Well, I know he didn't come home on Friday night, because I ran into his wife on the Saturday morning. She was totally distraught – terrified that he'd left her for someone else.'

Shell jumped up from the chair. 'Me! He is leaving her for me! We have arranged to meet on Saturday night, at my apartment in Diss.'

'And he didn't turn up?'

'No. Saturday, he doesn't come. Sunday, he doesn't come. Monday, Tuesday, Wednesday, still he doesn't come and there's no call, no message. I ring him a hundred times and nothing. *Rien.* Now it's Thursday, and I am going crazy. The police are no help. I filled in a form, but I know they'll do nothing. They say he's an adult and can do what he wants. But now I can wait no longer. I *must* find out where he is – what's happened to him.' She sank down onto her chair and leaned closer, eyes blazing. 'I love him, yes, but we are also business partners. We are involved in a property deal, and he was due to transfer the last of the money we need. We have a tight deadline to meet or the whole thing could fall through. Now tell me, why would he disappear now? Why?'

She had a point. From what I'd seen of Michael, he was a bread-head who wouldn't risk jeopardising a plum investment opportunity.

Shell lifted one slender hand to point at me. 'I must find him. And *you*, you are going to help me.'

'Me?' I said, the hairs on my arms prickling.

'Yes. You will look for him.' Her lustrous eyes narrowed. 'You *will*.'

'I'm not sure about that,' I said, thinking that Dad would go ballistic if I started making a nuisance of myself with the neighbours. 'Look, I've come here for a break. I don't think I can help you.'

'Why not? Over the years I've read some of your articles. Oh, not those ones about the *bêtises* of wealthy people. No, the ones before that. The investigations. They were good – *formidable*, in fact.'

'Do you think so?' A glow spread through my chest; it was a long time since anyone had complimented me on my investigatory skills.

'Yes. And I know you have lost your job. I read about it online.'

'Oh.'

'Pah! All journalists do that sort of thing. Politicians, too. You are just the idiot who got caught.'

Hallelujah! At that point I wanted to grab her and give her a kiss.

'I have a proposition for you. I must go abroad and I don't have time to look for Michael, but even if I did it would be difficult. I am conspicuous. I am different. And some people, they will refuse to talk to me because I am Black.'

No arguing with that.

'And so I want *you* to look for Michael – to find out where he has gone.' She leant forward, exuding a delicious scent of jasmine and rose. 'And I will pay you.'

I sat up straighter: this was more like it. 'How much?'

Her dark eyes looked deep into mine. 'You will supply me with firm information by Monday morning, and I will pay you £150.'

'£300. That's still only £100 a day.'

After a moment, she nodded. 'And if I am satisfied with your work, perhaps I will pay you to do more.'

'Done.'

We agreed I'd email her an invoice with my bank details later that day, and Shell filled me in on some background. She'd met Michael a year before when he showed her round some flats in Diss. She was looking to expand her buy-to-let portfolio, and they met several times over the next few weeks. Nothing happened for a while, but one day they got talking and discovered they both wanted to invest in property. Shell knew of a golden opportunity: a development in Antibes, close to Nice, whose builder was up to his eyes in debt, and needed to sell quickly. On the personal front, one thing led to another, and they started an affair.

Shell took a deep breath. 'I don't like to have an affair with a married man, but his marriage is not happy. He has told me his wife will be better off without him.'

And he'd be better off without her, I thought. Shell would be a much more attractive asset than the desperate, drunken girl who'd almost knocked me flying – especially since Patsy's despotic dad had refused to cough up the funds Michael needed to get Cleverly-Made off the ground.

'A week ago we met for coffee, and he told me he has got the money we need because he has sold a luxury house.' She fumbled in her bag and pulled out a printout. 'Look. I have booked the tickets for us to fly to Nice next week.'

'So he's booked some time off from his work?'

She made that dismissive gesture again, as if she was chasing away an irritating fly. 'No, he has left his job.'

'When? When did he leave his job?'

Shell drummed long fingers on the table. 'Friday! He has come home to tell his wife he is leaving and to pack a case.'

I nodded.

'But I think first he has gone to the pub.'

'Ah. Yes.' I hesitated, unsure of how much to say. If I told her Michael had been chatting me up, albeit to get money out of me, Shell would probably brain me with her Prada bag. 'Actually, I talked to him that evening.'

Her eyes widened. '*You?* You talked to him?'

'I'd travelled up from London and I went into the pub for a quick drink before coming here, to my dad's house. We just sort of … got chatting.'

Shell clasped her hands together and leant closer. 'And how was he? What did he say?'

'He talked a lot about Cleverly-Made. Said he was looking for investors.' Then another penny dropped. 'Did you send him a text?'

'Yes!'

I asked her about the money they'd been accumulating to fund their joint venture, and Shell said that they each had separate bank accounts. 'And *naturellement* he has one that his wife doesn't know about. I have arranged a loan for the Antibes development, but we need to put down a deposit of 60,000 euros each.'

'And he was expecting to be able to pay that this week?'

'Yes.' She shrugged. 'He was just waiting for his bonus.'

'Do you have access to his bank account?'

Shell tossed her head so that her hair swirled round her shoulders. 'Of course not! What do you think I am? An obedient little wife? No. We are lovers. We are business partners. But I have my own money and he has his. Now,' she said, standing up, 'we are agreed?'

'Yes, but I'll need some expenses,' I called, as she headed for the door, conscious that I could only liberate about £50 from my bank account before heading into unauthorised overdraft charges.

She turned, a frown creasing her forehead. 'Expenses? I only want you to ask a few questions.'

'Bus fares. Train fares. I'll need to speak to people who don't live within walking distance. And I might have to offer some people money to get them to talk to me. I'll keep receipts, and a note of everything I spend.'

She huffed. 'Oh, all right.' Opening her bag, she pulled out a matching wallet and extracted £40 from a fat wad of notes. 'Take this, then.'

I kept my hand outstretched. '£100, or I won't do it.'

With a loud sigh she added three twenties to the two in her hand. I slipped the notes into my pocket, enjoying the crisp feel of them as she vanished out of the door.

5

Rags

I was surprised that Shell remembered the story of my
downfall, because it had only occupied the media for a few
days. My crime? I'd read the private emails of a woman I
was investigating on the orders of my news editor because
he thought there was something fishy about her. I thought
so, too. But this wasn't just any woman: this was Jenny
Halliwell, mother of Felicity, a twelve-year-old girl who
went out to get a bag of chips in Peckham on a rainy Friday
night, and never returned. Jenny Halliwell had milked the
media for a good six months before the whisper started that
the girl wasn't missing at all. My editor suggested I get to
know the family. Pretend to be helping them find Felicity,
while nosing around and digging some dirt.

Mug that I was, I said yes, because by then I'd spent
nearly a decade on the celebrity news circuit, and was fed
up with hanging round nightclubs hoping to see some stick
insect in platform shoes fall over when she was out of her
box on MDMA and champagne. Given the chance to get
my teeth into a meaty news story, I jumped at it.

My way in was via Jenny Halliwell's younger brother,

an amateur boxer called Sean. I hung around his gym in Bethnal Green, took some beginners' boxing classes (and that was fun). Sean was easy to reel in, and within weeks he was taking me out for drinks. We even kissed a few times (too slobbery for my taste), but there was absolutely no sex, though he later invented a sordid sexual affair when he and his sister flogged the story to the gutter press.

I had to work on him with flattery and flirtation until eventually I got myself invited round to Jenny's house for Sunday lunch, and when I went upstairs to the loo, I saw a laptop open in Jenny's bedroom, displaying an email list.

Could you resist? I couldn't. I nipped in there, hoping to find proof that the story about Felicity going missing was invented.

Ah, but Jenny was several steps ahead of me. She'd rigged up a hidden camera and got some crystal clear images of me reading her emails. She and Sean nearly pissed themselves laughing as they threw me out of the house. Jenny made up some crap about a heartless journo (me) hacking into the computer of a woman grieving over her missing child (her), and flogged the pics and the story to a tacky Sunday paper, making a tidy twenty grand on the way.

I was out of a job a week later.

Dad found out – one of his workmates came across the story – and was mortified. Our next (and last) lunch date, a few weeks later, ended in the flaming row that had led to our two-year estrangement. I tried to explain, but he wouldn't have it. 'How could you *do* such a thing? I'm disappointed in you, Rags. Very disappointed.'

That had cut me to the quick. Worst of all, I knew there was some justification for his disappointment. I'd been compromising my fine, journalistic ethics for some time, and though I'd been conned by the Halliwells, I'd sailed close to the wind a few times in the preceding few years.

Well, now I had the chance to show him what I was made of.

After Shell left, I scooted upstairs and sent off an invoice to the email address she'd given me, to be paid on Monday after I'd delivered my report. Then, following a quick lunch of olives, camembert and crusty bread, I decided to make a start on talking to the occupants of The Terrace. I wanted to know if any of them had seen Michael on Friday night after he left the pub.

Dad had told me who lived in The Terrace, and, out of habit, I'd jotted them down in my notebook. I looked at them now.

1. Tim and Tracey Jones, Damon (3) and Roddy (8 months).

2. Dad's house

3. Freddy (Susan Fredericks) and Doll Perkins (partners)

4. Patsy and Michael Cleverly

5. Gerry (Geraldine) and Hector Goodchild, and Iona (15)

6. Alaric Veil

7. Judith and Alan Wright – second homers and seldom there

Number one had a kitchen looking out on the shared path, but the remaining six houses were built in pairs, with kitchens and yards that faced each other. Dad's kitchen window faced Freddy and Doll's. Michael's kitchen faced Gerry and Hector's. Alaric's kitchen faced that of the second homers. Gerry and Hector were most likely to have seen Michael if he returned home on Friday night, and Patsy's muddled account suggested that he might have come back to The Terrace, for a while at least. But all the houses had a good view of the path and back gardens from upstairs windows.

Dad had been out all evening, at a local history lecture, and so hadn't seen anything, but I needed to talk to the others.

I started with number one, since Tracey had been in when Shell passed the house an hour or so before. After some thought, I'd decided to tell people I was researching some features linked to local issues, and then slip in questions about Michael Cleverly, figuring they'd be more likely to let slip useful information if I approached them in that way. I'd tell Tracey I was talking to people about childcare provision. But I'd seen her slam the door in the face of a Jehovah's Witness, and from what Dad had told me about her (*Got a huge chip on her shoulder. Gives that husband of hers hell*) I was pretty sure I'd be sent packing, too, unless I could find a way to soften her up.

So I nipped back into town and bought a little soft-toy – a monkey – from one of the stalls. It was adorable, if you like that sort of thing, with chocolate brown eyes and a long tail. As I knocked on the back door, I could hear high-pitched wails – the same wails I sometimes heard, faintly, at night. The door was opened after a couple of minutes by Tracey, her face sweating and blotched red. She was wearing black leggings and a baggy tee-shirt that just about covered the hillocks of her belly and bum.

'Yes?' she barked, over the baby's squally cries.

'I'm sorry to trouble you. It's Tracey, isn't it?'

'Yes.' Her eyebrows drew together in a suspicious frown. 'You're not from Social Services or anything like that, are you?'

'No. I'm staying with my dad, next door.' I held up the monkey and waggled it at her. 'And I wondered if your little boy would like this. I bought it for a friend's baby, but he's got one already.' I waggled it again, and Tracey's scowl softened. 'It's safe for small babies. I checked.'

'Oh, all right,' she said, ungracious, reaching out to take the monkey, then added, belatedly, 'thank you.'

'My name's Rags.'

'Tracey.'

'What's his name? The baby?'

'Roderick. Roddy.'

'I'm a journalist, and I'm thinking of writing a feature on childcare provision in rural areas. Could I come in and talk to you for a few minutes?'

She sized me up. 'I suppose so. But I'm warning you, it's not very tidy in here.'

Understatement. The sink was piled with dishes and the draining board crammed with cutlery and plates waiting to be put away. The crockery was part of a set with a black and white pattern – the sort you buy in a chain store at a knock-down price. The kitchen table looked as if someone had emptied a waste paper bin on it, though when I looked more closely I could see scrawled drawings and crayons among the debris. A stale smell was wafting from a rubbish bin so full the lid wouldn't close.

Tracey waddled over to the high chair and waggled the monkey in Roddy's face. His cries died down then picked up in volume again. She unstrapped him and picked him up, murmuring into his sticky hair and stroking his back with the palm of one hand. Doing these things, she looked less angry, less clumsy. There was a grace to her movements and a tenderness in the way she bent over him, even when he was yelling in her ear. 'Aw,' I said, trying to sound sympathetic.

Tracey threw me a look heavy as a sack of coal, her eyes daring me to say something critical. 'He's not neglected or anything, you know.'

'I never thought ...'

'I know what people have been saying, but it's not my fault. He suffers from colic. That's all.'

'Hello, Roddy.' I moved forward gingerly. 'He's gorgeous,' I said, trying to hold my breath because he smelled like he'd just had an explosion in his nappy. As if he understood what I'd said, Roddy's howls dampened down to sobs and then shuddering sighs. He surveyed me with blue eyes shiny as marbles. Now he'd stopped yelling I could see that he was rather cute, with his round face and rose-petal lips. He gave a huge yawn and I felt a tingle of sympathy: it would be no joke to have belly-ache all the time.

'You've got another little boy, haven't you?'

'Yes. Damon. He's three, and a right little sod. What about you? Any kids?'

'No.' I put on a sorrowful face, but the truth was that I'd never had a burning desire for children. 'But I love them,' I added, which was not *quite* the truth, though I adored Carola's boys. 'So what can you tell me about childcare in Middleham?'

Tracey grunted. 'There isn't any, unless you're rolling in money or have grandparents who'll lend a hand.'

'Disgusting, isn't it?' I said, since childcare (or lack of it) *was* a bloody disgrace. 'Can you give me some more details? Tell me what you'd like done about it? I really want to get across the views of people like you.'

She weighed me up for a minute. 'Oh, all right. But I can only give you ten minutes. Let's go into the front room. It's a bit tidier in there.'

I followed her into a room furnished with a cheap sofa and armchair. An old-fashioned television took up space by the window. Toys were strewn around the floor – a plastic fire engine, model cars, a few battered teddy bears, sheets of paper covered in scribbles. Tracey made a half-hearted attempt to shoo the toys towards a plastic toybox, and sank down onto the sofa. I took the armchair, having removed a few lego pieces from underneath my bum. Roddy started to mew, so Tracey pulled up her tee-shirt and started to feed him. I busied myself pulling out my notebook and pen, telling myself it was ridiculous to feel embarrassed by the sight of a woman breastfeeding her child. In my defence, all my London friends who'd produced babies got them onto bottles within a few weeks, and hired a nanny so they could return to work to service their huge mortgages.

As we talked, I learned that cheap childcare provision was indeed lamentable out here, though it transpired that Damon had been at a reasonably priced play group based in a local church, but that Tracey had taken him out after another mother complained about him biting other children. 'But that's what kids do, isn't it?' she said, giving me a fierce look that defied me to disagree. 'Look. I've got to pick him up from my mum's in five minutes. Have you finished?'

'Yes.' I put away my notebook. 'Oh, before I go, I wanted to ask you about Michael Cleverly.'

'What do you want to talk about *him* for?'

I put on my best gossipy voice. 'Well, his wife almost knocked me flying last week, and since then she's gone to her father's and he hasn't come home. No one knows where he's gone. That's weird, isn't it?'

Tracey pulled down her tee-shirt and struggled to her feet with Roddy in her arms. 'Not really. He's probably gone on holiday, or something.'

'Well if he did, he didn't tell his wife,' I said. 'Did you see him last Friday night? Only I ran into him in The Rampaging Bull, but then he just vanished.'

'If he came back here, I didn't see him, but I wouldn't have in any case, because I was watching TV with my mum in the front room. He would have come round the back. We all do.'

'And what's he like?' I said, following her into the kitchen as she decanted Roddy into his buggy and strapped him in.

'Do you want me to be honest?'

'Of course.'

Tracey's face tightened into a scowl. 'He's a total scum-bag. He bullies people. He makes them feel small. He looks down his nose at everyone who isn't as smart or good-looking as him. No one can stand him.'

'Really? What sort of things does he do?'

Tracey thought for a moment. 'He gets to people – says things that make them squirm. Or he'll be nice as pie one day, then stab you in the back the next. For example, when he first moved in a couple of years ago, he got pally with my husband, Tim. Started to give him big ideas about how he should be doing this or that with the salon. Tim idolised him. He had a bit of a man-crush, I think.' She cracked a bleak smile – a smile soon quenched, as she went on with growing bitterness in her voice, 'But then he went to Tim for a haircut. There was nothing wrong with it, but Michael made a huge fuss – insisted Tim had made a complete balls-up. Since then he's been saying Tim's a crap hairdresser, and the business has gone down the tubes. It's all that bastard's fault.'

'That's terrible,' I said, though I couldn't believe Michael was single-handedly responsible for the decline in Tim's hairdressing business. I made a mental note to go in there for a trim. 'Anyway, I wondered if you had any idea why he's cleared off.'

Tracey gave a humourless bark. 'Probably made one enemy too many.'

'So he had lots of enemies?'

'Yeah, like I said, he's a scumbag.' And with that, she started to wheel Roddy's buggy towards the back door.

'And how does he get on with his wife?'

'Her? She's another waste of space. An alkie. She's had every advantage in life – her father lives in some million-pound mansion over in Fairham Market – and yet she mopes around drinking herself to death. They argue all the bloody time.' Tracey's eyes, dark brown and full of malice, skewered me. 'It wouldn't surprise me if Michael's run off with someone else. And now, if you don't mind, I've got to get going.'

6

Rags

Tracey's spiteful comments left me with a bad taste in my mouth. And yet I felt for her, too. My overall impression was of a woman with an underused brain in desperate need of stimulation other than bawling children.

It was only half three, so I decided to drop in on Tim while the conversation with Tracey was still buzzing round my head. I could pay for a trim out of the expenses Shell had given me and hopefully get him to gossip about Michael at the same time. Dad had told me that his salon, *Strands,* was round the back of the market and I found it within five minutes. It was a small place, with a blue and cream sign that needed a lick of paint. Through the steamed up window I could see a slight figure, with jeans hanging off his backside, blow-drying a woman's hair. That must be Tim. His client was smiling at him in the mirror as her grey hair settled into the severe, manly shape favoured by most of the women over fifty in this town. Another woman was having her hair coloured by a stylist with straightened blonde hair. I went into the fug swirling with the odours of hair products and peroxide as Tim turned off the hairdryer and started to poke here and there with a comb. Seeing me, after a brief word to his client, he came over.

'Hello. Can I help you?'

'I was wondering if I could have a trim.'

'Just a dry cut?'

I nodded. I had a niggling feeling that I'd seen him before, but couldn't put my finger on where.

'When would suit you?' He ran his finger over the page covered by names and crossings-out.

'If you had any time this afternoon, that would be fantastic.'

'Well, I've had a cancellation, so I could squeeze you in now.'

'That would be great. Thanks.'

'Take a seat. I'll be with you in a couple of minutes.'

I was able to take a good look at him as I waited for my trim. He was half Tracey's width, slightly built, with round-ed shoulders. His hair was fine and combed into sculpted spikes, and though he had a pleasant enough face, a weak chin kept him from being handsome. His tee-shirt, shoes and jeans were clean but well worn: he hadn't been clothes shopping recently.

When the woman paid and left it was my turn to take the chair. Tim tied the cape round me with a modest flourish and asked me what I wanted.

'Just a couple of centimetres off all round, please. It's getting a bit straggly.'

'OK.' He clipped swathes of hair up on top of my head and started to cut, fingers nifty. As he snipped, I asked him how long he'd had the salon.

'About three years. I bought the business off my old boss.'

'It must be great to run your own business.'

For the first time his genial face drooped. 'It's great when things are going well.'

'You seem to have plenty of customers today.'

'Today's a good day because of the market.' He forced himself to smile. 'Have you got any nice holidays booked, then?' he asked, trotting out the hardy perennial in the hairdresser's conversational repertoire.

'I'm on holiday right now. I'm staying in your street, actually, with my father, Graham.'

'Really?' The sharp blades of the scissors gaped wide open as he looked more closely at me in the mirror.

'Yes. Next door. Isn't that incredible?' I smiled at his reflection, and as I did the niggle at the back of my mind materialised into a memory. The pub! He was the weedy bloke who'd been cosying up to Michael at the bar. 'You're a friend of Michael Cleverly aren't you?'

Crunch. His scissors hacked off a chunk of my hair. I yelped. 'Careful! I don't want too much taken off.'

'Sorry.' Was it my imagination, or were his hands shaking?

'Didn't I see you talking to him in the pub last Friday? The Rampaging Bull?'

My hair had suddenly got much more interesting. He bent his head over it and snipped swiftly – a little too swiftly. 'No. I hardly know him. You've mistaken me for someone else. Apparently he's gone missing,' I said, keeping my tone light and gossipy. 'I wonder why.'

He didn't respond, finishing my trim in double-quick time and picking up the mirror so I could see the back of my head. Not bad: he knew his stuff. 'Sorry to rush you,' he said, 'but my next lady's due any minute now.' He whipped off the nylon cape and brushed the hair off me with one of those dinky brushes.

'Thank you,' I said, paying him. 'It was in a right old state.'

He replied with a weak smile. Something was scaring the crap out of him, but his next customer had arrived, and now was not the time to press him about it.

I was thoughtful as I left the salon. I'd not got a good look at the face of the weedy bloke at the bar with Michael, but I was pretty certain Tim was the same man. If so, why would he deny it? I could feel the buzz you get when you know someone is lying to you, though as I meandered home a perfectly reasonable explanation came to mind: Tracey. He'd probably lied to her and didn't want her to know he'd been to the pub. She was a harridan, that one, and would flay him with her tongue if she found out.

Well, that would be easy enough to check out. I'd ask her where Tim had been last Friday night.

As luck would have it, I came across Tracey on the way back home. As I approached the graveyard I could hear shouting. Over the hedge I could see a skinny little boy with black hair jumping on and off a low tomb in the churchyard, responding to Tracey's shouts of, 'Damon! Stop doing that at once!' with high-pitched yells of 'No! No! No!' Roddy was wailing in the buggy, struggling to escape from the straps holding him in. When Damon climbed up on the tomb again, Tracey burst into a run, caught him by the arm and shook him. 'Naughty boy. When I tell you to stop doing something, you stop.' Cue piercing wails even louder than Roddy's. I turned into the churchyard just as Tracey was dragging a scarlet Damon back to the gravel path.

'Can I help?' I asked, hurrying over.

'Just mind your own business.' Damon, silenced by curiosity, stared up at me with shiny eyes. He looked smart as sherbet: I wasn't surprised he led Tracey a dance.

'I'm sorry if this is a bad time, but can I ask you one more thing?'

Tracey straightened up. 'Look, just piss off, can't you? I've had enough of your questions.'

'Was Tim at the pub on Friday night?'

'Why do you want to know?'

'Just curious.'

A sly smile lifted one corner of her mouth. 'Tim never left the house. He was with me and Mum the whole evening.'

What a load of crap. Tim must have rung her and told her to back up his story. I was pretty certain it was Tim who'd been sitting at the bar with Michael but I wasn't going to get any more out of Tracey, so I headed back to The Terrace. I knocked on Freddy and Doll's back door, but got no reply. Ditto, at number four, though I didn't expect anyone to be there, having seen Patsy trundling off with her suitcase. I peered through the kitchen window: no sign of life, just a kitchen full of wooden units too big for the space. Nothing out of place, no plants, no ornaments. Soulless. But from number five, next door, I could hear the faint thump of a drum beat. Perhaps Gerry, the fitness fanatic I'd seen jogging up and down the path most days, was in and would be happy to talk.

7

Rags

I'd decided to tell Gerry I was researching a piece on people who go missing. It was half-true, in any case: if I turned up anything interesting about Michael, I could include it in a longer feature.

I nipped back to Dad's house to pick up two scones I'd bought at the market that morning. I was feeling peckish, and scones are always welcome, aren't they? As I approached the house, the music got louder. *You're simply the best! Better than all the rest* ... I allowed myself to stand for a minute on the path listening to Tina Turner's full-throated roar, then went in the back gate.

The neat yard of number five contained two large terracotta pots planted with inky blue lobelias. The yard was swept clean, with the bins fenced off in a small enclosure. On the kitchen windowsill stood two evenly spaced pots of marigolds. Through the window to the dining room I could see Gerry flat on her back, lifting a large pink exercise ball held between her ankles up and down. After a few of these manoeuvres, she placed her trainers on the ball, and lifted herself onto her shoulders, forming a bridge with her back.

She rounded off her routine by clenching the ball between her muscular thighs and doing a series of sit-ups.

Just watching her made me want to lie down and have a rest.

When the track finished, I tapped on the windowpane. Gerry looked over and bounded to her feet. She parked the pink ball on a stand in the corner of the room and came round to open the back door. Her pale auburn hair, cut into an elfin bob, glistened with sweat, and though her features were a little too gaunt to be pretty, hers was a kind, open face.

'Hello there,' I said. 'I'm Rags. I'm staying with my dad at number two. Thought I'd come and say hello.' I held up the bag of scones and rattled it. 'I've got some scones from the market.'

Gerry's mouth opened then closed. Too late, I realised that she'd probably die rather than eat a whole, buttery scone full of fat sultanas. 'Oh, thanks,' she said, without enthusiasm. 'What a lovely idea.'

'My dad has told me all about you.'

'Nice things, I hope,' said Gerry, with a nervous giggle.

'Of course,' I said, though Dad had moaned about Gerry mowing and strimming *like a blooming harpy* whenever he sat out in the sun.

'Come in then. Do take a seat and I'll make us some tea.'

A few minutes later she put a teapot, milk jug and fine porcelain cups on the table, along with two side plates, butter and strawberry jam. I fished out two scones the size of oranges. 'I'm going out for a meal later, with Hector, my husband,' said Gerry, swiftly, 'so I won't have a whole one, thank you.'

'They are a bit humungous, aren't they?' I said, cutting one scone in half, and dividing it between the two plates. I helped myself to the butter and jam and took a squishy bite.

Gerry broke a crumb off her half-scone and popped it in her mouth. 'So: how are you settling in?'

'Loving it. I'm enjoying the peace and quiet.'

'It's a nice little town. Hector and I have always been very happy here.'

I took a mouthful of tea and went into my spiel. 'Actually, I'm a journalist, and I've started work on a feature about people who go missing. I want to explore each individual's story, so they're not reduced to faceless statistics. And as you were his neighbour, I wondered whether you could tell me anything about Michael Cleverly. What sort of person is he?'

'Michael? He hasn't gone missing, has he? He's probably on a business trip, or something.'

'No one's seen him since last Friday, and his wife has no idea where he's gone.'

Her voice rose sharply. 'I don't know him that well. He's more of an acquaintance than a friend.'

'But he came to your party, didn't he? Dad said he talked to him there.'

'Oh, well …' Gerry flapped her hands in the air. 'I tried to be friendly with him and Patsy when they first moved in, but he was rather pushy. He was setting up a property company, and tried to get Hector to invest in it.' She gave another nervous giggle. 'He tried it on with everyone. I know he was hoping that Patsy's father would put some money in.'

'And did he?'

'Well, I couldn't say for sure, but I doubt it. You see, he never took to Michael. Because I live next door I could hear some of the arguments that went on when he came to visit.'

'And?'

'He called him a gold digger more than once.'

'Ah.' I nodded, though none of this was news to me. 'And did you see Michael last Friday?'

'Me? No! My husband and I went out for a meal, to the Red Anchor in Warsham. We were there until – oh – nearly midnight, because they had a quiz, for charity – the premature baby unit at the hospital – and we like to support that sort of thing.' She paused for a gulp of tea.

'I see.' I dabbed my lips with the paper-made-to-feel-like-cloth napkin Gerry had provided. 'And how do you get on with him?'

She paused before speaking. 'All right, I suppose, though I wouldn't say we were friends. But Patsy can be difficult.' She leant forward and said in a confidential tone, 'You know she has substance abuse problems, don't you?'

'I know she's fond of a drink.'

Gerry shook her head sadly. 'I feel so sorry for people who have addictions. It's an illness, isn't it?'

I avoided Gerry's glittering, green eyes. Talk about kettles and pots: Gerry was clearly an exercise addict with an eating disorder added on for good measure. I popped the last buttery mouthful of scone into my mouth.

'I've got a fifteen-year-old – Iona – and I worry about her going down that path – drinking, I mean,' continued Gerry. 'She acts all grown-up, but they need support at that age, don't they?'

I nodded, non-committal. At fourteen my mother had left me to get on with it while she cooed and fussed over Tarquin. Benign neglect was the kindest way of describing her parenting style.

'And she's been so difficult lately. She argues with me about *everything*.'

I murmured something consoling about Iona being a normal teen, ending with, 'She'll grow out of it.'

'I hope so.'

'Could I have a word with her?'

Gerry's face tightened up. 'She's not in at the moment.'

In a rush, she stood up. 'And now I'm sorry but I'm going to have to kick you out. I've got to sort out the ironing before Hector gets home. We're going out to the pictures tonight, you see, on a date.'

'Just one more thing,' I said, remembering a question that had been at the back of my mind. 'Does Michael have a car?'

She thought for a moment. 'I don't think so. He used to have a black VW, but I haven't seen it for a while. I think he uses his works car sometimes.'

I stood up. 'Well thanks for your help, and for the tea.'

'My pleasure.'

I went back to Dad's house and wrote up notes of my meetings with Tracey, Tim and Gerry. I had to admit that Michael didn't come out of it well. He was shaping up as something of a bully: Tim had been seriously rattled by my questions – so rattled he'd taken a chunk out of my hair. And then there was the fact that Tim denied having a drink with him in the pub last Friday. Sitting at the table, laptop open in front of me, I closed my eyes and tried again to remember just what I'd seen in The Rampaging Bull. I was 95 per cent certain Tim was the weedy bloke sitting with Michael at the bar. And Tracey hadn't mentioned he was at home when I first spoke to her. She'd just said she was watching TV with her mum. Yet they both swore he'd not been at the pub that night.

And there was something odd about Gerry: her voice had gone up an octave when I asked her about Michael. Perhaps they'd had a thing at some point? Even as I asked myself the question I pulled a face. It was unlikely. I couldn't see Michael going for someone like Gerry, and she was one of those annoying women who witter on about their husbands all the time. Even if she fancied Michael, she'd never get off with him.

Would she?

I sat there for a few moments. What now? Then it came to me: I'd go back to the pub and try to squeeze some information out of Wayne, the landlord. He'd know whether Tim had been there, and he might be able to tell me more about Michael.

Tina Turner had got me into a music mood. I settled on Stevie Wonder's *Talking Book*. What an album! Not just brilliant songs, but a production so huge and airy it sounded good even chirping out of an iPod. In between spells of dancing to *You Are the Sunshine of my Life* I changed into a powder-blue Whistles blouse and put some mascara on my eyelashes. Then I stood back and took a long look at myself: not bad. I'd picked up a light honey tan, and my greeny-brown eyes were brighter, the shadows beneath them gone. Life in the sticks was clearly doing me some good. I added some lip gloss and ran my fingers through my hair. Then I picked up the guitar and played along to *Maybe your Baby* because it was so damn funky.

When I glanced at the clock it was twenty to six: time to hit the pub. Late sun was gilding the gardens, and I found myself humming as I strolled along the footpath into town. Four minutes later I was in the beery fog of The Rampaging Bull. As it was market day, there were plenty of punters scattered around the benches – older couples sipping half pints and tonic waters, and stallholders sinking pints after a long day. A fleshy redhead was propped up behind the bar. As I approached, she broke into a coughing fit that made her cleavage tremble.

'Hello,' I said, not leaning too close. 'Is Wayne in tonight?'

The barmaid coughed again, and blew her nose. 'Sorry. Can't shake this off. He's downstairs, changing a barrel. Can I help you?'

'No. That's OK. I'll wait till he's free. Thanks.'

I ordered a glass of Sauvignon and took it to a small corner table – the same table I'd sat at last Friday. Sipping my wine in a slant of sun, I asked myself why Michael might have taken off. Having failed to extract the necessary funds from Patsy, I could well believe that he'd look for another woman with better prospects. Enter Shell. But he'd let her down – broken their arrangement. So perhaps he'd failed to raise the money for their investment, and cleared off rather than face the music. I could imagine someone like Michael wouldn't want to lose face. Or perhaps he'd found an even better prospect – a woman with more dosh than either Shell or Patsy. But Shell had been adamant that they'd been in love as well as business partners, and the expression on his face when he received her text made me believe that was true.

Looking up, I saw Wayne's bullet head appear behind the bar, and headed over to speak to him.

'Lovely evening,' I said, ordering a packet of plain crisps.

'Yup. Going to be good all week, they say.'

'Thanks.' I handed over the money, noting that even crisps were half the price they were in London pubs. 'I was in here last Friday,' I continued. 'It was rammed, wasn't it?'

He smothered a yawn. 'Yeah. Fridays are mental.'

'Do you know if Tim's coming in later?'

'Couldn't say.'

'He seemed like one of your Friday night regulars.'

That provoked a stony look. 'I can't remember everyone who comes in here.'

'Well I can see why you're so popular. This is an awesome pub!'

His face almost cracked into a smile. 'Glad you think so.'

'Everyone's so friendly. I got talking to – what's his name? – Michael, the guy who was sitting at the bar.'

Wayne's face snapped shut.

'Is he a friend of yours?'

'No,' he said, eyes cold as a fridge freezer.

'Only I want to get hold of him, because he was talking to me about his property business, and ...'

But Wayne cut me off before I could get more out of him. 'Look: much as I'd love to chat I've got to get on.' And with that, he turned away and busied himself with tidying some glasses that didn't need tidying.

I pulled a face at his broad back and took the crisps back to my sunny table, telling myself not to get wound up: Shell had given me until the end of the weekend to come up with something. No need to tear the arse out of it on the first day. And things were looking up for me, weren't they? Dad and I were getting on OK. I had a comfortable bed and some paid work. To celebrate the change in my fortunes, I headed back to the bar for another glass of wine. Wayne had disappeared and the snuffly barmaid was busy with a large order. In an adjacent room the local news was filling a large television screen that last Friday had been showing football.

The screen showed a river bank, looking impossibly beautiful with its sprinkling of kingcups, and, in the background, the river moving at a gentle pace. A white tent had been erected nearby, beside a gravelled track. The usual yellow tape had been strung between a couple of metal posts, and in front of it a blonde female reporter appeared, speaking into a microphone. 'In this serene corner of North Norfolk, on the outskirts of Middleham, Geoffrey and Peter Coles had a terrible shock while out fishing this morning: they found the body of an unidentified man in the River Rush. Police enquiries are continuing.'

A chill chased down my back. Behind the reporter, some distance from the white tent, I could see a shoe. A black shoe. A black Kurt Geiger shoe.

I got out my phone. Dialled Shell's number. Got her

answerphone and left a message asking her to call me back as soon as she could.

I'd found Michael Cleverly.

8

Rags

I knocked back the rest of my wine and hurried towards the river. I wasn't alone: at least a dozen nosy parkers had seen the item on the local news and were heading for the Rush – useful for me, as I could follow people who knew where they were going. The posse headed for a part of the river I hadn't been to before, joining the riverside path near the bridge over the main road into town. I traipsed along at the back of the crowd past a broken-down barn and some meadows in which a few bullocks were munching on lush pasture. After a few minutes a railway bridge came into view, and a hundred yards further on the yellow tape I'd seen on the news report, keeping the public away from a white tent, a police van and two cars which had bumped their way up a rough track. I looked around for the shoe I'd seen, but it was gone: the police must have found it since the TV report was filmed. I sneaked through to the front of the thirty of so people who'd gathered, and flashed my NUJ badge at the pimply police officer standing in front of the tape.

'Press. Can I talk to the investigating officer?'

'That's not possible, Madam. We'll be making a further statement in due course.'

I peered round his beanpole body, but could see only a man and woman in plain clothes talking quietly outside the tent. 'Can you tell me how long he'd been in the water?'

The officer looked at me with bored, brown eyes. 'All the information currently available has been released to the media.'

'And do the police have any idea of his identity?'

'As I told you, we'll be making a further statement in due course.'

'Do you happen to know if he's Michael Cleverly, the local man who's gone missing?'The pompous plod directed his gaze into the middle distance, but not before I'd seen a flicker in his eyes. So it *was* Michael. I moved along the tape to get a better view of where he'd been found. A few feet behind the white tent a mature willow tree growing on the river bank trailed leafy fingers in the slow-moving water. It looked as if Michael's body had got caught in the underwater roots of the tree, where the river bank soil had been eroded.

I'd seen all I could. On the way home I took a swift detour to Asda and bought a bottle of cheapo Sauvignon. I had a lump in my throat as I counted out the coins from my purse. I'd already drunk two glasses of wine in the pub, but what the hell? I felt wretched at the thought of that delicious man being nibbled by fishes for the past week, and needed some consolation. In my early days as a reporter on the crime beat in Halifax and Huddersfield I'd seen a couple of bodies that had been in the water for a while, and they weren't pretty sights. At home, I unscrewed the bottle and poured a hefty whack into one of Dad's half-pint tumblers. He had a set of rose-tinted crystal wine glasses in a small cabinet in the dining room, but I'd been informed that, 'they're only for best, so don't go using them.' As the alcohol hit my stomach I took a deep breath and found tears coming into my eyes. 'Don't be so bloody stupid,' I said to the empty kitchen, wishing that Napoleon was here, wagging his whole body with happiness. 'You'd only met him once. You didn't know him. Not really. And he sounded like a dodgy geezer.'

I took another hearty swig. I'd been off the crime beat for too long. Those years chasing after airheads with breast implants and trout pouts had softened me up. Then a truly selfish thought swam into my mind. Now that Michael had been found by the fishermen, Shell might refuse to cough up the £300. Plus, she'd want her expenses back. 'Oh, crap,' I muttered, before knocking back the rest of the tumbler of wine.

I fumbled for my mobile. I needed to talk to my oldest friend. Carola had been away, on some hideous team-building exercise in the Scottish highlands, but was coming back to London today. She answered on the second ring. 'Hello, babes. I'm just on my way home from the tube, covered in midge bites and longing for my own bed. How are you getting on in the back of beyond?'

'Well, it was all hunky-dory until about an hour ago. You're not going to believe this, but an Amazonian woman promised me 300 quid to find her missing boyfriend.'

'And?'

'And the stupid man has turned up dead, in the river.' As I said this, the sobs I'd been holding back came rushing out.

'Dead?' I heard the sound of Carola's footsteps change as she turned into the gravel path that led to her front door. A bus grumbled past, giving me a huge pang of homesickness for London where, despite my lively lifestyle, no one I'd almost kissed had turned up dead in a river a week later.

'Yes,' I said, through satisfying snuffles. 'And I knew him.'

Carola's door slammed shut. 'Oh, I'm so sorry, sweetie. Was he an old school friend, or something?'

'No.' I paused. 'I only met him last week.'

'Rags?' The woman was a bloody mind-reader. 'He wasn't one of your little adventures, was he?'

'If only.' And then I told Carola the whole peculiar story: the meeting with Michael, the almost-kiss, his disappearance, the arrival of Shell, and the discovery of his body in the river. 'But something funny's going on,' I continued, articulating this aloud for the first time. 'First of all his wife, Patsy, runs home to her horrible father. And then there's the fact that Tim, the weedy hairdresser, is lying to me.'

'I agree. Something smells funny.'

A warm feeling filled my chest. 'Oh, it's so good to talk to you. I mean, Dad's been doing his best, but he keeps making little digs about how my career has gone down the plughole.' I sniffed again. 'And now Shell might pull out of our little arrangement, and I was counting on that money,' I added, glad I could be selfish in front of my oldest friend.

'Oh, sweetheart. I'm sorry. It all sounds really difficult.'

I could hear Carola switching on the kettle and ached to be in her kitchen, looking out at the small garden crammed with pots full of geraniums and pansies. 'It is,' I said in a feeble voice, thanking the goddess for good friends.

'But surely this woman – Shell – will want to know what happened to him. My guess is that she'll want you to carry on.'

'Do you think so?' Through the fog of wine I glimpsed a glimmer of hope.

'Yes.'

'I hope you're right,' I said, releasing a long breath of relief, because Carola had impeccable judgement.

'Now tell me what else has been going on.'

So I gave her the rundown on Dad and Napoleon – which made Carola laugh. 'I can't believe you actually *like* a dog. You've always shunned them before – even poor old Karl Marx.'

'I know. But Napoleon's different. He's – he's full of the joys of life,' I said, tactfully not adding that Karl Marx, her black Lab, smelled to high heaven and slobbered all over me whenever we met. I chatted to Carola for a while, and it was bloody lovely. By the time we said goodbye I felt much better.

Shell rang me back half an hour later and I delivered the news that Michael had been fished out of the river, dead.

'And are you sure it's him?'

'There's been no formal identification, but it seems highly likely. I'm so sorry,' I said, glad I'd had my meltdown while talking to Carola and now sounded cool and composed. 'It looks like he fell in the river while he was drunk.'

Shell, made of sterner stuff than me, didn't dissolve into sobs: her voice became a blade, sharpened by fury. 'Michael was never drunk. Never. He liked to drink some wine, yes, but never to excess. Someone has done this to him, and *you* will find out what happened to him and *you* will tell me. And then *we* will make those people pay.'

'So you want me to carry on with my investigation?'

'Of course. For every extra day you work, I'll pay you another £100. Is this agreeable to you?'

I took a deep breath. 'I've got another suggestion. From now on I think it's better all round if I bill you on an hourly basis. I've been checking out the rates for this sort of work, and I'll do it for £30 an hour.' Carola and I had discussed this and, being a solicitor, she'd pushed me to take this approach, as it was easier to record and justify. Though £30 was cheap as chips, we'd agreed it was a good rate for the time being, as I was a rookie at this lark. 'And that's very reasonable.'

A long pause, that made me wonder whether she'd been checking out the going rate, too. Then: 'All right.'

I punched the air. 'Thank you. And I might need more money for expenses.'

'OK. Keep records and send me receipts. Text me if you need more funds.'

When I'd hung up I released a long breath of relief. Poor Michael might be fish food, but I'd found a way of making some money.

Yes, folks, I'd become a private investigator.

Investigating stories was where I'd begun. At university (York) I'd worked my arse off on the student newspaper, truffling out scoops: a scandal involving a university chaplain who'd been siphoning off money from the collection bowl was my greatest triumph. These stories helped me get onto a post-grad journalism training course with a group of northern newspapers. (Yes, they existed in the 1990s, and you even got paid.) I did the rounds of the magistrates' courts and local nicks, and learned the ropes of news reporting, but what really floated my boat was investigative journalism where I could follow a hunch and dig for details. My big break came when I got an anonymous call about a local councillor who was taking advantage of young people on a youth employment project. I tracked down a few of the kids on the scheme, and found there was indeed something nasty going on. The councillor, with the help of a dodgy youth worker, was passing on vulnerable girls to a woman who ran a beauty parlour which allegedly offered additional services from two rooms at the back of the salon. I asked a few questions and got nowhere, but then had a stroke of luck. Sadie, the woman running the beauty parlour, fell out with the councillor, and suggested we meet. I had to soften her up over a couple of boozy lunches at the local wine bar, but eventually she spilled the beans and admitted what was going on.

My editor published the piece, and to my amazement I won a young journalist's award. On the back of the prize I got a reporting job with a London weekly, and then a national daily, and the world was my oyster.

Until I screwed it up.

I made sure I was in bed before Dad came in, and, like a guilty teenager, hid the empty bottle in my room. I'd dispose of it at a bottle bank: if I put it in the recycling box Dad would see it and treat me to one of his disapproving looks. Though I fell asleep straightaway, I woke up when Dad opened the back door. Napoleon's feet scurried up the stairs and paused outside my bedroom door. He sniffed a few times before trotting onto Dad's room and his own comfy bed with the red fleece blanket. For some reason that made me feel like crying all over again.

My sleep was troubled that night: in one dream Michael was running his hands over my breasts and I woke up with a start, feeling uncomfortably sexually aroused. No, I didn't want to get turned on by a dead man. In another dream I saw his bloated body bobbing down the river, and a crowd of onlookers were pointing and laughing at it.

I woke up late, with a mouth like a hamster's cage, reminding me that there was a price to pay for finding solace with Sauvignon Blanc. There had been years when I'd started most days with a hangover, but I'd left that behind when I lost my job and my regular income. I heard the back door close and bobbed downstairs to make myself a mug of tea to find a note from Dad saying he was going to do some errands in Holt, and would be back early that afternoon.

The rain had started up after a week of dry weather, and the spits and spots dashing against my window added to my blue mood. But half a pint of tea will do wonders, and after

I'd drained my mug I sat up and pulled my laptop onto the duvet cover.

It was time to map out a plan of action.

First, I needed to attend the inquest, so I could suss out whether the police were going to investigate further – unlikely, since it was obvious that they thought it was a paralytic-man-falls-into-river scenario (death by misadventure). And if that was confirmed by toxicology tests, they'd do bugger all. The website for Norfolk Coroner's Court showed that most inquests were dealt with pretty swiftly. As the body was found on a Thursday, the inquest would probably be opened early next week; I could find out the exact date by keeping an eye on the list posted on the website. The results of the autopsy might be in by then.

What else?

- *Where did Michael go after leaving the pub on Friday night? Talk to the other residents of The Terrace.*

- *Finances: was Michael in debt? Did he have large sums of money stashed away (as Shell suggested)?*

- *Work: check when and why he left his job.*

- *Family background.*

As I looked at the list I realised that maybe – just maybe – I was doing something worthwhile.

9

Tim Jones

Early – too early – after a night broken, as usual, by Roddy's crying, Tim Jones woke with a jerk. A sick feeling swirled round his belly. Last Friday Michael Cleverly had been up to his usual tricks, slapping him on the back, calling him 'my old mate'. Oh yes, Michael Cleverly thought it was a great laugh to lift up his glass and say, 'Cheers!' while his eyes were laughing at you and crowing, 'Loser! Loser!'

And now the silly bastard had only gone and fallen in the river and drowned.

Tim groaned under his breath. It was no good. He'd have to get up. With a sigh he rolled out of bed, away from his wife's sizable backside, and crept along to the bathroom, where he had a long, satisfying pee. As he washed his hands, bleary, brown eyes stared back at him from the mirror over the sink. With a sudden intake of breath he leant closer and fiddled with his hair. Was he going thin at the temples? Oh Christ, he hoped not. His dad had been bald by thirty and Tim was nearly twenty-six. He didn't want to be bald: he didn't have the right sort of skull. When he'd been a little boy head lice had spread like wildfire round his class, and his mum had shaved his head. The bumps and lumps that had appeared had scared him to death. When he burst into tears she gave him a clout (but not a hard one) and told him to stop being a nancy boy. These days his hair was his calling card. He had standards to uphold. People who came into the salon wanted a hairdresser who had funky hair, who looked the part. They didn't want some spindly git who'd gone prematurely bald.

A wail erupted from along the landing, making him wince. Roddy had woken up again from his twitchy, red-cheeked sleep. The doctor said it was colic and would soon pass, but after eight months of wailing sharp enough to shred his eardrums, Tim was exhausted. He heard a thump as Tracey heaved herself out of their bed. Her footsteps clumped along the landing. He sighed: Tracey had never been a sylph, but she'd put on the pounds since she'd had children, and she was so bloody sensitive he couldn't even make a joke about it when she nearly crushed him if she climbed on top during sex.

Guilt brought a flush to his cheeks: Tracey was stressed because they were short of money, and when she was stressed she ate. Her voice drifted from Roddy's bedroom, frayed by fatigue. 'Hush now. Hush up. Give us a break. Come on now: come to me. Have a feed. That'll cheer you up. That'll calm you down.' And indeed the wails subsided. Sometimes that worked. Sometimes he'd feed for a bit and drop off to sleep.

He knew he should have been able to keep his wife and children as they deserved, but people were having their hair done less often now that money was tight. The mortgage was due next week, and he'd have to go overdrawn again. But at least he wouldn't have to resort to taking out a loan from the payday lender who drank in the British Legion and was always hinting that he could help out.

Thank goodness he'd had a little extra to tide him over this month.

He shook his head – what was done was done – and crept back along the corridor to the roomy bed that was a cast-off from his parents. As he sank into the odour of Tracey's milky breasts and her salty, feminine body, he told himself to stop being a big girl's blouse.

He'd done nothing wrong – not really.

* * *

Doll Perkins

Doll was thinking hard as she prepared breakfast. Freddy's face was transparent as a window pane, so you could see her internal weather without even having to try. Today it was dismal drizzle and the threat of thunder. No doubt about it, she was out of sorts, but Doll couldn't work out what was up. It couldn't be because Michael had been found dead in the river, could it? Surely not. For a start, Freddy had hated Michael – hated him with a venom Doll had never understood. And though they'd both been shaken up when they heard about the discovery of Michael's body, Doll knew that something else was at the root of Freddy's foul temper – something which had been brewing for several days now. In fact, ever since Doll got back from a visit to Beth, her God-bothering daughter, Freddy had been a beacon of doom and gloom. It couldn't go on.

'Now,' said Doll, as she brought the warmed croissants to the pine kitchen table. 'I want to know what's wrong. And don't tell me you're distraught about Michael Cleverly, because you couldn't stand the man.' Then, when Freddy grunted but said nothing: 'I want some answers.' Doll's voice was low but firm: she hadn't been a school secretary for thirty years without learning how to deal with recalcitrant children, and Freddy was like a child sometimes – a neglected, bumptious child who can't handle her feelings. Doll knew this and loved her all the same: loved her loyalty and protectiveness; loved the red roses, bottles of perfume and packets of scented soap Freddy gave her; loved Freddy's warm mouth running over her skin, and the press of her body in their queen-size bed with its top of the range mattress to support Doll's arthritic hips.

'Nothing's wrong.'

Doll broke off a piece of her croissant and popped it in her mouth, enjoying the buttery flakes. 'Yes, there is. You're fretting over something.'

'I'm not,' mumbled Freddy, through a mouthful of crumbs. She'd devoured her croissant in thirty seconds – a sure sign she'd got something on her mind.

'Then why are you behaving like this?'

'Like what?'

'Grumpy. Sullen.'

Freddy stood up abruptly, banging her leg on the table as she did, so that the royal-blue glass vase holding a clutch of white roses in the centre of the table wobbled, fell, smashed on the kitchen floor with a splash of water and a scatter of blossoms. 'Oh! I'm so sorry, Doll. Why am I so bloody clumsy?' Dashing to the cupboard under the sink, she pulled out a dustpan and brush and swept up the pieces, wrapping them in newspaper before putting them in the bin. She mopped up the spilt water and started to jam the roses into an ugly, chipped jug.

'It's all right. It's only a vase,' said Doll, though it wasn't all right – not really – as the vase was one of a pair left to her by her grandmother. With a sigh, Doll dispatched the last of her croissant and laid the knife neatly on the plate. 'Now please come and sit down. Talk to me.'

Freddy's back remained turned. If a back could glower, it did. 'Stop getting at me.'

Doll counted to ten under her breath then stood up. 'I don't know why you're in a foul mood, but I'm going to leave you to it and do some gardening.'

'No!' Turning round, Freddy threw her arms around Doll and clung to her. After a few moments, Doll let herself sink into Freddy's embrace, which was a little too tight for comfort and scented with *Eau Savage*. 'I'm sorry, Doll. I don't know what's got into me. Let's go out. Let's drive down to Holkham and have a long walk. We can take the binocs and look for the marsh harriers. Please. Please, Doll.'

'We're not going out until you tell me what's up.'

Doll waited. After a minute or two Freddy pulled back and looked at her with desolate eyes. 'We got a poison pen letter. It came while you were away.'

So that was all it was! 'Well, show it to me, then.'

'I don't want you to see it. It's disgusting.'

'Oh, I can handle disgusting.' And she could. She'd spared Freddy the details of the last decade of her marriage, when Ron had morphed from a miserable sod into a full-blown bully who shoved her around and surfed the internet for pornographic sites featuring golden showers and worse. Freddy would never know about these things: they'd upset her too much. And Doll could live with them because Ron was history: he'd dropped dead six years ago, courtesy of a heart attack after an August Bank Holiday dinner when, as usual, he'd had two helpings of everything.

Freddy's cheeks reddened. 'I don't want you to read nasty things about us. People have talked behind my back all my life, but you – you've lived a normal life.'

Doll gave Freddy a quick kiss on the lips. 'Show it to me.'

With a groan, Freddy lurched to the kitchen drawer full of the hefty, silver-plated cutlery they never used. She pulled out a folded piece of paper and handed it over.

Doll slipped on her specs and smoothed it out.

You're a couple of dirty old Lezzos. Wait till I tell everyone about you. 'Well, well. Someone's been spying on us.' Doll couldn't keep a smile from her voice; she rather liked being called a dirty old lezzo – her, with her round face and white bob of hair, and comfortable skirts that covered her curves.

'It's not funny.'

Doll took Freddy's hand and gave it a squeeze. 'OK, it's nasty, but surely everyone round here knows we're a couple and they don't give a damn. In fact they quite like having a couple of old lesbian lovebirds as neighbours.'

Freddy's shoulders, hunched with tension, relaxed a fraction. 'I suppose you're right.'

'Course I am. Come here.' They stood up and hugged, rocking a little on the spot. 'There. That's better, isn't it?'

Freddy started to run her hands up and down Doll's back and round her arse. Doll was just thinking it might be a good idea to go back to bed when they heard a polite tap on the back door. Immediately, she felt Freddy's shoulders tense up again. 'Don't worry. I'll get rid of them,' she said.

But when she opened the door, Rags, their new neighbour, stood there, in a white cotton dress, with chestnut hair tumbling over her shoulders.

'I'm a journalist,' she said, showing them her NUJ card, 'and I'm researching a series of articles on issues of local interest. Dad told me you were members of the local horticultural society, and I wondered if I could talk to you about that.'

With a smile, Doll invited her in. They sat around the table and chatted. Rags jotted some notes in her little book, and Doll filled her in on the forthcoming horticultural show.

'It'll be on the third weekend in July, and there are competitions for cakes, flower arrangements and photography, as well as prizes for the best flowers and vegetables.'

'Sounds fantastic. I'll make sure I come,' said Rags, closing up her notebook.

'I can introduce you to the chairman of the committee, if you like.'

'Great.' Standing up, Rags thanked them for their time. But just before she reached the door, she turned. 'Oh, before I leave, I wanted to ask you about the night Michael Cleverly disappeared. An editor in London has asked me to look into his tragic death. Did either of you see him that night?'

Aware of Freddy's face freezing over, Doll said smoothly, 'I can't help you, I'm afraid. I was away, visiting my daughter, Beth.'

'And I didn't see or hear a thing,' muttered Freddy. 'I was watching TV.'

'Did he have any enemies that you know of? Anyone he might have got into a fight with?'

Out of the corner of her eye Doll saw the flush rising up Freddy's neck. 'No,' she said firmly, ushering Rags out of the door. 'You'll find that we're a peaceable lot in The Terrace. If he did get into a fight, it wouldn't be with anyone from the street. I mean, we're all one big family, aren't we Freddy?'

To which Freddy grunted in assent.

Rags's visit plunged Freddy back into gloom, and Doll no longer wanted to go upstairs to bed. Instead they both went into the garden to do some weeding and pruning. The early morning drizzle had stopped and the garden, lit by soft sunshine, was rich with the scents of damp earth and honeyed buddleia.

'You've kept the garden so nice while I was away,' said Doll. Then, in a rush of gratitude for the life they shared:

'Think how lucky we are. We have each other, our house, our life together. No one's going to take that away from us.'

Freddy didn't reply.

10

Rags

As I came out of number three after my conversation with Freddy and Doll, I saw Alaric, the eco-warrior dude from number six, wheeling his bike along the shared path towards his house. Good. I could catch him and ask a few questions. But first I needed to find a way in. I went into my house and flipped through the notebook to see what Dad had told me about him. *He's a miserable so-and-so but get him talking about wildflowers and birds and you can't shut him up.*

OK: that was the approach I'd take. I'd noticed that his back garden was full of meadow flowers: cowslips, scabious, campions, cow parsley. And in the patch cut short beside the path bird's-foot trefoil and scarlet pimpernel bloomed beside daisies and violets. I could introduce myself by talking about them. I know my wildflowers, thanks to my rare outings with Gwendolyn.

A few minutes later I found Alaric in his backyard, cleaning the chain of his upended bike in a battered saucepan of murky oil, feeding the links through one by one as he teased out gobs of black muck.

'Yes?' His blunt voice cut through the fragrant air.

'I was just admiring your garden,' I said, pointing at the embroidery of small flowers threaded through the grass. 'It's almost a meadow, with all those wildflowers.'

'It *is* a meadow, though Gerry, next door, calls the flowers weeds.'

'Well I love them.' I stepped into his yard, but didn't hold out my hand to shake his, as I normally would, since his were covered in gooey muck. In any case, he'd returned his attention to the bicycle chain, nimble fingers feeding the links through the darkening pool of oil. 'I'm Rags,' I said. 'I'm staying with my dad at number two.'

'I know.' His eyes lifted and held my gaze for a few seconds. Dark brown with specks of moss-green, they had the same shuttered quality as the rest of his face. Yet it was not an unattractive face, with its long nose and sharp bone structure.

'I'm a journalist researching stories about local issues, and I'd like to do a piece on the work of the Coastal Nature Reserve, focussing on the marsh harriers,' I said, recalling that Dad had told me Alaric was *barmy about those blooming birds*. 'Could we have a chat some time?'

He blinked dark lashes and gave me an intent look, as if he were seeing me for the first time. Straightening up, he wiped his hands on an old tee-shirt. 'When?'

'Today, if you're free.'

He rolled his shoulders and stretched his arms, showing muscles sleek beneath the skin. A shiver ran up my thighs. Behave, I told myself. He's a surly git who's got trouble written all over him.

He gave me a half smile which lit up his face. 'All right. I've got the day off, so how about we go for a drink this lunchtime? The Green Man in Penfield has a nice beer garden.'

A tingle found its way into my knickers. 'Great. What time?'

'One o'clock?'

'Sounds good.'

'Can I meet you there? I've got a few things to do in town first.'

There was a sway to my step as I sauntered back to the house. Oh, sweet, sweet sex fizzes up the dullest day. I'm a feminist – you have to be stupid *not* to be a feminist – but a feminist who enjoys sex with men (and the occasional woman) – good, straightforward sex with no funny business. I'd tried all sorts, but the outer limits leave me cold. Once, in my early days as a journalist, I'd spent over an hour dying for a cup of tea when some effete politics professor left me trussed up to his bedpost while he ran out to give a lecture on semiotics. Any desire I might have felt had died a death by the time he returned.

Dad was back, sitting on the garden bench, throwing the ball for Napoleon. I joined him, knowing I needed to talk to him about the discovery of Michael's body, and my investigation.

'Did you hear about the body in the river?' I said, sinking down beside him. 'They've confirmed that it's Michael Cleverly.'

'Yes. I heard the news on the local radio. Very sad. Such a young man, too.'

We sat in silence for a while then I spoke again. 'Dad? I've taken on some work and it's a bit unusual. Someone has asked me to look into what happened to Michael – how he ended up dead in the river.'

'Shouldn't you leave that to the police?'

'The police enquiry will take weeks, and this person wants answers as soon as possible.'

'And who is this person, may I ask?'

I summarised my meeting with Shell, and the arrangements we'd agreed, asking him to keep them confidential.

He made a raspberry sound with his lips. 'I thought it would be some girlfriend. It usually is.'

Ignoring this, I ploughed on. 'So I'm asking people in The Terrace questions about Michael. I just thought you should know.'

'Well, I hope you know what you're doing.'

My hackles rose. 'And what does *that* mean?'

'You can upset people, asking too many personal questions.'

'I promise I won't embarrass you.'

'Oh, I'm not too worried about that. It's you I'm thinking about.'

A shiver lifted the hairs at the back of my neck. 'What do you mean?'

He gave me a stern look. 'Michael turned up dead, didn't he? I'd hate anything to happen to you.'

I burst into a fake laugh. 'Dad! I'm unlikely to be in danger in Middleham. It's not exactly the crime capital of the country.'

Dad picked up the ball and threw it again for Napoleon. 'Have it your own way, but you might be better leaving things well alone.'

Bristling – what right did he have to tell me what to do? – I went upstairs, fired up my laptop and ran a search on Michael Cleverly. His handsome mug shot came up on the website of Gordon and Gordon, independent Diss estate agents 'specialising in luxury homes of distinction'. The site clearly hadn't been updated in the last week, since there he was: dressed in a black suit and wine-red tie, with hair shorter than when I met him, under the heading 'Residential Sales'. I checked the address of the office, and ran a search on the best way to get there from Middleham. A couple of buses would do it – slow, but easy enough. I'd go over there Monday or Tuesday and nose around a bit.

What else? I sat feeling the cogs of my brain turning in a way they hadn't since I'd left proper investigative journalism. From my experience at the magistrates' courts when I was a cub reporter I knew that most murders and violent attacks were committed by someone close to you or in the same criminal fraternity. Did Michael have a criminal record? There was one way to find out. It would cost a bit, but Shell had made it plain that she wanted answers ASAP, and this would go on expenses.

I dug out my mobile and scrolled through to a number I hadn't used for a while. It was picked up immediately.

'Paddy? It's Rags.'

'Hello stranger. How's my favourite girl?'

'Not bad. Not bad.'

'I heard you got yourself in a spot of bother with that dodgy Halliwell bird.'

I felt my mouth settle into a smile. Paddy McKee hadn't changed a bit: he was still the same, unreconstructed ex-police officer with ginger hair and jug ears who'd helped me out more than once when I needed information. He'd always had a soft spot for me: we'd fallen out of a few Soho pubs together when I was first in London and he was still with the Met. He was such good company that I'd almost ended up in bed with him, but had stopped myself because I thought he might fall in love with me. And that would have been a disaster.

'I'm looking for some information on a guy called Michael Cleverly. Until last week he was an estate agent working in Diss and living in Middleham in Norfolk. Now he's dead – fished out of the river. I need to know whether he has a criminal record or any criminal associations – people who might want to be rid of him.'

'Tut, tut. You know I can't help you with anything like that,' he said, going through the form of words we always used.

'Not even for a pony?'

'Not even for four ponies. Sorry, sweetheart. You'll have to try somewhere else.'

Good: he'd do it. I told him what I knew about Michael, and as we caught up on each other's news I visualised him sat in his cosy office in Shepherd's Bush (a shed in his back garden) with his feet up on the table, puffing on a cigarillo and drinking the evil instant coffee that fuelled him throughout the day. He'd get onto an old pal in the Met. I'd send him a hundred quid in cash. Done deal.

'How are you doing, babes? Uncle Paddy's been worried about you.'

'I'm OK.'

'I heard you got pally with a certain editor, and he got you into the Halliwell mess.'

'You heard right.' No point in denying it: Paddy's sources were impeccable.

'He's a complete arse. You're better off without him – good girl like you – smart, too.'

'It's a while since anyone's called me that,' I said with a sigh, thinking of my professional reputation in tiny shreds around my feet.

'Bollocks. You were conned, that's all. And it sounds like you're back on track now.'

I pulled a face. 'I wish. I can't get a proper job for love nor money. I'm freelance now.'

'That's not a bad place to be you know, sweetheart. Take it from Uncle Paddy. I've never been happier since I retired from the Met. No more bollocks, no more form-filling, no more late nights scraping drunks up off the pavement.'

As we chatted, I realised he might actually be right.

When I came off the phone I sent Shell an email asking for her to transfer a hundred quid to my account so I could pay Paddy, emphasising that his information was blue-chip.

Then it was time to spruce myself up for my lunch with Alaric. I put on four outfits and took them off again before settling on a primrose-yellow dress, made of soft, well washed cotton and cinched at the waist with a white belt. No, it didn't have a fancy label – I'd bought it from a charity shop and the label had been snipped out – but it showed off my figure (and, yes, I have a decent pair of breasts, which I don't call my 'tits' or 'boobs' because those words make a joke of them) – and fell in folds round my knees. I put on a pair of white sling-back sandals with kitten heels – Jimmy Choo copies bought off eBay, but not half bad – and some more eye make-up. My hand hovered over my Givenchy III cologne – I was pretty sure Alaric wouldn't appreciate a woman drenched in scent – then picked it up and sprayed some under my hair, and on my wrists and knees. Its perfume was light and summery, and would have softened to a flowery hint by the time I got to the pub. A quick rummage in the drawer of the table I used as a desk produced my small digital recorder. So far I'd just taken notes, but I didn't want to spend all my time with Alaric scribbling shorthand.

Before leaving I did a swift Google search on marsh harriers. They were magnificent birds, coloured chestnut, bronze and fawn, with curled wing feathers and fierce beaks. I decided I'd write the article in any case, and get it placed in a local magazine. Couldn't do any harm, and those birds deserved coverage.

Alaric was sitting at a table in the sun by the time I got to the pub, after a stroll through town and along a country lane to Penfield, a village half a mile from Middleham. As I approached, he reached up and pulled off the band holding his hair up. Rich brown curls fell round his face, softening his sharp, suspicious features. Oh my lord, I could just imagine those curls tickling my bare skin as he bent over me and …

'Hello there! What's a nice girl like you doing in a place like this?' Jason, my friend from last Friday, who'd regaled me with tales of the musical genius of Quo, was sitting at a table with four other shaven-headed men.

'Just meeting someone for a drink,' I said, noticing out of the corner of one eye that Alaric was yanking his hair back into its ponytail. Bugger. I was beginning to realise that in a small town like this you couldn't go out of your house without running into someone you knew.

'Friend of yours?' said Alaric, as I approached him.

'Just a guy I got chatting to in the pub. I think he took pity on me because I didn't know anyone.'

'Do people usually take pity on you? You don't look the type.'

I side-stepped that one for now. 'Can I get you another drink?' I said, gesturing to his almost empty half-pint glass.

He considered for a moment then threw me a smile that gave me goose bumps. 'All right. As you're asking, I'll have a pint of Shires.'

I went into the cool of the pub and got a pint for him and a glass of Sauvignon and some tap water for myself, most of which I glugged straightaway as I was hot and thirsty after walking in the sun.

'So what brings you to this part of the world?' asked Alaric, lifting his pint to clink my wine glass. 'You're not from round here, are you?'

'What makes you say that?'

His gaze ran over my body before moving down to my feet. He pointed. 'Those shoes, for a start.'

'I've been living in London for a while, but I was born and bred in King's Lynn. And what about you? I bet you're an incomer.'

'What makes you say that?'

I laughed. 'You've got hair, for a start.' I gestured to the table of men with shaved heads. 'That's not the fashion round here.'

'True enough.' He took a long swallow of beer. 'I was brought up on the south coast, studied Environmental Sciences at UEA, and moved here about seven years ago. I love it – the quietness, the space.'

'The marsh harriers.'

'Yes. The marsh harriers.'

And so it went on. Conversation ran between us easy as breathing. Alaric went into the pub to buy more drinks. I looked out at Penfield Common, which was fringed with shoots of rosebay willowherb, and imagined kissing him – that moment of connection when stars explode in your veins and you urgently want that person to touch you.

But as soon as he sat down again he looked at his watch and said, 'We'd better get started on the interview. I've got to be somewhere in an hour.'

So I packed away my desires and got out my digital recorder. He spoke fluently about the conservation programme, and gave me literature about the Coastal Reserve and a page of website addresses where I could find further information. 'And we've got an open day with a slide show at the beginning of September, so you could tie the feature in with that.'

'Will do.' It was a joy to talk to someone so smart, so on the ball.

'Where are you thinking of placing the feature?' he asked. 'Because the EDP magazine or *Norfolk Living* would probably carry it.'

'Thanks. That's helpful.'

He looked again at his watch. I still hadn't asked him about Michael. Better take the plunge. 'Before you dash off, can I ask you about something else?'

'What?' he said, a smile softening his mouth.

'Michael Cleverly.'

His face soured. 'What about him?'

'Did you know him? Was he a friend?'

'Why do you want to know?' He stared at me with cold eyes before leaning close enough for me to smell his odour of spicy soap and sweat. 'He's the reason you wanted to talk to me, isn't he?' he said, his voice quiet.

A blush seared my face. 'I'm looking into what happened to him. What's wrong with that?'

'I saw you sitting with him in the pub that night. You were all over him. Well, for your information, the man was a total arsehole.'

I moved so close our mouths could have kissed. 'Well, for *your* information, we were just talking, and I'd like to know why you don't give a shit about the fact that he's dead. In fact, you seem to care more about your bloody birds.'

He pulled back as if I'd hit him and gulped down the rest of his pint. 'You never were going to write that feature about the marsh harriers, were you? This was all about poking your nose in where it doesn't belong because you think there's a juicy story there.'

'I *am* going to write about the bloody marsh harriers, and I'll poke my nose wherever I want. It's called journalism.'

With a jerk that shook the table he stood up. 'Christ, you sound self-righteous!'

'Hark who's talking. Mr Right-On who's soppy about birds but doesn't give a flying fuck that a man has died.'

'That's it. I'm not going to sit here and listen to this.' He jammed his bicycle helmet on his head. Beneath it, his face looked pinched and mean.

'Yeah, that's right,' I crowed, because now I was livid. 'Fuck off when someone challenges you. Fuck off to your precious birds.'

He jabbed a swift V-sign into the air and rushed over to where his bike was slumped against the pub wall. Without a backward glance he pedalled off. I sat and stewed, feeling my heart pump rage round my body.

'Excuse me?'

I looked up to see one of the balding men who'd been sitting with Jason, the Quo fanatic. 'Yes?' I barked.

'Only I heard you asking about Michael Cleverly, and I used to go to school with him.'

I refocused my attention on the mild, sunburnt face looking down at me. 'Oh. Sorry. Please take a seat.' He did, introducing himself as Billy. 'So you knew Michael Cleverly when he was a boy?'

'Yes, but he didn't call himself Michael Cleverly back then. His name was Scruggins. His family lived on the Meadow Lea council estate on the outskirts of Horningham. I don't know the address, but they probably still live there.'

I took a sharp breath: it was often like this – a nasty knockback was followed by a stroke of luck. 'And what was he like?'

'Quiet. Kept himself to himself. A bit scruffy – his mother didn't keep his clothes clean, and he got stick for that from the other kids. I wasn't surprised when he changed his name because the family were – well, they had a reputation.'

'What for?'

'Nicking from shops. Burglary. Nothing major. The Old Bill were always round their house.'

'Was he involved?'

'Probably.'

'And was he popular? Did he have friends?'

'Not that I remember, but I was a few years older than him, so I didn't know him well.'

'And did you keep in touch?'

'No. Haven't spoken to him in years. I live out near Sandringham now, so our paths never crossed.' Billy paused.

'But I saw him around town once in a while, and I was gutted when I heard he was dead, because even when he was a kid he had *something* about him, if you know what I mean.'

I did.

11

Rags

I left the pub as soon as I'd finished my drink. Though still smarting from the dressing-down I'd got from Alaric, the fresh lead had buoyed me up. So Michael had changed his name. And I'd found out where he'd grown up. A visit to the Meadow Lea estate was in order.

When I got home I scoffed a cheese roll, and changed into a comfortable pair of jeans and a T-shirt. I checked out the buses to and from Horningham, a middling-size market town a dozen miles from King's Lynn and found I could get to the town in forty minutes and then catch another bus or peg it out to the estate. I decided to go the next day – Saturday – as I'd have a good chance of finding members of his family at home at the weekend. Deciding I'd done enough detecting for one day, I caught up on some Bee Cool work. An email had come in from the features editor of *All For You*. She wanted to commission *Sex Toys: Play Dates for Grown-ups*. Yawn. They were only offering £220 (tight-wads) but I accepted it, as I needed every penny I could get.

I rang Paddy McKee again. He didn't pick up so I left a message asking him to check out Michael Scruggins, formerly of the Horningham Meadow Lea estate, as well as Michael Cleverly, shit-hot estate agent of Diss. Then I pootled downstairs, made myself a cup of tea and, since Dad was out at the library, turned on the television to watch an old episode of *Columbo*. Carola and I had got into watching reruns of the show when we were at university and should have been writing essays; we'd both adored Peter Falk's glass eye, wonky features and tatty mac – and the way he was always smarter than the murderers.

I must have drifted into a doze, because the next thing I knew Dad was talking to me from the doorway. 'Make yourself comfortable, won't you?' But he sounded less grumpy than earlier in the day.

I stretched and yawned. Columbo was just about to reveal who'd shoved a glamorous model into the deep end of an empty swimming pool. 'Hello, Dad. I hope you don't mind me watching this rubbish. It'll be over in a few minutes.'

'Of course not. Watch what you like when I'm not here.'

Napoleon burst through the door and leapt onto the sofa next to me. 'Hello, handsome,' I said, stroking his head as he snuggled into me.

'He seems to like you, all right,' said Dad, his voice softening as it did whenever he talked about Napoleon.

'He's adorable.'

Dad shifted from foot to foot, looking awkward. 'I sometimes get fish and chips on a Friday night. I could get some for you as well, if you like.'

'Thanks, Dad. That'd be fantastic,' I said, hungry after not eating much apart from a cheese roll all day. Besides, I appreciated his gesture of conciliation. 'Shall I go and get us a bottle of wine or some beers?'

'No, you're all right. I've got some in the pantry out back.'

And so, at six-thirty that evening, I sat down with my dad and ate fish in golden, crispy batter and proper chips, washed down by a stonking bottle of Barolo he'd been hiding away in the little shed beside the back door. We didn't talk about the investigation. Instead we chatted about inconsequential things – the market, the weather, Napoleon. When we'd finished our meals and were sitting in a chip-induced daze I asked Dad what period of history most interested him right now.

'Ancient Greece.' He looked a little shy then said, 'I've signed up to a free online course to study the Ancient Greek Hero in literature, history and song.'

'Good for you, Dad,' I said, then winced inwardly at my patronising tone.

But he didn't seem to notice. He collected up the plates and we went through to the lounge to watch a documentary on The Tudors. It was good to feel at ease in each other's company – something that had seldom happened since my mum left him. Yet I know they'd been happy together once upon a time. I remember him bringing her a huge bunch of bluebells when I was a small child, and her jumping up and hugging him. Open-mouthed, I'd watched Dad's arms close round her back, as his head with its springy, dark hair bent down so he could kiss her.

After Gwendolyn whisked me off to Devon I only saw him once or twice a year. When I grew into a stroppy ad- olescent we often locked horns. After I moved to London we met up for lunch now and then but I always got the impression he thought I was too big for my boots. Several times he accused me of being just like my mother – some- thing I thought was monstrously unfair, since Gwendolyn had always been an idle, spoiled mare, and I'd worked my arse off to get where I had. But I had her neat nose and wide mouth. Like her, my hair fell into long, loose curls. When I was younger we looked so alike that people had taken us as sisters. Perhaps that was what got Dad's goat.

I was so sleepy after the meal and the Barolo that I forgot to charge up my phone. On Saturday morning I woke up just before eight – hadn't slept so well in ages – and found it had run out of juice. I plugged it in but tripped over the charger lead on the way to the loo, and the screen flickered then died on me. I pulled the charger out of the socket and discovered I'd broken the lead. Shit: I'd have to buy another one. Needing to check bus times, I switched on my laptop. It whirred and rattled into life before that screen, too, went blank.

'No, no, please no!'

I switched it off then on again. This time the whirring and rattling was louder than before. Nonetheless the icons slowly stopped break-dancing and settled on the screen. I checked the bus times to Horningham – plenty of time for granary toast and coffee – and swiftly ran through my emails. Nothing urgent, though Carola had emailed to say she was heading off again, this time to Nigeria to teach an intensive postgraduate course on international human rights law. Just reading her email made me realise how much I'd slowed down, and how much I liked it. When I called goodbye to Dad he was pottering in the garden, weeding the rows of bright marigolds, with Napoleon flopped in the shade of the bench.

Before heading for the bus, I dropped into the phone shop in town to buy a replacement charger, but the sales assistant with slicked back hair shook his head when I showed him what I wanted. 'We haven't supported that phone or charger for a couple of years. Can I interest you in taking out a contract?' I politely declined. My phone was a primitive

Nokia pay-as-you-go: I didn't have the funds to service a monthly phone contract.

I caught the bus by a whisker – a single-decker that rocked along lanes fringed by verges frothing with feathery grasses. Though the bus was nearly full, I found a seat near the front and watched the lanes curving in front of the bus through low-slung fields in which barley or vegetables were shooting up. Clouds scudded across the sky, obscuring the sun then letting it beam down on the rolling landscape. Hey, guess what? I was happy, in a quiet sort of way.

When I got into Horningham I checked out a phone shop, but got the same story on the charger as I'd had in Middleham. I had a mini-tantrum, stomping along the road muttering, *fuck, fuck, fuck,* under my breath, then told myself to get over it. I could order one online: it would arrive in a day or two. I consulted a town map stuck up in the bus shelter. The Meadow Lea estate was a mile or so out of town. It was a sunny day with a fresh breeze, and I was wearing jeans and comfortable trainers, so decided to peg it. About twenty minutes later I came to a row of six shops on the edge of the estate, three of which were boarded up. One of the others was a bookies, and the remaining two were a newsagent and small supermarket fronted by sturdy metal grilles, partially raised. I felt my shoulders hunching and realised I hadn't felt like this since I left London. Telling myself not to be a wuss – I'd traipsed across numerous dodgy council estates in the past twenty years, and never been robbed or attacked – I went into the shop to try and find out where the Scruggins family lived. They weren't listed in the phone book and I hadn't found them on the electoral roll, but the name was distinctive and if the family were still around, someone would know where I could find them.

A stocky man with a bald head was reading the sports section of a newspaper behind the counter. When the doorbell pinged he looked up then returned to his examination of the football results. I nosed around the shop, finding the usual high prices and limited selection of fresh produce for this sort of shop, though there were local potatoes, carrots and cabbage on sale. I picked up a small bottle of Evian and took it to the till.

Just as he was giving me my change the door pinged again and four teenage boys, faces hidden in hoodies, bundled in the door, joshing and shoving each other.

'Hey, you! Pack it in!' the man yelled.

But the four boys were converging on the sweets and crisps section and in less than a minute had grabbed some and rushed out the door, braying in half-broken voices. The shop keeper dashed out from behind the till and hurtled out of the front door. I hotfooted it after him, only to see the boys scattering at the nearby crossroads. The man skidded to a halt then turned round.

'Little bastards,' he spat, coming back in the door and banging it shut behind him.

'Oh dear,' I said – a feeble comment, but all I could muster. 'Are they always doing that?'

He looked at me properly for the first time, and I could see that he was older than I'd first thought – in his late fifties, perhaps, with a boxer's broken nose and tired eyes. 'I haven't had any trouble for a while, but the biggest one recently got out of borstal or whatever they call it these days, and he's a bad influence on the others.' He let out a noisy sigh and rolled back to his perch behind the counter. I followed him.

'I wonder if you could help me with something. I'm looking for the Scruggins family. I'm a journalist, writing a piece on Michael Cleverly, the man who was found dead in the Rush a couple of days ago. Someone told me he was related to them.' I pulled out my NUJ card and flashed it in front of his face.

His lugubrious face showed a flicker of interest. 'If I don't tell you, someone else will. The boy who was leading the gang of toerags nicking stuff from my shop is the son of one of the Scruggins girls. He's got a different surname, but he's from the same rotten barrel. His mother lives on Meadow Rise. Name's Leeanne.'

'Do you know the number of the house?'

'No, but there's an old banger in the drive and a washing machine on the lawn. You can't miss it. Her mother lives next door, in the last house in the street.' Then, after a pause. 'Do you want to take my photograph? For the article, I mean.'

I told him I didn't have my phone or camera with me, but thanked him for his information.

All the houses on the estate had gardens, and some of those gardens were dancing with colour. One or two featured gnomes on toadstools fishing in small ponds. But the gardens got barer and the houses more forlorn as I walked further down Meadow Rise. Leeanne's house had an old Fiat rusting in the drive.

I decided to start with her mother, next door.

The bell was broken, but when I knocked I could hear scuffling and breathing from inside, though the door remained shut. After knocking a couple more times, I called through the letterbox, 'Hello? Can I please talk to you about Michael?'

Abruptly, the door was opened by a gaunt woman in a saggy dress clutching a balled-up tissue in her hand. 'What do you want now? Can't you leave me alone? I've already told the inspector everything I know.'

'I'm not from the police. My name's Rags Whistledown. I'm a journalist, looking into what happened to Michael.'

She stared at me, then at the NUJ card I was holding up for her to see.

'There are lots of unanswered questions, and I want to find out the truth. Please.'

Her shoulders slumped. 'I suppose you'd better come in, then. I'm Michael's mother. Amanda. Amanda Bates.'

Her nose and eyes were swollen from crying and the story she told was a pitiful one. Last night the police had contacted her with the news that they believed Michael had been found dead – drowned in the river.

'And they said they couldn't find his wife, so they dragged *me* down to the hospital first thing this morning, even though I'm not well. I have agoraphobia and acute anxiety. Then, when I saw him dead, like that, I couldn't stop crying. You see, I was only fifteen when he was born. My mum kicked me out. His dad was married, and didn't want anything to do with him. And then when I got married a few years later, Bobby, my husband, took against him.'

She convulsed into sobs, pressing the balled-up tissues in her hands against her eyes to dam up the tears. A lump came to my throat: I'd been away from the raw, bleeding edge of journalism for a long time. At least I had clean tissues in my rucksack. I pulled out a couple and handed them over. 'Here. Take your time. I know it's difficult.'

'It's just, just … I don't know how I can help you, because I hadn't seen Michael for years. He wouldn't come here, you see, because of Bobby.' She went over to a table littered with old newspapers and coffee cups, yanked open a drawer and pulled out a blue envelope hidden under a pile of magazines. With a shaking hand she held it out. 'But Michael still loved me. Here. Take a look at this.'

I opened the envelope. In it was a note written in flowing, royal-blue script on thick, cream paper.

Mum, here's a little something to tide you over. Don't let that bastard Bobby get his hands on it. Michael.

There was no address or phone number at the top.

'He sent cash,' said Amanda. 'Usually a fifty-pound note. Sometimes more.'

'How often?'

'Every few weeks.'

'And what did Bobby think of the arrangement?'

'He doesn't know about it. He's always at work when the post comes. I give the money to Leeanne so she can buy a few little things for herself and Jimmy – that's her son.'

'Does she live next door?'

'Yes.'

'And have you got any other children?'

'Two more daughters with Bobby, but they've moved away.' Her lips curved into a quivering pout. 'They live in bloody London. Don't know how they can stand it. I never hear from them. Never.'

So, like Michael, they'd escaped. 'Can you think of anyone who might have held a grudge against Michael?'

Her red-rimmed eyes snagged on mine. 'Why do you want to know that? It was an accident, wasn't it?'

'I want to explore all angles.' She shrugged. 'Like I said, I hadn't seen or spoken to him in years. Leeanne might know something. She and Michael were thick as thieves; she's only eighteen months younger than him.'

'Thanks. I'll talk to her.'

Amanda followed me to the door. 'You might have to knock a few times. She's just come out of rehab and they've given her these pills that make her sleepy.'

'OK.'

'And you'll let me know what you find out about Michael, won't you? Here.' She scribbled her phone number on the back of an envelope and handed it over.

'I promise I'll keep you in the loop.'

'And tell me about the funeral?'

'I'll do what I can,' I said. 'But it'll be a while, because there'll be an inquest, to determine how he died.'

When I knocked on Leeanne's front door I got no reply. I knocked again, louder than before, then a third time. A sound behind me made me spin round: the tall boy I'd seen in the shop was watching me from across the road, straddling a bike too small for his lanky legs, stuffing crisps into his mouth. I took a sharp breath: with his hood half down he was giving me a good view of high cheekbones and bright blue eyes. His features hadn't quite settled into adulthood, but his resemblance to Michael was striking. When my eyes met his, he turned and cycled away at speed, dropping the crisp packet as he went. I bent down and peeped through the letter-box; all I could see was a brown carpet with unopened envelopes strewn across it. I walked round to the front window and looked through a gap between the half-closed, mustard coloured curtains. A pair of slender legs and bare feet were propped up on a sofa.

I tapped on the window lightly, then harder, calling Leeanne's name. The legs moved as someone sat up, and a woman's face came into view – a beautiful face, similar to Michael's despite its lines and weariness. Slowly, her eyes focused on me. She struggled off the sofa, made her way shakily towards the window and opened it a crack.

'Who ..? What ...? What do you want?'

'I'm looking into Michael's death. Can I please come in?'

Immediately she was more alert. 'Come round the back.'

I hurried round the side of the house to the back door, which she opened a moment later. 'You from the police? Have you got any more news?'

'No. I'm a journalist, trying to find out how and why he

died, and I hope you can help me. You want to know what happened to him, don't you?'

She blinked, still dazed. Large eyes the colour of a wintry sea searched my face. I felt a pang of sorrow for this young woman: she was as gorgeous as any of the airheads I'd pursued over the years, and wouldn't have looked out of place on the cover of a glossy magazine, but she was stuck here, drugged up to the eyeballs. How had Michael got out? Then the feminist at the back of my brain reminded me that it was easier for men. They couldn't get pregnant, for a start. Leeanne must have had her son, Jimmy, when she was in her teens.

'Course I do. Come in. Can I make you a cup of coffee? Sorry I'm so out of it.'

I followed her into a kitchen that was bare but clean, where she put the kettle on and pulled out a cafetiere and fresh coffee. 'Have you talked to Mum yet?'

'Yes.'

'I bet she was weeping and wailing. She hasn't stopped carrying on since she heard he was dead, but she was a bloody useless mother. The things she let happen to Michael were criminal.' When she turned to face me, her eyes were brilliant with anger. 'Bobby used to thrash the life out of him. I bet she didn't tell you that.'

I didn't reply: I'd worked that out for myself.

'So it was no surprise he fucked off as soon as he could.' With a flounce of hair she turned to pour water over a mound of grains. The rich aroma of good coffee filled the kitchen. 'I'd have gone, too, but I had Jimmy at fifteen. Plus I was an addict by then. I expect she told you that, too.'

'She said you were clean at the moment.'

'Did she? Well I am. I've been in rehab. Got out of the clinic two weeks ago.' A tear rolled from one of her beautiful eyes. 'Michael paid for it. Again. This is my fourth go, and

I'm determined to stick at it this time.' Her head drooped forward for a moment, then she pulled herself together and started putting cups, milk, sugar, coffee, on a tray. 'We were close, you know – not like him and mum. We talked on the phone every couple of weeks. We had the same dad, and that gave us a special bond, even though the bastard never had anything to do with us.'

'Did Michael tell you about what he was up to? His plans?'

'Nah. Not really. He just asked me how I was doing, and whether Jimmy was going to school. That sort of shit.'

'Did you ever meet up with him?'

'Now and then. I met him for a drink a couple of months back. He told me he'd fallen for some Black woman and was going to leave his wife. I tried to persuade him not to. I mean, Patsy's a dozy bitch, but she's got money, hasn't she?'

'Did he tell you this woman's name?'

'Yeah. Something stupid like Seashell. He kept going on about her – said she was his soulmate – all that sort of crap.'

I kept myself busy writing in my notebook. What she was saying supported Shell's story, and I was pleased about that. Leeanne took the coffee through to the living-room and became more talkative under the influence of the caffeine. When I asked her if she knew anyone who might hold a grudge against Michael she wrinkled her forehead in thought. 'Well, he rubbed people up the wrong way because he was ambitious, but I can't think of any enemies as such. Not from round here, anyway.' She confirmed that her half-sisters lived in London, but said she didn't have much to do with them. 'Just Christmas and birthday cards. They think they're better than me.'

I was subdued on the bus ride home. What had I learned? That Shell was telling the truth about their relationship;

that Michael had paid for Leeanne's rehab not once but four times; that he'd had the determination and balls to turn his life around.

But I couldn't for the life of me see any reason why Amanda or Leeanne might want him dead.

12

Tracey Jones

Tracey banged the saucepan full of potatoes down on the stove, in a serious huff. She didn't ask much of Tim. She was stuck looking after the boys while he waltzed off to the salon and sat half the day twiddling his thumbs because the business was going down the tubes. She did all the shopping, cooking and cleaning – and making the household budget stretch wasn't easy, particularly when Damon kept grabbing plastic fire engines and tractors from the shelf of every shop they went in, crying, 'Me want this! Me want this!' They shouldn't put them down there, on a level with a small child's eyes. Toys like that should be high up, where the little sods couldn't reach them.

Today they'd had a rare chance for you-know-what, while her mum took the kids out to the park, and Tim hadn't delivered.

He'd got home at the usual time – just after six – and she'd been waiting for him, squeezed into the lacy bra and G-string he'd given her for Valentine's day three years before. Sex calmed her nerves, put her in a good mood. When they were first married, before the kids came along, they'd

103

done it like rabbits. This afternoon, giggling, she'd pulled him upstairs and pushed him down on the bed. Normally he'd get a hard-on straightaway, and after a bit of foreplay she'd let him climb on top. Lord knows, he didn't have to do anything fancy, because she came as easily as falling off a log.

But today he couldn't get an erection. Nothing. Not a dicky bird, whatever she did. She'd tried touching him – had even gone down on him, though she wasn't keen on the rubbery taste. It was all so bloody humiliating. In the end she'd shoved him away, tugged on her clothes and run downstairs.

It was probably because she'd got so fat, she thought, hacking away at a few tired carrots. Men didn't like fat women: they pretended they did, but what they really wanted were bony girls with big boobs. Perhaps Tim didn't fancy her any more. Perhaps he fancied the snotty cow who'd come round asking questions about that bastard Michael Cleverly. This thought was so devastating that Tracey thumped down on a chair and blinked back furious tears. If she found out that Tim had been off with someone else she'd kill him.

'Trace?'

She rubbed her nose vigorously but didn't look at him. 'What?'

'It's not you.'

'What do you mean?'

'I mean it's not ... it's not because ...'

'Not because I'm *fat*. Not because I'm bloody enormous. Is that what you're trying to say?'

'I love you whatever size you are.'

Rounding on him, she snarled, 'Oh, yes! You *love* me, but you don't *fancy* me. You don't want to *do it* with me.' Despite her rage her clitoris buzzed at the sight of him, slender as a reed, with his belt still unbuckled, leaning on the wall beside the kitchen door.

'I do. I do fancy you. I've just got things on my mind.'

'What sort of things?'

'The business. That sort of thing.'

'Crap! That never stopped you before. The business has been going downhill for years, but it never made you *impotent* before.'

* * *

Alaric Veil

In his kitchen, washing brown rice in a sieve, Alaric was feeling distinctly uncomfortable for the same reason as Tim. After the blazing row with Rags, he'd cycled off to meet Jenny at their usual place close to the reserve, where Jenny had a small holiday let, usually empty because it didn't have the oversized, chrome bathroom fittings most guests required. She was as immaculate as ever, her tawny hair blow-dried into thick waves, her skinny white jeans spray-painted onto a pair of legs women thirty years younger than her would have killed for. She'd been wearing one of her expensive bras, too – one that gave uplift to her breasts and normally gave him an erection even before he'd hidden his bike away in the holiday home's patio garden.

But today: nothing. He hadn't felt turned on. And though she'd done her best – Jenny was a skilful lover who knew her way around a man's body – he hadn't been able to get, let alone keep, a hard-on. Not that she'd gone without. He'd brought her to orgasm with his mouth – no great hardship as he loved the salty taste of her body and the way her vagina contracted around his fingers.

She'd asked him what was wrong and he'd said he didn't know. Just a few things on his mind. These things happened now and then. Blah-di-blah. All rubbish, of course. This had never happened to him before. Never. And he knew what was causing it. Rags. That bloody woman had got him stirred up with her questions about Michael Cleverly. Why couldn't she just leave it alone?

With a sigh, he took a long swallow from the bottle of Black Sheep beer in his hand. He'd been enjoying his affair with Jenny: apart from the excellent sex, he enjoyed getting one over on her husband, and he liked the fact that he didn't have to tiptoe round her. Sasha, his former girlfriend, a brainy beauty he'd met while doing his MSc at UEA, was forever asking him how he was *feeling*, was he *OK*, which was code for her wanting him to ask her these questions. When he did, she went into a litany of complaints, usually about some look he'd given her, or some remark he'd made days before and had completely forgotten. When she had PMT she was strung so tight she'd scream at him if he put a foot wrong.

Since they broke up he'd been coasting along nicely: good job, good house, good sex.

Until Rags came on the scene.

Taking a long swig of his beer, he turned down the gas under the brown rice and looked out at his mini meadow, not seeing the tangle of wildflowers that normally gave him such pleasure. He was thinking.

Thinking hard about the last time he saw Michael Cleverly.

13

Rags

Sunday morning dawned bright as the marigolds in Dad's back garden. At about nine I moseyed downstairs in my pyjamas to make myself a mug of filter coffee. My dad was sitting at the dining room table, gazing intently at the screen of his shiny MacBook. I stood for a moment, watching him, able to see him as others did – a good looking, older man, curious and eager to learn.

I cleared my throat. 'Morning.'

He looked up, pushing reading glasses up into his clipped white hair. 'Morning. I was just taking a look at my new course.'

'Can I see?'

He gazed at me for a moment, with a hint of wariness, then gave a small smile. 'If you like. It's well organised. I'm impressed.'

Pulling up a chair beside him at the dining room table, I watched as he scrolled through the various screens. The twelve-week course was run from the USA by the prestigious Mid-Western University, no less. There were weekly teaching sessions, with supporting texts and questions to discuss. Students submitted two assignments: one halfway through, and a longer essay of up to 3,000 words at the end. A chat room gave the students a chance to swap comments about the course, and to post drafts of their assignments. A reading list directed them to where they might find out more.

'Wow. I didn't know stuff of this quality was available for free.'

'It's good, isn't it? And it keeps my brain ticking over. There are some face-to-face courses in Norwich, but that's a bit of a trek, so I thought I'd give this a try.'

I wanted to tell him I was proud of him. I wanted to tell him that he'd changed, and for the better, but the words wouldn't come to my mouth, so I left him to make my morning coffee. I use an old-fashioned cone and filter paper, so I can make it strong and fresh. I drink it black unless I'm feeling weedy and need a hit of milk. After feeding the water slowly through the coffee, I added a quarter-spoonful of brown sugar, took a sip and held the bitter-sweet liquid on my tongue. Ah. All my London friends had bought the coffee machines that required little sealed packages of coffee. Coffee for wimps, in my opinion, delivering a mean measure of caffeine and a lot of huffery-puffery. A rip-off, too, and ecologically suspect.

Taking my cup upstairs, I got out my notebook and found myself jotting down some ideas for a short story. I'd written some in my early twenties, and even got a couple published – one in *The London Magazine* – but had given them up once my career took off and I found my time more than filled with work. Seeing my dad this morning had started up an itch at the back of my head: why didn't I do something creative? A long time ago I'd thought of writing a novel about a young journalist who gets in too deep when she's pursuing a story about crack cocaine dens. Something like that happened to an old friend of mine, who'd ended up with a serious crack habit and a scar running down one side of her face. She'd got her life back on track, but following her in and out of rehab had almost destroyed her family. My book wouldn't be all gloom and doom: it would have dancing, and love, and sex in it – the highs as well as the lows. I sketched out a few notes for characters, enjoying the whirring of mental cogs that had been idle for a long time. After a few minutes I put the notebook down and sat, quiet, letting sunlight wash over my face. When did I last study, or take a course? When did I last push myself as a writer?

I drained my coffee – enough navel-gazing for the time being – and pulled on a pair of loose, linen shorts and a white, sleeveless tee-shirt. It was Sunday, and I'd decided to take the morning off from the investigation. Time to hit Holkham. Downstairs, when I told Dad of my plans, he surprised me by asking if I wanted some company.

'Napoleon could do with a run on the beach, and we haven't been down there for a few days.'

After a quick slice of toast, we were ready to go. I'd expected to catch the bus, but Dad surprised me by saying that we could go in his car, 'as it needs a little run to charge up the battery.'

'I didn't know you had a car.'

'I don't use it often, but it's perfect for a run up to the coast. It's in a garage round the corner. Come on.'

We walked up to King's Road, turned left and into a long grassy drive. It occurred to me that Michael might have kept a car here, and checked that with Dad.

'He rented the first garage for a while. I saw him driving an old Golf a few times, but I think he sold it a few months back when he started using his works car.'

Napoleon knew where we were heading. He ran, barking, until he reached the farthest garage in a row of five, where he started to scratch at stout doors recently painted with creosote. 'Stop that,' called Dad, at which Napoleon dropped down onto his bum and waited for the slow-coaches to catch him up. Inside the garage sat a shiny black Mini, about ten years old, and in excellent nick. I gave a whistle of approval.

'Bloody hell, Dad. It's gorgeous.'

Dad beamed. 'It's my pride and joy. Napoleon likes it, too. Can you hang onto him while I get it out?' I obliged, and moments later climbed into an interior that smelled faintly of creosote and leather upholstery. 'Do you mind having him on your knee? He likes to look out of the windscreen.'

'I'd be delighted.'

So we pootled down the 'dry road' to Wells-next-the-Sea, with Dad explaining that it got its name from the fact that there was not a single pub on its eight miles. 'It used to be a toll road,' he added, pointing out a four-square house that stood where the toll house had been located. We looped around the edge of the town, heading for Lady Anne's Drive, where we could park close to Holkham beach. As we turned right into the long drive, Napoleon started to quiver with excitement. Dad parked fifty metres from the path to the beach, instructing me to keep a firm hold on Napoleon's lead while he got a ticket from the machine, 'because he can get over-excited and I don't want him running off.' For this outing, Dad had strapped a harness on Napoleon, 'because it's more comfortable for him if he goes nosing around in the bushes.'

I felt a small twinge of envy: I couldn't remember Dad ever taking such tender care over me. I'd been expected to dress myself from when I was a small child, and to iron my school blouse. Then Napoleon looked at me with expectant joy in his eyes, and my resentment blew away like the small, white clouds scudding across the sky.

Once Dad had placed the parking ticket on the dashboard,

Napoleon shook his body from his black-button nose to the tip of his tail and gave me a look that said, 'Come on, then! Let's get going.' The wind was stronger here, by the coast, rippling the tall grass in the water meadows, and I was glad I'd brought a jumper with me. Dad took over Napoleon's lead, and we headed for the beach. As we tramped up the wooden boardwalk, and the broad sweep of the beach opened up before me, I felt a tremor run through me like the breeze stirring the creaky pines: I'd been here before. The sound of our shoes on the boards recalled a time when I was reaching up to hold someone's hand, and was scooped up and placed on a pair of shoulders high above the ground, with just a head of springy black hair to hang on to. That *must* have been Dad. Looking at the back of his neck, the hair clipped into a neat line above tanned skin, I almost said something, but didn't, since any conversation about when he was married to Gwendolyn caused him to shut down, and I didn't want to break the thread running between us.

Let off his lead once we reached the beach, Napoleon tore off in a westerly direction along a broad, sandy path between swathes of salt marsh on which samphire and sea lavender were growing. I dawdled, breathing in air scented with salt and, faintly, with the resin of the pine trees that formed a barrier between the beach and the water meadows beyond. Dad was marching ahead at a steady pace. I jogged to catch up and, on impulse, hooked an arm through his.

He looked at me. 'What's that for?'

'Just enjoying being with you.'

We walked out to the long line of waves breaking in white ripples. Small birds ran to and fro on the wet sand exposed as each wave retreated, leaping into flight when the wave returned. 'Sanderlings,' said Dad. 'Lovely little things, aren't they?' He knew the best route to avoid sinking into wet sand, but at the water's edge I took off my sandals to feel the cool lap of the waves around my toes and ankles. As we strolled back through the woods, between pines and spreading holm oaks, Dad told me the history of these woods – how they were planted in the nineteenth century to protect farmland from inundation. 'And an earlier Lord Coke, who lived over there,' pointing to a monument rising above the trees in the nearby Holkham Estate, 'was an agricultural innovator.'

We finished the morning with a coffee at the handsome, flint-faced Victoria pub. As we relaxed on a squashy leather sofa, I told Dad briefly what I'd found out about Michael's family the day before, adding, 'whatever his faults, he was still looking after his family.'

Dad nodded, then said, 'It looks as if you're doing a good job, Rags, but just be careful, won't you?'

I said I would. We bowled home around noon, and I offered to make us a bite to eat, but Dad said he was meeting a friend for lunch.

'Do you mind looking after Napoleon while I'm out? I should be back by four.'

'Course not.'

After a chunky Gruyere and rocket sandwich, I brought my computer downstairs so I could work at the dining room table while Dad was out.

I spent twenty minutes checking emails and Facebook, (my way of keeping tabs on old friends, though I seldom post anything myself). Carola had put up an old photo of herself and her boys having a picnic on Hampstead Heath, with the comment, 'Missing you guys so much. Can't wait to see you when I get back from Africa next week.' I pondered the difference between Carola's involvement with her boys, and my own growing-up. Basically, I'd been left to get on with things: to organise my school work, sort out my social

life, and arrange after-school activities. I'd never been ferried
to and from drama and music lessons. Instead I'd caught the
bus or walked the mile and a half back home when I was
rehearsing after school. If I say so myself, I was a pretty good
Mercutio in *Romeo and Juliet*. Not that Gwendolyn saw me
tread the boards: she was too busy cooing over little Tarquin.

I gave my head a shake. What was the point in dwelling
on all that? I'd been a fully functioning, independent adult
since I left home at eighteen.

Another email arrived, this time from the posh Oxford
graduate who commissioned features for *All for You*. 'Hiya!
Soz to hassle you on a Sunday, but we've got a Code Black
emergency here. We've had to pull one of the features for
our next issue, and I'd just LOVE to replace it with your
Sex Toys piece. Only snag is I need it by 6 o'clock 2morrow
. Soz about that! But I can pay you an extra £50. Pleeze let
me know if you can do this. Tabby.'

'Yes!' I punched the air. I'd made some preparatory notes,
and should be able to pull the whole thing together in a
couple of hours. Humming *I Will Survive*, I jumped up to
make myself a cup of tea.

But when I returned to the table, the laptop screen was
jumping up and down like a geriatric at a 60s disco, until
with a final whir the computer subsided into silence and a
blank screen. 'Oh, no, no!' I banged my clenched fist on the
table, then rubbed my throbbing wrist-bone, hearing in my
head Carola's measured voice telling me, as she had many
times when we shared a house at university, that I shouldn't
do that, as it didn't help. I did the usual – turn off, unplug,
plug in, turn on. No joy. It was well and truly dead. 'Now
what?' I asked the universe, and got a sympathetic whine
from Napoleon, who'd been dozing in his downstairs basket
before I started my tantrum.

I sat drumming my fingers on the table. Why did the
bloody machine have to conk out now? I could probably

get it repaired, but not on a Sunday, and I certainly couldn't afford a new laptop. But I couldn't pass up this piece of work. I needed the money.

Then my eyes alighted on Dad's MacBook, dormant under a clean, checked tea towel on a side table. He wouldn't mind if I banged out my piece on it, would he? He'd let me look at the online course this morning. People used other people's computers all the time, particularly when they were staying in their houses, and this was an emergency, wasn't it?

In a hurry, before I could think too much, I picked up the laptop and opened its spotless lid.

14

Graham Whistledown

Graham found himself in a right two-and-eight as he drove along the coast road towards his rendezvous.

Early this morning, when he'd opened up his laptop and clicked his way to Findlove, he'd found he'd had thirteen views since yesterday. Well, well, well. He must be doing something right.

His profile picture, taken by an amateur photographer pal he used to work with, made the best of his strong nose and decisive jaw. His white hair had been trimmed into shape by Tim, at *Strands* in town. 'I suppose I don't look too bad,' he muttered now, glancing in the car's mirror and thinking that his skin was reasonably free of the blotches and bumps that bubbled up on the skin of most men his age. In his mind he ran over the words he'd put beneath 'About Me': *Young at heart mature man seeks easygoing woman for companionship and romance. I have no commitments. I'm fancy free.*

Was that right? Did he have no commitments? Oh, he had no relationships hanging around – no unfinished business – but what about his pesky daughter? What about Rags? She'd given him the fright of his life, turning up like that, but, more than that, she'd disturbed the easy calm he'd found since he retired. Last night, wide awake, listening to the chimes of the church clock, he'd been worrying about her latest cock-eyed venture: playing detective. What the heck did she think she was doing? But she wouldn't be told. In fact trying to argue her out of it would probably make her even more determined to continue. As the chimes struck, two, then three, he'd alternated between fuming and worrying. What a bloody nuisance she was! He shouldn't have to be thinking about her at this stage of his life. And she'd brought all her problems – the debts, losing her flat – on herself, hadn't she? Why had she done it? Why had she got herself into such a pickle? Why couldn't she be *sensible*, like that nice lawyer friend she'd brought to lunch in London one time?

As he signalled right and turned up a lane bordered with hollyhocks taller than his head, his heart gave a sudden squeeze. It wasn't simple, you see. She got on his wick, but he loved her to bits. He'd enjoyed the walk they'd taken that morning. He took pleasure in her company and having a female presence in his house. It had been many years since he'd allowed himself that. After Gwendolyn left he'd had a rebound relationship with a clingy accounts clerk called Helen who'd driven him round the twist with her fussing and hints about marriage. After five years he'd called it off. Life since then had proceeded down one long motorway of singledom, broken occasionally by a few lay-bys and service stations of brief affairs that went nowhere.

And now, just as he was hoping to embark on a romantic adventure, Rags had turned up out of the blue, stirring up all manner of emotions.

They'd not been close for years, but when she was a little girl she'd been his companion, his game little helper, buttering toast, hanging out washing, while her useless mother lolled around on the sofa. He'd adored her. And when Gwendolyn took her off to Devon it had broken his heart! A far-off summer evening drifted into his mind, when he'd been sitting at the kitchen table on his tod, eating baked beans on toast, realising that he missed her talk and her silly jokes, missed the way she helped him with the weekly wash in that dreadful old twin-tub, missed her greeny-brown eyes which often looked like they knew things a nine-year-old shouldn't know. Oh, she was smart as mustard, even then. She could see things weren't right between him and Gwendolyn. Then, after she left, he sank into a trough like a cold bath you can't get out of. He longed for her visits, but when she came he was grumpy and cross. He criticised and carped. Told her off all the time. Couldn't tell her he loved her and missed her.

When she was a teenager, things went from bad to worse. On her summer visits he couldn't say a word without her arguing with him about it. She'd argue about anything: politics, music, the environment, the best way to do the washing-up. He'd found the changes in her body alarming, too. She left one summer as a little girl and came back the next year with a grown-up figure and a new wardrobe that was just short of indecent. The length of those skirts! And, of course, she wouldn't hear a word of advice from him. 'Gwendolyn lets me wear them,' was her mantra. Bloody Gwendolyn. The odd thing was, she'd always got her head stuck in a book.

He'd been proud as punch when she started working as a journalist. Upstairs, in his bedroom, he had an album of her early articles. But then she moved to London and started reporting on so-called celebrities he'd never heard of. What a bloody waste of talent! And then, when she lost her job for hacking into someone's emails, he'd been so furious he could hardly speak.

When they met for lunch in that bloody awful restaurant where they served rabbit food she took umbrage because he told her she'd let herself down. She told him to mind his own business. He lost his rag and told her she was a bloody disgrace. That was it. She went berserk. She told him to F off. Told him he had no right to preach to her. Told him she never wanted to see him again. Now, thinking of her face on that day – the flash of eyes that held tears as well as temper – he groaned. He was her father. He should have been the grown-up one. He could see that now.

A Hooray Henry in a four-by-four beeped at him for going too slowly along the winding lane. 'All right, all right,' Graham huffed, pulling over to let him pass, and, with an effort, dragged his thoughts back to his upcoming date. He was on his way to meet *Not so Plain Jane*, and he was going to enjoy it if it killed him.

A few years back he would have scoffed at anyone resorting to a dating website. In fact he'd pronounced more than once, 'They need their bloody heads examined.' But something had changed in him. First of all, when he was coming up to retirement, he'd sold the poky house in Gayton where he'd lived with Rags and Gwendolyn – didn't know why it had taken him so long – and bought the house in The Terrace. He'd thought he'd be bored to tears after forty-five years at the same company, working his way up from the shop floor to the heady heights of credit control, but after retirement he'd got Napoleon on an impulse, and found his heart was opened up by the little dog. He'd discovered the pleasures of looking after another creature, and the dog got him out and about. Soon his days were full of walks, half pints in country pubs, thrifty lunches, doing little jobs around the home. He had his books, his online course, and the HD television he'd bought when he moved here, so he could enjoy watching nature programmes and documentaries.

The only thing he missed was company. He couldn't be doing with the church, or bowls, or suchlike, and he'd never been one for making a pig of himself down the pub with a group of barracking men. He still met up with a few mates from work on a regular basis, but, if he was honest with himself, he wanted a woman in his life, and after yet another solitary Christmas chewing his turkey in front of the TV, he'd decided to give online dating a go.

It had taken him a couple of months to set himself up with a computer and pluck up the courage to do it, but, lo and behold, since he put his profile up on the site three weeks ago, he'd had a flood of women writing to him. Some were obviously a sandwich short of a picnic, but he'd been emailing a few, and had whittled the field down to three possibles, (*Lovely Legs*, *Wake up Little Susie*, and *Not so Plain Jane*), all in their fifties and surprisingly well preserved. He'd met *Lovely Legs* for coffee a couple of days ago, and while her legs were not quite as lovely as he'd hoped, she'd been pleasant enough – an ex-teacher, with a winning smile and a blonde bob. Nice figure, too. But she'd been a bit dull: she'd droned on about pupils she'd taught, the way teachers often did. He wasn't sure he wanted to meet her again, and had decided he'd see all three of his possibles before taking any decisions.

As he turned right onto a winding road that would lead him to The Woodside Bell gastro-pub, a frown gathered on his forehead. Sooner or later a woman might expect him to take her to bed. And it had been a long while. He hoped it was all still in working order. And if they went to bed in his house, what would they think of Napoleon, who slept in a tidy wicker basket in his bedroom? He sighed and signalled to turn into the pub's car park. It would be a good test, wouldn't it? If they didn't like Napoleon, they could sod off. Anyway, nothing was going to happen any time soon, not while Rags was here.

He'd die of embarrassment if she found out what he'd been up to.

Not so Plain Jane was a good-looking woman with fine, sandy-coloured hair and big blue eyes, but she was one of those bony females who won't eat more than a few lettuce leaves. She wouldn't eat the artisan bread in a basket, wouldn't drink a glass of wine, and chose a green salad from the menu for her lunch. *A green salad*. That made him feel like a glutton as he tucked into an excellent steak and ale pie while she picked at her rocket and water cress. She'd said she was interested in history, but it turned out she meant her family history, so he had to sit through an hour of her yakking about how her great-greats were distantly related to the Cokes of Holkham Hall. Graham tried to be patient – he knew he had a tendency to make snap judgements – but he found himself looking forward to getting away from her droning voice. As soon as he could get rid of her, he'd visit a couple of bookshops in Kelling and Wells-next-the-Sea. Then he'd relax in front of the TV with Rags and Napoleon.

Not so Plain Jane pursed narrow lips when he said, over coffee, as tactfully as he could, that he didn't think they were suited, but he wished her well.

'Well, I was going to say the same thing. For a start, I think you're a little old for me,' she said.

Graham glowered at her.

'I'm in my fifties,' she continued, 'and I think you're probably a little older than you've stated on your profile.'

'That's none of your business,' snapped Graham, who'd chopped two years off his age, because sixty-five sounded better than sixty-seven. 'And you can pay me for that green salad.'

Pottering around the bookshops after lunch didn't lighten his mood. He felt stung by her observation about his age.

Bloody cheek! He'd bet a tenner she was older than she said on her profile. Fifty-four: I don't think so. Knocking sixty, he reckoned. By the time he got back to Middleham just before four, he was tired and cross. He'd been stuck behind a tractor the size of a shed for five miles, and was gagging for a decent cup of tea.

But as he walked up the shared path towards his house, thunder clouds gathered on his brow. Napoleon was in the garden, *on his own*, with no Rags in sight. He'd *told* her not to let him out unsupervised in case he chased after a cat and got onto the main road. Then, as he turned in the back gate, through the window he saw her sat at the dining-room table, with his MacBook open in front of her. A scarlet wave of anger flooded his head. She'd been snooping! Humiliation and a choking rage combusted in his head. He hurtled in the door and pulled the laptop away from her, slamming its lid shut.

'What the bloody hell are you doing?' he roared. 'I *told* you not to use my laptop. *And* you've left Napoleon out in the back garden on his own. He could have chased after a cat and been run over by a car!'

Rags stood up and held up her hands. 'Just cool it, Dad. I can explain. I needed to …'

'I don't want to hear your explanations. Two things! Just two things I asked you not to do, and you've done them both.'

'Dad, please! I …'

He found himself pushing and shoving her out of the back door. 'Out! Get out! I don't want you in my house.'

'But, Dad …'

'You can come back in a couple of hours, when you're ready to apologise.'

And he slammed the door behind her.

15

Rags

I stood in the backyard, shaking. Jesus: how dare he treat me as if I were a snotty kid? Yes, I'd been taking a liberty using his computer, but he hadn't given me a chance to explain. As for Napoleon, he must have nipped out the back door when I wasn't looking. Perhaps I'd left it ajar after throwing the ball for him in the back garden when my brain ached from looking up information about inventive vibrators.

Oh shit. Dad would see that I'd been writing about sex toys. That would go down well, wouldn't it?

Now what? I'd got no phone and no money on me, so couldn't ring someone or head for a cafe. I'd have to go for a walk.

I took the route I'd taken with Napoleon once or twice: a circuit of the little park opposite The Terrace, then past The Rampaging Bull and round the town. Walking soothed my jangled nerves, and I was interested to see how swiftly strange places became familiar. Just over a week ago I'd been hunkered over my desk in Stoke Newington Church Street, not expecting to leave the big city, yet now I recognised that particular beech tree trailing coppery branches, and the creaky tune played by the sign of The Rampaging Bull. I turned right into Norwich Road, and made my way to the square where I'd sat having coffee on the day I met Shell. I thought of having an espresso and asking them if I could pay later, but walked on: my nerves were strung tight enough as it was.

I hadn't yet gone into the church. I pushed open the heavy wooden door as quietly as I could, though there was unlikely to be a service going on at 4.30 in the afternoon. The church was empty except for two women: one was tidying up an exuberant flower display, removing a couple of drooping delphiniums, and replacing them with cornflowers. The second woman, wearing a light coat and a bubblegum pink beret, was sitting in a pew near the front of the church, with her head bent in prayer. Neither of them took any notice of me as I walked up the aisle, admiring the high beams and richly coloured windows behind the altar. Though not a believer, I found myself envying these women their quiet certainty that there was a God and that He would always listen to them.

I walked back to the door via a side aisle and went out into the porch. A few notices showed that the church was well used. Apparently it ran an annual art exhibition, and a Christmas tree festival. There was a playgroup once a week, and something called 'Mess and Muddle', which encouraged children to come and make a noise and a mess if they wished. I wondered if the playgroup was the one Damon had briefly attended.

The visit to the church must have affected me, for as I walked past the shady graveyard, on my way back to The Terrace, I felt the first twinges of guilt. I could have waited until Dad got home and asked him if I could use his laptop. I could have waited until Monday and gone to the library to use a computer there (though that might have been awkward if anyone looked at what I was writing and researching).

Why didn't I *think*?

Oh well. It was done now, and I'd just have to wait until Dad had cooled down enough to let me in. I knocked tentatively on the back door, but there was no reply so I decided to leave it a bit longer. The sun was still warm, so I went to the bench in the garden and sat with my face upturned and eyes closed, rehearsing what I might say.

'Hello there.'

Shading my eyes from the late afternoon light I looked towards Dad's garden gate.

Alaric.

My stomach clenched. Great: someone else who thought I was a piece of shit.

'Can I join you for a moment?' he said, walking towards me.

'Please don't have a go at me. I've just had a horrific row with my dad, and I can't face another bollocking.'

I felt the heat of his body seeping through his faded green tee shirt as he sank down on the seat beside me. 'Actually, I've come to apologise. I flew off the handle and that wasn't fair. It's just that the mention of Michael Cleverly's name makes my blood boil. And I know it's pathetic to be furious with someone who's dead, but he wasn't nice. Not nice at all. And I'd like to explain why, if you'll let me.'

Doused in shadow, his eyes were dark as ink. Hair was snaking loose from his ponytail in silky tendrils lit up by the sun behind him. The muscles in my face relaxed a fraction. 'OK. But in return you must believe that I'm going to write the piece about the marsh harriers. That wasn't just a ploy.'

'Friends?' He held out a suntanned hand, and I shook it.

'Friends.'

He invited me to his house for a drink, which I accepted, grateful. Entering the kitchen, I noted the plain, pine dresser and shelves, and the butler sink. 'My ex had the kitchen replaced with all this vintage stuff,' he said, when he caught me looking round. 'I rather like it, though I wouldn't have bothered to do it myself.'

'I like it too.'

With a swift grin he pulled two cold bottles of Black Sheep artisan beer from the fridge and popped off the caps. I took a sip: bitter, hoppy, but clean on my palate. We took our beers through to the living room, whose walls were covered with photographs of wildlife. And, yes, the marsh harriers featured in three photographs showing a bird perching on a bush, lifting off, then soaring in flight, the feathers at the end of the wing-span curled like eyelashes. The furniture was basic – a leather sofa and armchair, pine table and four upright chairs – but the room had a male, spartan energy I liked.

'What a cool room.' My eyes caught his, reviving the tingle I'd felt the day before. 'And I don't see a television.'

'I don't bother with it. I watch films and catch-up on my computer,' he said. 'Anyway, take a seat and I'll fill you in on a few facts about Michael Cleverly.'

I sank into the squishy armchair, taking a mouthful of cool beer.

Dropping onto the sofa, Alaric took a deep breath and began to speak. 'OK. So here's why I hated that bastard,' he said, his face darkening. 'I came across him and some of his mates lamping on the nature reserve. You know what that is, don't you? They drive out there at night, park their cars, turn the headlights on full, then shoot or set their lurchers on the hares in the field. They think it's a great laugh to slaughter one of our most beautiful wild animals for sport. So forgive me if I wasn't his biggest fan.'

'Are you sure it was him?' It was on the tip of my tongue to say that it sounded like something Michael Cleverly would run a mile from, but the red spots of rage on Alaric's cheeks stopped me.

'Of course I bloody am! I live almost next door to him and, though it was dark, I recognised him before they scarpered.'

'One-hundred per cent certain?'

Alaric looked at me steadily, then shrugged. 'All right. Ninety-nine per cent certain.'

'And when did it happen?'

'A couple of weeks ago.'

'Only I have an idea of someone else who might have done it – someone who looks very like Michael,' I said, treading as carefully as I could.

Alaric took another swig of his beer but kept his gaze on me. As before, I was struck by the intelligence in his eyes. My god, I'd missed the company of an intelligent man! My last boyfriend had been a lanky drummer who seduced me with his paradiddles, but bored me rigid with tales of drummers, kits and sticks. He even had a black dog named Ginger, after Ginger Baker.

'Go on,' said Alaric.

'On Saturday I met his nephew, and he's almost his double. Same height, same build, similar features. He got out of approved school a few weeks back. And he's the sort of boy who might do things like lamping.'

We sat in silence for a while, then I asked, 'Can I talk to you about something, in confidence?'

'Of course.'

I had a gut feeling about Alaric. Yes, he was a hothead, but he was sound. So I told him about my unexpected meeting with Shell, my acceptance of the work Shell offered, my visit to Michael's relatives, my conversations with other occupants of the Terrace. As I talked, I felt the weight of his steady attention.

'And you think there's something dodgy going on?' he asked, when I'd paused to take a swig of beer.

'Yes. For a start, I'm sure I saw Tim talking to Michael in the pub on the night he disappeared, but he insists he was at home.'

'Of course he was in The Bull. I saw him.'

Hallelujah! My heart gave an extra thump. I'd *known* I was right about that. 'So why's he lying about it?'

'I don't know, but I can't see that he'd shove Michael in the river. He's not the type – too much of a wimp. Now Tracey's another kettle of fish. I wouldn't want to get on the wrong side of her.'

We sat for a moment, thinking.

'And do you believe what Shell has told you?'

'Yes, I do. For a start, what she told me was confirmed by Michael's sister. They were in a relationship, and he was planning to jump ship from his marriage to Patsy. He and Shell were just about to invest in a property development in the South of France.'

'And you say the police think he fell in the river when he was rat-arsed.'

'Yes, but I'll know more once the inquest has been held, and the toxicology results released.'

'Perhaps he was celebrating and overdid it.'

'He didn't seem paralytic when I spoke to him. Merry, yes, but not drunk.'

'Hmmm.'

We sat in an easy silence. I could get used to this, I thought, then roused myself as Alaric started talking again.

'Rags? There's something else I need to tell you – something else about Michael. You might be right about the nephew, but Michael was a nasty piece of work.'

'In what way?'

Alaric looked down at his hands. 'This is a bit embarrassing. I'm having an affair with someone I shouldn't be having an affair with, and Michael knew about it, though I don't know how. And when I confronted him about the lamping, he said he'd tell her husband if I didn't fuck off and shut up.'

That made sense. Michael would have guessed his nephew was involved, and would do anything to stop him getting into trouble again.

'It's nothing serious,' continued Alaric, 'but I'd be in deep shit if word got out.'

'Why?'

Alaric looked up at me through thick lashes, a spark of mischief in his eyes. 'Because she's married to the pompous, pain-in-the-arse landowner of half the reserve.'

'Ah.'

'And he'd find a way to get me sacked if he found out his wife had been doing a Lady Chatterley.'

'And she's worth it, is she? Worth the risk?' Despite my smile, I was disappointed he was involved with someone.

'She's a nice woman, and we've had a lot of fun.' He drained the rest of his bottle. 'I expect you see me as an earnest do-gooder, but I like taking risks.' His face opened into a proper grin. 'Besides, the sex is pretty bloody good.'

'Too much information!' I called, laughing.

'Sorry.' He stood up and waved his empty bottle. 'Another one?'

'No, I'd better get back and do penance.'

'Have another beer. You haven't told me what the quarrel with your dad was about yet.' Intense eyes looked full into mine. 'And I'd like to know more about you.'

'Really?'

'Really.'

So I accepted another beer, and told him everything, without the bullshit. I told him when and why I'd been sacked from my job. I told him I'd been evicted from my flat. I told him about the bailiffs. I told him about the sex toys article and about using Dad's computer. It took a while – so long I'd almost finished my second beer by the time I'd finished.

He gave a long whistle. 'I'm impressed.'

'Why?'

The mischief was in his eyes again. 'I'm impressed that you're writing an article about sex toys.'

'I don't put my name to those articles. They're written under a pseudonym.' I couldn't bring myself to tell him that they were written by someone called Bee Cool. 'I can't stand those glossy magazines full of inane advice for women who are wearing themselves out trying to be perfect.'

'And how is that different from writing about botoxed celebrities?'

'I've left all that behind me. Even if someone will have me, I'm not going back to that cess pit.'

He laughed.

'Seriously, though, what am I going to do about my dad? He took me into his house, even though we'd hardly seen each other for years, and now I've been a complete arse.'

'No, you haven't. You were thoughtless, and you didn't show enough respect for his house rules, but no serious harm was done, was it?'

I thought for a moment. 'No. I suppose not.'

'Then get back there and grovel. He'll come round. You'll see.'

I found Dad throwing the ball for Napoleon in the garden. Sitting down on the bench beside him, I took a deep breath, so I could get it all out.

'Dad, I'm so sorry. I was completely out of line. What I did was thoughtless and disrespectful. Please forgive me.'

He wouldn't look at me. Instead he called Napoleon over

and started to stroke his head and ears. 'I just wanted some privacy. I didn't want you laughing at me.'

'Laughing at you? What are you talking about?'

'The website. You must have looked at it.'

I took his arm and shook it gently. 'I haven't got a clue what you're talking about. The only websites I looked at were ...' And here I hesitated, not wanting to mention vibrators, handcuffs and masks, '... related to my article.' Dad made a harrumphing sound of disbelief and stroked Napoleon harder. 'Dad! You have to believe me. I know I'm selfish and thoughtless but I would never look at someone else's browsing history. Never.'

He looked at me with bruised eyes. 'That didn't stop you hacking into that women's computer, did it?'

'I didn't hack into her computer! I only looked at her emails, which had been left on the screen. It was a sting, Dad. I was conned. I was too full of myself, and I thought I was cleverer than they were.' I touched his arm briefly. 'I swear I didn't look at anything on your computer.'

'So you didn't see anything about – about internet dating.'

'No!' Ah. So that was what he was worried about.

'Well that's not so bad, then,' he said, and released a long sigh. We sat in silence for a minute or two before he went on, 'I might as well tell you now. You'll find out sooner or later. I've signed up to a site called Findlove. I expect you think I'm a sad old git. At my age!'

'Of course I don't think you're sad. Most of my friends are on dating websites as soon as they're single.' I didn't mention the fact that lots of people used Tinder and Grinder just to get laid. 'And no one thinks they're sad. It's what people do these days.' I squeezed his arm. 'And I'm delighted you're thinking of meeting another woman. You're a good catch, you know?'

Dad made a raspberry sound.

'Can I make you dinner, to say sorry? I cook a mean vegetable curry.'

'As long as it's not too spicy.' He threw the ball for Napoleon, avoiding my eyes. 'And I'm sorry I flew off the handle. I should know how to control my temper by now.'

I pulled him round so we were facing each other. 'Dad? We're two of a kind: that's why we fight. But I'm proud of you.' There: I'd managed to say it. 'And I'm glad I'm here.'

16

Rags

The next morning, before catching the bus to Diss to inves-tigate the estate agency where Michael had worked, I took my laptop to a small firm that repaired computers from an office above the vegetable shop in the High Street, praying they'd be able to fix it by the time I returned that afternoon. If they couldn't, I'd have to finish my Bee Cool piece in the library, hoping no one read it over my shoulder. A cheerful young man with a ginger beard the size of a squirrel said he'd take a look and would probably be able to sort it out that morning. Or, if it couldn't be repaired straightaway, he'd extract the data from the hard disk. 'I could lend you a computer in the meantime, or find you a second-hand one for fifty quid. It'll be an old desk-top but it'll work all right.'

Thinking of the aggro I'd been through trying to get *anything* repaired while living in Stoke Newington I almost kissed him on his beardy cheeks, but confined myself to thanking him very, very much.

I had plenty to think about on the long bus ride to Norwich. For a start, there was what Alaric had told me about Michael. I didn't believe for one minute that he'd been involved in the lamping, but the more I learned about him, the more he was revealed as a nasty piece of work – an operator who knew how to manipulate and control people. And then there was Alaric. I found him attractive, and if he'd been unattached, I might have made a move – and he might have responded. But that wasn't on, was it? He was having an affair with someone else, and I had the feeling he wasn't tacky enough to be unfaithful, even though his lover was married. Mind you, that was no bad thing, I thought, as the bus swirled around the back streets of Middleham and onto the road to Norwich. My romantic trajectory in recent years had gone something like this: meet someone, sleep with them, head for the hills.

It hadn't always been like that. I'd lived with Matt, a TV documentary producer, in my twenties and early thirties. We'd met at university, lived in Yorkshire and moved to London together. We'd been an item that everyone thought would last forever. Hah. Fat chance. Matt had wanted children at a point when I'd been on my way up the slippery pole and had been offered a to-die-for job writing features for a national daily. 'You'll never leave me,' I'd taunted, with a smug toss of chestnut hair that had no need of the dye bottle back then. Oh, but he did leave me, a few months later, for Felicity, his docile, pregnant secretary. And he broke my heart into tiny little pieces and stamped all over them by telling me in blunt detail exactly what he thought of me.

'You've changed: you're not the person I fell in love with. You're too bloody selfish. Too bloody vain. You don't care about *anything* except work.'

Our break-up had destroyed something in me, and I'd not had a serious relationship since. As soon as things got tricky or intense, I scarpered.

Things were different out here, in the Back of Beyond.

Take my relationship with Dad. In London, after a row like the one we'd had yesterday, I'd have stalked off and drowned my sorrows with a few mates in Shoreditch or Soho. Or I'd have cut him off, as I did after we had our monumental row two years before. But that wasn't possible out here. I'd *had* to talk to him. Had to work it out.

The bus took forty-five minutes to hit the sprawling suburbs of Norwich, a city I hadn't visited since I was a child. On the way we passed through unremarkable countryside – mainly huge fields growing grain and vegetables. The traffic wasn't bad but I was glad to get off the single-decker and stretch my legs when it finally hit the bus station. With half an hour to spare, I headed to John Lewis to cruise the bed linen department. My pulse quickened as I feasted my eyes on a cream Egyptian cotton duvet cover decorated with a border of sage-green vine leaves. Then I told myself to stop it: no way could I afford any of this lovely stuff. In any case, I had plenty of bed linen stored in black bags in Carola's cellar. I had a quick squizz round Waterstones, then had to sprint back to the bus station to jump on the bus to Diss, after finding that the centre of Norwich was bigger than I'd thought.

I decided that the A140 was a seriously boring road, then reflected that Dad would probably love it as it was so straight it must have been built by the Romans. Diss was a buzzy market town, larger and more trendy than Middleham. The offices of Gordon and Gordon were on a street corner opposite The Mere, a lake set in a grassy park. Willows trailed graceful fingertips in the greenish water, and a row of cheerful cafes and shops ran alongside the lake. I earmarked the Copper Kettle as a possible meeting place if anyone in the estate agents was prepared to talk to me. Having sorted that out, I crossed the road, pinged the door of Gordon and Gordon open and strolled over to a desk occupied by a girl with coal-black hair.

She looked up with a professional smile. 'Can I help you? Are you interested in buying or selling a property?'

'I'm interested in Michael Cleverly.'

'Oh.' The cheesy grin vanished from her face. 'I'm afraid he doesn't work here any more.'

'I know.' I leant closer. 'What happened to him was tragic, wasn't it?'

The girl looked down at oyster-pink, manicured nails. 'Yes. It was terrible.' When she looked up her eyes were brilliant with tears. 'But I can't help you. Mr Gordon senior has told us not to say anything about Michael.'

I dropped into a chair and leant forward. 'Look. I was a friend of his, a close friend. I just want to know a little more about his life. I want to understand how he could do a thing like that.'

'Like what?' The girl's hazel eyes, framed by false eyelashes, burned with curiosity.

'Like …' I strung out the dramatic pause. 'Like throwing himself in the river.'

The girl's mouth fell open. 'He didn't, did he? I thought it was an accident.'

I moved a bit closer. 'They don't know, do they? No one knows for certain. Look. I don't expect you to tell me anything confidential – nothing about Gordon and Gordon – I just want to get a feeling for how he was in the last few weeks. I need to talk to someone who knew him well. Like you. I'm sure he mentioned you …' reading the name plate on the desk, '… Sarah. He said you were a close friend.'

'Did he?'

'Yes.'

The door opened and closed and an angular, besuited man with austere grey hair marched in. 'Sarah?' he called on his way past. 'Has Mrs Macarthur called about Field Drive?'

'Not yet, Mr Gordon.'

'Then can you please try to get her on the phone for me? Now.' He took his seat at a large desk at the back of the office and started rearranging the ink blotter and pens.

'I'll come back later,' I said. Then, in a whisper, 'or we could meet for a coffee at the Copper Kettle when you take your lunch break.'

Sarah nodded and mouthed, 'Twelve-thirty.'

Sarah was punctual, running across the road with her dark mane bobbing up and down – a sturdy pit pony in a navy blue jacket and skirt. I beckoned her inside the cafe and led her to a quiet table at the back of the room. 'Coffee?'

'Yes, please. Cappuccino with chocolate sprinkles.'

I ordered an espresso and brought the drinks over.

'Did he really say I was a close friend?'

'Yes,' I said, telling myself the lie was harmless. 'He said you helped him unwind when the pressure got to him. I mean, selling luxury homes must be stressful: he told me that some nights he couldn't sleep for worrying about his sales targets.'

'Well,' breathed Sarah, 'he was so motivated. He put his heart and soul into the job.'

'But he was successful, wasn't he?'

'Oh, yes! I mean, the lady customers adored him.'

I bet they did, I thought, continuing, 'He told me only last week he was working on a big sale and looking forward to closing the deal.' I pretended to blow my nose and dab away tears. 'We were going to celebrate with a few drinks – just as friends, of course. But he didn't get in touch, so perhaps it didn't go through after all.'

'Oh, it went through all right, but Mr Gordon took all the credit. He always did. He made Michael do all the viewings for the expensive properties, then he did the final negotiations and got the commission.' Her voice trembled as she spoke.

'Really?'

'That's not right, is it?'

'No.' I fished two clean tissues out of my bag so Sarah could blot her eyes. 'So Michael didn't get any commission from the sale?'

'Not a penny.'

'And that was why he left?'

Sarah's eyes sparkled with tears. 'Yes.'

I had a difficult conversation with Shell while I was waiting for the bus to take me home.

'He definitely didn't get a fat bonus from his work last week. Can you think of any other way he could have raised the necessary funds for the property deal?'

'Why are you asking *me*? I told you before: Michael and I have our own money. We are not in each other's pockets. Perhaps he made a sale this girl didn't know about. How he raised the funds is not important.'

'But it *is* important if he was involved in dodgy activities – drugs, for example – and fell out with some dangerous people.'

'What rubbish! Michael was not interested in drugs. A woman knows these things.'

'Not taking them – dealing in them. That's one way to make large sums of money fast.'

'It's preposterous.'

'Well then, if he wasn't setting up a drugs deal, how did he get the money?'

A cold silence ran down the phone line. 'I am paying *you* to find the answers, but I can assure you that the Michael I knew was not a criminal.'

Yes, but what about the Michael she *didn't* know?

In the synchronous way these things happen, Paddy McKee called as soon as Shell hung up on me. 'You wanted to know about young Michael Scruggins, I believe? Well, he's got form all right, starting with TWOCing at thirteen and progressing to shoplifting. He did four months' youth detention. Got out at seventeen. After that, he's off the radar.'

'Thanks, Paddy. You're a diamond.'

When I got back to Middleham I was hugely relieved to find my laptop had been repaired. The guy in the computer shop would only accept £20. I thanked him and scuttled home to finish off the article before my deadline. Fortunately I'd emailed a rough draft of *Sex Toys: Play Dates for Grown-ups* to myself shortly before Dad stormed in and confiscated his MacBook. (Emailing drafts to myself every half hour was a habit I'd got into after losing a long piece when I spilled a latte over my keyboard a few years back.) I knocked the article into shape and sent it off just before five. Sod it: they'd given me so little notice that it would have to do.

I also found a charger for my phone on eBay and ordered that.

A steady rain had started to fall. Dad was working his way through a course module. I typed up my notes from the visit to Diss, and longed for Alaric to knock on the back door and ask me out for a drink.

He didn't.

Just before six Dad asked me if I'd like a glass of wine. I accepted gratefully. As he brought it over he said, 'Why don't you bring down that guitar from your room? Play me a song or two. You've got a face as long as a giraffe's neck.'

I sighed, not wanting to admit to Dad that I was feeling daunted by the investigation.

'Go on. I've heard you practising.'

So I got the Epiphone from my room, wondering what to play. My renditions of Joni Mitchell still left a lot to be desired and lots of men were not keen on her vocal style. Then it came to me: Bob Dylan. Dad would know his songs, wouldn't he? Perhaps he'd join in. I struck up *Blowing in the Wind* and Dad joined in on the refrains.

'Can you play the drunken sailor song?'

Of course. I'd forgotten we used to sing it on Saturday afternoons while we did the washing. I hadn't played it before, but managed to work out the chords by ear, and after a couple of experiments settled on A minor to G. I strummed away, and we sang through the verses we knew, and made a few up of our own. Then we moved onto *How Much is That Doggy in the Window* (for Napoleon) and by the end of that my shoulders had relaxed and my mood had lifted.

17

Rags

On Tuesday morning I was on the swaying bus to Norwich again. I'd checked the list of inquests scheduled for the Coroner's Court, and confirmed that Michael's was to be opened on that day. Proceedings were brisk. The coroner, a trim woman with a severe haircut, got through cases at an impressive rate. Michael's came up at just after eleven. She presented some preliminary findings: toxicology tests showed that Michael Cleverly had nearly four times the drink-driving alcohol limit in his blood. He'd probably drowned soon after hitting the water. He had a superficial head wound and minor lacerations to his hands and arms, which could have been caused by him falling over while intoxicated. However, his movements after 9 pm on the night he was last seen alive were not clear, and so the inquest was adjourned. It would be resumed once 'further enquiries' had been made.

On the bus home I thought back to that first evening. Had Michael been paralytically drunk? He'd not been sober, but I'd got up close and personal with various drunks over the years, usually collecting material for versions of the binge-drinking on a Saturday night story (yawn), and the drunks I'd seen had been slurring, vomiting, or passed out on the pavement. Michael hadn't been like that. Yes, he'd been tipsy, but his breath hadn't carried the vinegary blast of the seriously drunk.

I'd seen him drink three glasses of wine – no more – over a period of an hour and a half.

I didn't like it. Didn't like it one bit.

When I got back to Middleham, I went straight to the police station, having decided it was time help them with their 'further enquiries'. I told the glum desk sergeant that I'd got information about Michael Cleverly's movements on the day he disappeared. He left me sitting on a hard chair for twenty minutes, then came back to say that DI Chloe Cooper, the investigating officer, could see me for a few minutes.

Chloe Cooper had honey-blonde hair pulled back into a neat bun. Sharp-featured, thin-lipped, she was clearly from the 'no-nonsense' school of coppers. She showed me to a seat, took my name and address, and asked me what information I had.

'I spent some time with Michael Cleverly on the night he disappeared. I've just come back from the inquest, and heard that he had a high blood alcohol level when he died.'

'And?'

'And I wanted to let you know that he wasn't excessively drunk when I was with him.'

She swallowed a sigh. 'And you feel qualified to judge how drunk he was?'

'I'm a journalist. I've seen a good few drunks, and at the

time I saw him, he was not out of his head. Merry, yes, but not totally pissed.'

The detective regarded me with sharp, green eyes. 'Leaving aside the possibility he could have drunk a bottle of spirits after you saw him, we've talked to others who were in the pub, and they've confirmed that he was very drunk – so drunk he could hardly walk straight.'

'What others?'

'I can't give you names, but several witnesses reported that he was swaying on his stool. And the landlord confirmed that he was drunk when he arrived at the pub, and had been drinking steadily ever since he got there – shots of vodka as well as glasses of red wine.'

'I didn't see him drinking any shots.'

'And you got there, when?'

'About half past seven.'

'So you can't say how much he'd been drinking before you arrived.'

'No. But I can say how much he drank while I was with him – and that wasn't much. I was sitting at the bar, talking to him, and in about an hour he drank only two glasses of red wine. I think he'd had one other glass before that.'

Chloe Cooper made a couple of notes on her pad then looked at her watch. 'I can't give you any more time now, but thank you for coming in. Our enquiries are continuing.'

'But you think it was an accident, don't you? You think he got blind drunk and fell in the river.'

'As I say, our enquiries are continuing.' Standing up, she gestured to the door. 'Good day, Miss Whistledown.'

I left the police station in a bad mood, but when I got home my new charger had arrived. I ran upstairs and plugged in my phone. It started charging up. Wahoo! I did a happy dance round the bedroom. With my phone and computer working again, I was reconnected to the world.

It was a beautiful afternoon, so I asked Dad if I could take Napoleon on an outing. I fancied catching a bus to the coast, then picking up the Coasthopper service to the Cley Marshes nature reserve. If I was to write a feature on marsh harriers, I should learn more about bird life on the North Norfolk coast. Plus I'd heard they had a mean eco-cafe there, with a roof sprouting grass. The next time I met up with Alaric, I could show him that my interest in bird conservation was serious.

'He's got to you, hasn't he?' said Dad, without looking up from his library book about Athens and Sparta.

'Who?' I felt myself start to blush, wondering how my father knew I'd been thinking about Alaric.

'Napoleon. He's like that: even people who don't like dogs go soppy when they get to know him.'

'He's adorable,' I said, relieved. Then I sighed, because I was beginning to get a sense of the complexity of the job I'd taken on.

Dad pushed his specs up into his hair and looked at me properly. 'Is something upsetting you?'

I took a deep breath. 'I went to the opening of the inquest on Michael Cleverly's death this morning.'

'Oh.'

'And toxicology reports show that he was extremely drunk.'

'Well, that settles it, doesn't it? It's like those youngsters who get blind drunk and fall in the river. There was a young girl who did that last year in King's Lynn. Blooming idiots.'

'He didn't seem drunk when I was talking to him.'

'But the toxicology reports will be correct, won't they?'

I pulled a face. 'Yes. They'll be correct.'

'So you can tidy this whole thing up. Report to that lady

who asked you to look into it, and get on with finding a proper job.'

'I'm trying to find a proper job,' I said, struggling to keep the frustration out of my voice. 'I applied for one only last week.'

Dad's mouth opened then closed. I knew what he was going to say: *Well, you've only got yourself to blame.* But instead he said, 'Could I come to Cley with you? I'll drive. I fancy stretching my legs, and it'll take you a while to get there on the bus.'

Grateful, I thanked him, and we set off with an excited Napoleon.

From the cafe, where we stopped off for a quick coffee, we enjoyed a good view of Cley Marshes. The patchwork of pools and lagoons glistened like mercury in the afternoon sun and, beyond them, waves tumbled onto the beach. Dogs were not allowed in the reserve, but a lovely walk took us around the edge in the direction of the sea. On a long, extendable lead, Napoleon seemed happy enough snuffling around in the grass verges.

'He understands he's not allowed to run around the bird nesting sites,' said Dad, proudly, and though a week ago I'd have doubted his boast, I was coming to believe that the little dog was far more sensitive than I'd given him credit for. When we finally reached the shingle beach, we let him off the lead and threw sticks for him. A salty breeze blew away the last scraps of my frustration and doubt. Dad and I avoided talking about the investigation; it was enough to enjoy this place, enjoy the birds, the clouds, the music of the waves.

I promised myself I'd come back here with a good pair

of binoculars and spend some time in the hides watching the birds.

When we got home I decided to take myself down to the river, to the spot where Michael had been found: I wanted to see if there was anything the police had missed. The bank was still trampled and muddy, but otherwise the spot had returned to its sleepy state. The current was strong and steady: strands of weed stretched out in the river's flow, reminding me of Ophelia's hair in Millais' painting. Michael's hair had been short – a sharp, stylish cut I was sure hadn't been delivered by Tim. And Tim had lied. Why? I decided to talk to him again. And I hadn't yet talked to Patsy. I'd pay a visit to her father's house in Fairham Market. See if I could track her down.

I noted with a little pang that there were no bouquets, no flowers, no cheesy messages. It seemed that Michael had been unloved in this town. Then, as I turned to go, I saw a drooping bunch of flowers collapsed against a tree: roses, delphiniums and lupins that looked like they'd been nicked from people's gardens. I went over and found a card in a spiky hawthorn hedge a few feet away, probably blown there by the wind.

I will love you forever XX

Was this another lover? I looked closely at the handwriting – the rounded letters. On the front of the card, a teddy bear was weeping huge blue tears.

Then it came to me: this had been left by a child.

18

Rags

I got home to find Dad, in a striped apron, putting a steak and kidney pie in the oven to heat up. New potatoes sat in a pan with a sprig of mint, ready to be boiled, and he was busy de-stringing and chopping runner beans. 'Thought you might be hungry,' he said, gruff.

'Thanks, Dad.'

'I suppose you're going to carry on, then?' he said, with his back still turned.

I stifled a sigh. 'Yes. Apart from anything else, I need the money. But more than that, something's not right. People are not telling the truth.' Dad gave a *harrumph*, which I ignored. 'I need to talk to Patsy. Do you know where her father lives?'

'Somewhere in Fairham Market. Patsy once told me it was a gloomy old dump, and she was glad to be out of it.'

'Have I got time to pop round to Gerry's? She might be able to give me the address, since she knows everyone and everything.'

He took a quick look at his watch. 'Yes. Tea will be on the table at about half six.'

Gerry opened the door so quickly I was sure she must have seen me approaching.

'Hello there,' I said. 'Sorry to bother you again, but I wondered if you could help me with something.'

'Of course,' she said, with a nervous grin.

'Terrible news about Michael, wasn't it?'

'Heartbreaking.' Tears filled her eyes. 'I still can't take it in.' Bony hands reached out and clutched mine. 'It was so out of character. I mean, Patsy was always the one who liked a drink.'

Before I could respond, a man appeared at Gerry's shoulder – a tall man with a lock of sandy hair falling over his forehead, and broad, regular features. Dressed in a turquoise cotton shirt and faded jeans, he was carrying a bit of extra weight, but this didn't detract from his good looks. 'Hello there.' He held out his hand. 'I'm Hector, Gerry's husband. I don't think we've met.' His grip was firm and perfumed with sandalwood soap.

'Rags Whistledown. I'm staying with my father, at number two.'

'Ah yes. Gerry told me we had a new neighbour. How are you finding our little town?'

I found my mouth responding to the smile beaming from his mouth. 'I rather like it. It makes a welcome change from London.'

'And how can we be of help?'

'I'm trying to get in contact with Patsy. I'm writing a piece about what happened to Michael. It started off as an article about people who go missing, but now …'

Hector's face became serious. 'Yes. Such a tragedy. It's hit us hard.' Another gulp from Gerry. 'Look,' he said. 'Why don't you come in? No need to talk about this standing on the doorstep.'

'Thanks.'

We went through to the lounge, where Gerry sank into the armchair and sniffed into a handkerchief. 'I'm sorry,' she said, her voice wavering on the brink of tears. 'I don't know what's come over me.'

Hector patted one of her knobbly knees. 'Of course you're upset, darling. He was our neighbour.' He turned towards me. 'I know Michael had his ups and downs with other people, but we always got on. Whenever I ran into him, he told me about his plans for his property company. And, do you know what? I think it was going to be a success. We thought of investing in it, didn't we, darling? If I hadn't been expanding my practice we would have done.'

Another gulp from Gerry.

'So you think he was a good businessman?'

'Well, he was an excellent salesman. The last time I spoke to him he said he was waiting to have a loan approved, and then he could launch his first development. I congratulated him.' He gave me that easy smile again. 'I admire someone with get up and go.'

'And did you see him on the Friday he disappeared?'

Hector shook his head. 'Gerry and I went out for a meal, didn't we, darling? Didn't get back until about midnight.'

'I'm hoping to have a word with Patsy. Do you know her father's address?'

Hector and Gerry exchanged glances and shook their heads. 'Can't say I do,' said Hector. 'I have my practice over there, but he wasn't one of my patients.'

'Do you know his name?'

'Something Scottish – Macduff or Macdonald, or similar. But if you go over to Fairham Market someone will be able to direct you to his house. It's a small community – everyone knows everyone.'

'I'll do that.' I stood up. 'And thank you so much for talking to me.'

Hector stood too, and shook my hand again. 'My pleasure. And you must come round for a drink some time. Gerry and I love to entertain, don't we darling?'

After another gulp, Gerry managed to force out, 'Yes. Of course.'

As I left their yard and walked up the shared path, I was sure someone was watching me from an upstairs window.

The delectable smell of flaky pastry met me as I came in the back door. Dad, prodding the potatoes with a fork, turned to me. 'Oh, I've found out where Patsy's father lives. I rang a pal who used to do some gardening for him: Sea Lane, just off the High Street. He says you can't miss it: it's a Georgian farmhouse – the only one in a sea of bungalows. His surname's Macdonald. Says there's no sign of Patsy's mother.'

I dashed over and gave him quick hug. 'You're a diamond, Dad. Did you know that?'

He gave me an embarrassed smile and shooed me away. 'Lay the table, will you? This food won't be long.'

19

Rags

There was no Macdonald in Sea Lane, Fairham Market
listed in the phone book – he must have opted to be ex-di-
rectory – so I couldn't ring, but I decided to head out there
in any case. I caught the bus that left just before nine the
next morning, having decided against asking Dad if I could
borrow his car: I might be pushing my luck after our latest
row. And imagine if I dented the bumper or scratched the
paintwork! Until recently I would have had my own car –
an old but decidedly classy black Beamer. In fact I would
have driven from London, swooshing through Brandon and
Swaffham until I reached the quiet roads of North Norfolk.
But I'd flogged the car a year ago when I could no longer
afford to keep it on the road.

The bus was fine. It bumbled through rolling countryside
towards the tang of the sea, glimpsed now and then as a
glitter of pale blue beyond grey-green salt marsh. Fairham
Market was set a mile or so back from the coast, but there
was a breath of salt in the air, and a keen breeze ruffling the
cottage gardens crammed with roses, delphiniums, stocks
and geraniums. 'I could live here,' I muttered, sizing up

the deli groaning with luscious olives and cheeses. After a pleasant half an hour nosing around pricey dress shops, a scrumptious cake counter, a crammed second-hand book shop and a couple of art galleries, I wasn't so sure. Prices were high, and the accents of the people buying suggested that some of them were related to the socialites I'd been following around for the past decade.

Nice place to visit, though.

I set off up Sea Lane. As Dad had said, Patsy's father's house was easy to find, set back from the road, a few minutes' walk from the shops. Though the building was a handsome double-fronted farmhouse, it was overshadowed by trees in a front garden conspicuously short of flowers. Instead the beds were stuffed full of gloomy, spiky shrubs. The whole place had an air of stinginess and austerity that gave me the creeps. It was obvious there was no Mrs Macdonald in residence: the place had the same forlorn air as my dad's old house.

I walked up the gravelled drive and rang the bell. From inside the house I heard a shrill ring, but no footsteps or sound of occupation. I rang again. Nothing. After a quick look over my shoulder, I bent down and peeped through the letterbox. Post was piled up on the mat. I decided to snoop a little more: no point in wasting the whole trip. A path led round the house to a back garden larger than the front, but similar in its preponderance of looming trees and overgrown shrubs. A small stone patio held two urns that contained only dry soil. Peering through the locked French windows I saw a room containing a battered leather sofa and two armchairs. No sign of bookshelves, and no photographs or personal items on display. I went to the other side of the house and, on tiptoe, looked into a kitchen that was surprisingly modern, but lacking any sign of occupation. No plants, either, and everything tidied away. One thing was certain: no one was here. I retraced my steps to the front of the house. I'd ask around the local shops; I was sure someone would know where Patsy and her father had gone. People noticed; people gossiped.

But I didn't have to go as far as the village. An elderly man had paused at the gate to catch his breath, leaning heavily on a walking stick. He called to me as I approached, in a voice stronger than his bent frame. 'If you're looking for Major Macdonald, you won't find him. He's off abroad. Cyprus, I think. Won't be back for a few weeks.'

'Oh, thanks. I was actually looking for his daughter. Do you know if she's gone with him?'

The man made an odd sound that might have been a laugh. Shrewd, watery eyes squinted at me through thick lenses. 'Gone with him? Not likely. He has a lady friend out there, and doesn't want Patsy playing gooseberry.'

Ah. I liked the major even less. 'Patsy's husband died recently,' I said. 'Did you know?'

'Yes. Blooming shame. I know she was over the moon when they got wed. She didn't get on with her father, you see, and I often heard them arguing. I live next door,' he said, pointing his stick at a neat, white bungalow. 'And during the past week the two of them have been going at it like hammer and tongs, just like they used to before she got married.' He paused for effect. 'She's gone now. They say in the village that he's put her into a private hospital, or clinic, or whatever they call them, up near Hunstanton.'

So Daddy had arranged rehab; Patsy was drying out. 'She must have been in a bad way.'

'She was. You've never heard such a noise: caterwauling, shrieking, breaking things. A spell in hospital might do her good. She's not right, that girl. Never has been since her mother died and he packed her off to boarding school.'

So her mother had died. Poor Patsy, left to the tender

mercies of an unloving, despotic father. No wonder marriage to Michael had been so appealing. There was a long pause, filled by the man's wheezy breaths. Sensing he had more to say, I said, 'Do you mind me asking you a personal question? What did you think of Major Macdonald?'

'Bloody horrible man. Ran over my cat and never so much as said sorry. Nasty to his daughter, too. Oh, she's a ruddy menace when she's drunk, but she was a nice little thing once upon a time.'

'Do you know the name of the clinic she's in?'

His face screwed up with the effort of trying to remember. 'No. Can't say I do, but you'll find it easily enough on the internet.'

'Thank you, Mister ...'

'Edward. Just call me Edward.' He held out his hand and I shook it. The skin was satiny over swollen knuckles.

'Look.' I fished out my card. 'Will you please give me a call if Patsy or her father come back to the house? I'm a journalist, looking into what's happened to Michael.'

He peered at the card, holding it close to his eyes. 'I doubt either of them'll be back any time soon, but I'll do it if you do something for me.'

'What?'

'Join me for a drink down at The Railway Arms some time. I get right bored on my own, and I'd appreciate some female company.'

'Done. Give me your phone number and I'll give you a bell when I'm coming over this way.' I scribbled it in my notebook, thinking that the old boy might be good for local gossip.

I had a half-hour wait before the next bus back to Middleham, so took another stroll round the village. On the corner of a side street I saw a sign for a dentist's surgery and wondered whether this was Hector Goodchild's emporium.

I went over. His name was on the sign, below the words *A Certain Smile*. I nodded in appreciation; it was rare to run across a man who knew the works of Francoise Sagan. I strolled into a spotless reception area, with not a hint of the antiseptic smell that usually pervades dental surgeries. In this room, the air was perfumed by a huge bunch of white roses and lilies in a glass vase that would break a bone if you dropped it on your foot.

The receptionist, a beautifully groomed woman in her twenties, with ebony hair pulled back into a loose chignon, gave me a professional smile. 'Hello. Can I help you at all?'

'I'm looking for a dentist, and wondered if you were taking on new patients,' I improvised.

'We do have some vacancies on our list, but I'm afraid we don't take NHS patients. However, we can recommend some dental treatment plans.' She pulled a brochure from her desk. 'Perhaps you'd like to look at some of our literature?'

'Thank you.' I sank into a white armchair and leafed through the glossy pages. Hector Goodchild's handsome face beamed out from the first page. Smaller photos of two other (female) dentists were printed below his pic. On the next page was a photograph of two shiny dental nurses, smiling to show flawless rows of teeth. There was no sign of prices. 'Do you have a list of your charges?'

'Of course.'

The receptionist handed over a smaller, printed list. Not cheap.

'And perhaps you'd be interested in our pamper day? We're launching a whole new range of beauty treatments and are inviting people in for a glass of fizz next Saturday. Here.' Smiling, she passed me a leaflet decorated with balloons and popping champagne corks.

'Thank you.' I took the leaflet, though I loathe the word 'pamper'. It's such a squashy, infantile word – a brand name for nappies. The idea that women need special pampering days sets my teeth on edge. I like a massage as much as the next woman, but surely women need good treatment all the time? Besides, why aren't *men* invited to pamper days? Answer: because they usually have a woman running round after them picking up their dirty socks and ministering to their needs. You seldom see a man run ragged by domestic duties.

Inner rant over, I ran my eye down the list of beauty treatments. They included teeth whitening (£595) and Botox (£350 a pop). Compared to London prices, these were reasonable enough. I had a feeling they might be popular with the ladies of Fairham Market.

A door at the far end of a corridor opened. A trim dental nurse escorted a woman in her sixties with a smooth face out of the room, saying, 'I do hope everything is to your satisfaction, but please come back to us, if not,' in what might have been a Russian accent. Behind her, I caught a glimpse of Hector before the door closed. I glanced at my watch: time to get back to the bus stop. 'Thank you so much,' I said to the receptionist. 'I'll take these away and think about it, if I may.'

20

Rags

I needed to tackle the residents of The Terrace again. Needed to find out whether they'd remembered anything more about the night Michael went missing, and whether they could think of anyone who might hold a grudge against him – a grudge serious enough to kill him. So far I'd come up with bugger all.

Then I had a lucky break. As I was walking home along the footpath, a lanky teenage girl caught up with me and dragged me towards the graveyard. 'I've got to talk to you,' she said, her voice trembling. 'Everyone's been telling lies about Michael, and I want you to know the truth.'

'And you are?'

'Iona. I knew him – knew him properly, not like Mum and Dad, and all the other losers in the street.'

A penny dropped. 'You're Gerry's daughter?'

'Yes.'

She pulled me over to a bench shaded by a clump of yew trees. Nearly six foot tall, with glossy sheets of strawberry-blonde hair and blue-green eyes, Iona was a beauty in the making. She had the easy good looks of her father combined with the striking colouring of Gerry. Her grubby white tee-shirt had *Girl Power* scrawled over it in black letters. A pair of denim shorts barely scraped her bum. Her long, long legs in black tights were stuffed into Doc Martens boots, with half undone laces.

'So, what do you want to tell me?'

'Michael was nothing like people have been saying. He was – he was nice to me, and he helped me out and, and ...' Her words stuttered to a halt as she tried to hold back her tears.

'So what sort of relationship did you have with Michael?' I asked. 'Did you …?'

Iona turned a furious face on me. 'No! Of course not. He was my *friend*. He met me one day on the path to town when I was being all pathetic, crying, because I'd had a shit day at school and then Mum had got on my case about my room, telling me it was a mess and I should clear it up, and he asked me if I wanted to come for a drive to the coast, and we drove down there in his car and he let me talk all the way and he listened – really listened – not like Mum who says she's listening and then gets it all wrong. And then he bought me an ice cream and we walked along the quay at Wells and it was totally fucking magic, man. And he told me that he was all mixed up when he was young but that it got better when you got older. He was *mega*. He was *awesome*.'

'And did you do it again? I mean, was this a regular thing?'

Iona looked down at her hands. 'No.' Her young, earnest face lifted. 'But I sometimes bumped into him on a Friday night, and he was *never* drunk. *Never*. That story about him being pissed is total fucking bullshit.'

'And did you see Michael on the night he died?'

'Yes.' She took a long shuddering breath. 'I was in the park when he came out of the pub, and I saw someone ride past him on their bike and shove him over – I mean, how sick is that? So I went over and asked if he was OK, and he said yes and I asked him if I could, like, take a walk with him and talk – just talk – but he said no.' Her eyes filled with tears. 'And I argued with him. I *shouted* at him.' She dropped her head in her hands and sobbed so hard her whole body shook.

After a couple of minutes I touched her gently on her arm. 'Do you know where he went?'

She swallowed hard and took a deep, shuddering breath. 'I followed him for a bit, and I'm sure he was going towards the high school, not the river. I mean, why would he go there?'

Good question.

'But then I ran into Debbie near Asda, and we went to her house.'

'Did you leave the flowers for him, on the river bank?'

'Yes. No one else cared, except Patsy, and she was always pissed out of her head. You'd think his wife would leave flowers for him, wouldn't you?'

'I don't think she was around when his body was found.'

'But she could have come back, couldn't she?' cried Iona. 'I bet her dad wouldn't let her. I know he hated Michael. He's a total fascist. Why do women let themselves be bossed around by ugly old bastards?'

There was no easy answer to that

Grabbing my arm, Iona continued, her voice rising, 'Michael was *murdered*, wasn't he? I *know* he was. Mum keeps telling me I'm crazy, but I *know* he was.'

While I was wondering how to respond to that I heard footsteps on the gravel path: Gerry. With another of those anguished gulps she threw herself down on the bench and clasped Iona in a bony hug. 'Hush, darling. You don't know what you're saying. You're just upset.'

Iona struggled to free herself and stood up, shouting, 'You and Dad never listen to me! I *hate* you!'

With that, she burst into a run towards the footpath, with Gerry in pursuit.

Wow. I felt like having a stiff gin to fortify myself after that, but instead went home to a lunch of mushroom soup and a ham sandwich with Dad. I wanted to confide in him – this investigation lark was hard when you didn't have an editorial team and a whole pack of fellow journalists to swap ideas with – but knew he'd worry about me if I told him Iona was sure Michael was murdered. Carola – wise, sensible Carola – was tied up teaching her course in Nigeria. Then I thought of Alaric. Should I? Would he think I was chasing him? Oh, sod it. I rang his mobile and left a message asking him to join me for a drink in The Rampaging Bull after work.

Over lunch Dad was fidgety. I wondered if I'd upset him (again), but after he'd dabbed his lips with his napkin, he asked me if I'd take a look at one of the profiles on the dating website.

'I'd love to.'

'And you won't crack jokes, or make fun of me?'

'Of course not,' I said, though Carola and I had rolled around cackling at some of the profiles when I'd had a brief go at internet dating. I'd hated it – the way everyone bigged themselves up, the disappointment when someone turned up six stone heavier and ten years older than they'd said on their profile. The couple of dates which seemed to be hopeful fizzled to nothing. No, it was not for me.

But lots of people have met partners through dating sites and apps, and perhaps it would work for Dad.

'You see, I've met two ladies,' he said, opening up his computer and avoiding my eyes. 'The first one was nice enough, but the second one was a complete washout.' He clicked and brought up a profile. 'So this is the third lady I'm thinking of meeting. What do you think?'

I scanned down the profile picture and information. *Wake up Little Susie* was a shapely redhead with a warm smile. Her interests were listed as *country walks, country music, countryside*. 'I like that,' I said. 'She's witty. What does she do?' Scrolling down I saw she was a volunteer at the box office of a local theatre. 'Dad, she sounds great.'

'But she might be mad on people like Johnny Cash, and he's not my cup of tea at all.'

'And she might not. Country music has changed, you know.'

'Has it?'

'Yes.' I pulled up a chair. 'Can I play you something?' When he nodded, I called up Kacey Musgraves on YouTube and clicked on *Silver Lining*, a song I'd learned on the guitar, and played when I needed to give myself a lift. 'See?'

'I suppose it's not so bad,' he admitted, still looking dubious. 'But suppose she wants me to go to a concert with her?'

I laughed. 'Just meet her for a coffee or a drink. If you like her, you can suggest going on to have something to eat. If she's not for you, just wave goodbye.'

'The last one would only eat lettuce leaves. It was a blooming waste of time.'

'But this woman might be different. Give her a go.'

I left Dad one-finger-typing a message to *Little Susie* and set off for Tim and Tracey's house. Taking a deep breath, I rapped on the back door. Heavy footfalls announced Tracey's approach. The door jerked open, and when she saw me her face screwed up as if she'd just trodden in dog shit. 'What do *you* want? Stop harassing me. That's illegal, that is.'

'A man has died and I'm trying to find out what's happened to him. Is that so bad?'

'We know what happened to him; he got rat-arsed and fell in the river. And you should be leaving that to the police and not poking your nose in where it's not wanted.'

'Why did you and Tim lie about him being in the pub that night?' I yelled, as Tracey started to shut the door.

'Piss off,' she shouted as the door slammed.

'Cow,' I muttered under my breath, smarting at being so thoroughly trounced.

I stomped along to Doll and Freddy's house. When I knocked, the door was opened by a smiling Doll with a gleaming grey bob.

'Is Freddy in? I'd just like to have a few words with her about Michael Cleverly. I'm wondering if she's remembered anything more about the night he went missing.'

'Oh, I'm sorry, dear. Freddy's not here. She's gone on one of those retreats in the middle of nowhere. She goes once a year, to replenish her spirituality.'

Replenish her spirituality, my arse. Freddy was keeping out of the way. 'Could I ring her?'

'Oh no, dear. Even I'm not allowed to call her.'

'And when will she be back?'

'I'm not entirely sure. The retreat is for a week, but after that she might go and visit some relatives in the north.'

'And did she tell you anything more about that Friday night?'

'No, dear, she didn't. And now I'll have to send you on your way, as my daughter's going to telephone any minute. Goodbye.' And, with that, still smiling, Doll closed the door quietly but firmly in my face.

No joy there, then.

I knew there was no point in going round to see Gerry and Iona at the moment, so I slouched back home to find Dad putting the phone down. He turned to me, face lit up. 'I've just spoken to Susie. We're meeting for a coffee later, in

Fairham Market. She's a dog lover, so I'm taking Napoleon along.'

Great. My *dad* was going on a date, and the only offer I'd had was from an octogenarian. 'That's brilliant, Dad,' I said, willing myself to be gracious. 'I really hope it goes well.'

He said he was going out on a couple of errands and would be back later.

Right. What was it Samuel Johnson said? Something like, 'If you're solitary, be not idle.' Time for Bee Cool to roll up her sleeves. I spent three hours researching a couple of pieces: one on sexy foods, the other on bondage (*All Tied Up with the One you Love*). I was pretty certain *All for You* would take the bondage article, as they'd jumped at the one on sex toys. The other feature (*The Food of Love*) might be picked up by a more mainstream mag. I also searched the job advertisements, but most of them were for posts in social media, which was not my bag of bananas. Face it: I was turning into a dinosaur at the age of 43. I typed up pitches for both the Bee Cool pieces, and sent them out. Within a few minutes an email pinged. Bingo! *All for You* were interested in the bondage piece, and wanted me to pitch another two, so they could do a three-part series on how to spice up your love life. They were offering £850 for the three – an increased fee. I replied, saying I'd email over ideas for the other two articles in the next couple of days. Then I returned to the subject that really interested me: Michael Cleverly. It was time to summarise what I'd found out so far and send it to Shell with an invoice. Drawing on my notes, I wrote a report for Shell. My concluding points read:

• *At the inquest the post mortem report revealed that Michael died from drowning in the River Rush while he was intoxicated, but he was seen walking towards the high school that night – the other direction to the river.*

- *Toxicology results show that he was extremely drunk, but you've told me he never drank to excess and others have confirmed this. I'm sure he wasn't drunk enough to fall into a river and drown at the time I parted from him.*

- *When he was found he had a minor head wound and lacerations to his hands and arms. Though these were explained at the inquest as being consistent with the wounds a very drunk person can sustain by falling over, banging into things, etc. this seems questionable to me.*

- *He was unpopular with his neighbours and workmates, but none of them appear to have a motive for killing him, though it's possible one of them killed him accidentally, perhaps while they were arguing or fighting. I've visited his mother and sister, and found that he was supporting them financially. They had no motive to harm him.*

- *I've learned that his wife Patsy is in a clinic in North Norfolk, being treated for alcoholism. I propose that I visit her, as she may be able to help with the questions below.*

- *I'm not convinced that Michael's death was accidental. I've talked to the police, but they don't believe that his death was sinister. They won't investigate further until I can provide them with more clear evidence.*

The following questions urgently require answers:

- *How and where did he get so drunk?*

- *How and where did he sustain the wounds on his head and his hands?*

- *Who had a motive to harm him?*

Please confirm that you want me to continue with my investigation.

I emailed the report to Shell, together with an invoice for 12 hours' work: £360.

Send.

I must have dozed off on my bed listening to Radio 4 because a quiet tap on the door woke me up.

'Come in.'

Dad stood there, in his striped fisherman's sweatshirt and ironed jeans, immaculately shaved and groomed. 'Do I look all right? I'm just about to head off, and I'm nervous as a blooming kitten.'

'You look bloody gorgeous.' I jumped up and hugged him. His hands waved around as if they were uncertain of what to do, then closed round my back.

After Dad had left, trailing wisps of manly aftershave, I footled around with a few things. I started drafting a piece on the marsh harriers, enjoying writing about something other than female sexuality. At about 7 o'clock my phone pinged. Shell had replied.

Continue with your investigation. I'll transfer payment for your invoice.

Wahoo! For the first time in two years I'd earned over £500 in a week. To celebrate, I poured myself half a glass of Muscadet from what was left in a bottle in the fridge. As I was taking my first celebratory sip, my phone rang. It was Billy, the guy who'd known Michael when he was a child. He said he'd remembered something about Michael, and did I want to meet up for a drink?

I pulled on a pair of white Levis and a loose, flowery Karen Millen shirt. Five minutes later I was out of the door and on my way to The Rampaging Bull.

21

Tracey Jones

Tracey watched Rags' trim arse pass beneath her bedroom window with a sneer. 'What's she up to now?' she muttered, for Tracey was firmly of the opinion that all incomers were troublemakers, and this one was in the premier league of troublemakers because she'd upset Tim. She must have said something to him because he'd been a nervous wreck ever since he cut her hair, biting his nails (bad for business when you're a hairdresser), hardly sleeping, shouting at Damon, when it was usually Tracey who did that.

And then there was that business with the pub. Tim had sworn he wasn't there on the night Michael Bloody Cleverly went missing, and she'd backed up his story, though she suspected he was lying to her. Well, when he got home she was going to get it out of him. She was going to find out what was going on.

She didn't have to wait long. He slunk in the back door ten minutes later, shoulders slumped, looking cowed and beaten. Tracey wanted to yell at him: why was he such a bloody wet blanket? Why couldn't he show a bit of get-up-and-go? But she swallowed her temper and sat him down at the kitchen table. Roddy was asleep. Damon was out on a play date with another terrible three-year-old. She opened a can of beer for him and told him she wanted to know what was up.

'Nothing.'

'Nothing, my arse! You've had a face like a slapped backside ever since that cow started poking her nose into Michael Cleverly's affairs. Has she upset you? Did she say something to you when you cut her hair?'

Tim shook his head rapidly. 'No. Nothing. I'm just worried about things – about the business.'

'Bollocks.' Despite her harsh tone, Tracey reached out and took his hand. She squeezed it gently. 'I know you. I've known you since our first day of school. I've been married to you for five years. You're hiding something from me, and I want you to tell me what it is. If you're having it off with someone else I'll chop your balls off, but if it's anything else I'll forgive you, and we'll work it out. Together.'

And then he told her. He told her what he'd done, and how worried he was. And she listened, nodding now and then.

When he'd finished she squeezed his hand again.

'Don't worry. I'll fix it,' she said.

* * *

Doll Perkins

Doll was running a Hoover round the carpets, getting the place ready for Freddy's return. She'd missed her in their large, comfortable bed – missed her strong arms, missed their drowsy chats, missed their love making. At Doll's urging, Freddy had spent the past few days on a horticultural course. She'd told Rags a little white lie when she said that Freddy would be away for a week at a spiritual retreat, because she didn't want Freddy to be pestered, and because it had been fun to watch the disbelief on the girl's face.

With a jab of her foot she switched off the Hoover and put it away in the cupboard under the stairs. There. All nice and tidy for Freddy. She hoped she'd be in a better mood when she came back. Oh, she'd known Freddy was moody when she got involved with her, but that was as nothing compared to her good qualities – her kindness, loyalty, and the boundless love she sent Doll's way. And, yes, Doll basked in it, after enduring thirty years with a husband who was more affectionate to his Golden Retriever than he was to her.

A throaty engine roar told her that Freddy had turned into the unmade road at the end of their gardens. Doll rushed to the back bedroom: the red MG Midget was disappearing into the garage. Doll's heart fluttered. She checked her teeth and hair in the mirror and dashed downstairs. Throwing open the back door, she waited with a blazing smile to greet her partner, her beloved.

But Freddy had a face like thunder on her as she stomped up the path, oblivious to the rich purples of the delphiniums coming into bloom.

'Hello darling!' Doll called, hoping a traffic jam had caused her lover's bad mood. 'Was the journey terrible?'

'It was all right,' said Freddy, coming into the yard. 'And I've asked you not to advertise our relationship like that. Don't call me "darling" so loudly that every Tom, Dick and Harry can hear.'

'And nice to see you, too,' said Doll, her voice turning to ice.

'Don't have a go at me. I'm tired. I've had a long journey. I just want to unpack.'

'Do you, now? Well you can just think again. I'm not having you talking to me like that. Sit down!' Doll pointed to a kitchen chair. 'You're not leaving this room until you tell me why you've been like a bear with a sore paw for the past week. What the hell has got into you?'

Freddy clenched her fists.

'And if you hit me, I'm leaving and never coming back.'

With a groan, Freddy sank onto a chair and buried her head in her hands. When she looked up, Doll could see the lines of exhaustion on her face. 'If I tell you what I've done you'll leave me in any case.'

'Try me.'

And Freddy did, though with a number of false starts and digressions.

When she'd finally spat it out, Doll came and sat next to her. Put her arm round her. Said, 'You're a good person. You're the person I love more than anyone. And you're not alone in this. We'll sort it out. Together. I'll do anything not to lose you.'

* * *

Gerry Goodchild

Hector was tucking into roast chicken and potatoes while Gerry picked at her steamed cabbage. The skin from her chicken breast lay wrinkled on the side of her plate, looking like a collapsed scrotal sac. It made her sick to look at it. She sawed off some white meat and put it in her mouth; chewed it mechanically and swallowed. Took a swig of sparkling water at the same time as Hector raised a glass of fruity Malbec to his lips.

'So, I've got all the finances in place now, and I'm sure that the procedures will pay for the new equipment within the year. After that, I'll be into profit.'

'Will you?' said Gerry, trying to inject some interest into her voice.

'Yes. And the launch event is going to be a howling success. I just know it.'

'Do you?'

'Yes.'

Gerry sighed. Hector had been droning on about the pamper day launch event for the past half an hour. He'd had posters and leaflets printed and distributed, set up a Facebook page, and emailed his considerable client base. He already had fifty or so patients signed up for the event. Most of them had already had their teeth bleached, capped and straightened, but they were up for more improvement – and willing to pay through the nose.

'You could get involved, you know, love,' said Hector, pouring another generous libation into his empty glass. 'You could become a personal trainer and help them sort out their weight problems. I'm sure that private gym in Fairham Market would let you run sessions there.'

'I'm not qualified.'

'Then take a course. It's not rocket science, is it?' As Hector beamed at her, Gerry wondered for the umpteenth time where he got his optimism from. Nothing dented his confidence – nothing. And, though she adored him, his positivity was getting on her nerves right now.

'We can't afford it.'

'Don't be daft: of course we can.'

'We can't, Hector. I've looked at the books. We're mortgaged up to the hilt.'

For the first time Hector looked a little uncomfortable. 'We've taken out loans, yes, but we need the money to expand the business.'

You need the money, thought Gerry, who'd been happiest when Hector was starting out in a busy but friendly NHS surgery in Middleham. Of course, the funding system had changed and he'd had to go private, but why couldn't he be content with what he'd got? If only he hadn't run into his old pal from Dental School at that reunion last year. The old pal (Andy? Aaron?) had bragged for two hours solid about how much cash he was raking in by offering beauty treatments as well as dental work. 'It's so much easier than dentistry. Needs bugger-all skill. You should give it a go, old man.' And Hector, a little bored by his dental practice, and not making as much money as he'd like, had come back fired up with enthusiasm. He'd talked about nothing else for the past year. He'd attended courses on the procedures and returned radiating enthusiasm. The most recent one had been on Platelet Rich Plasma treatment: he'd laughed aloud as he told her it was also called the Vampire Facelift.

And then there was Iona. Gerry was worried sick about her.

'Is anything the matter, love?' asked Hector. 'You seem miles away.'

'Of course something's the matter!' snapped Gerry. 'Since Michael died, our daughter has locked herself in her room. She doesn't speak to us, doesn't eat with us – just runs out of the house with her school bag. Don't you care?'

'Now calm down. Don't get yourself in a state.' He put his hand over hers.

Gerry pulled her hand away as if it had been stung. 'Don't you tell me to calm down! Iona's having a nervous breakdown, and you're rabbiting on about fillers and Botox.'

Hector gave a long sigh and took another mouthful of wine. 'She's not having a breakdown. She's a teenager. Teenagers stay in their rooms. They like to be on their own. If you gave her some space she'd probably come out and talk to us.'

'But she's so *angry*. She used to be so affectionate, so sweet.'

'Like I said: she's a teenager.'

'And she's heartbroken over this Michael Cleverly thing. I found her talking to that nosy Rags, telling her that Michael had been murdered.' Her heart was tumbling, racing now, so fast she had to stop to catch her breath. 'He wasn't murdered, was he?'

'Murdered? Good God, no. It was in the newspaper: he got drunk and fell into the river.' Hector stood up and went to the sideboard. Pulled out a packet of pills. 'Sweetheart, you've been getting overwrought. Why don't you take one of these? They're just mild sedatives. Go on.'

'I don't want a sedative.'

'Oh, I think you do.' He walked over, the packet in his hand. 'You've been nervy lately. Stressed. These will help you relax.'

'Will they?' Relief flooded through Gerry, because she *had* been feeling jittery, and wound-up, and confused. She'd been awake for hours at night going through what happened on the night Michael vanished and telling herself over and over again that *she did nothing wrong.* And now Hector – clever, handsome Hector – was going to save her from this purgatory.

'And don't worry, darling,' said Hector. 'Everything's going to be fine. Trust me.'

22

Rags

Billy was waiting for me in The Rampaging Bull, spruced up in ironed jeans and a blue and white check shirt. He insisted on buying me a large glass of Sauvignon and we sat down at a quiet table.

'So, what do you have to tell me?'

'It's about his work. A friend of mine ran into Michael a few weeks ago and says that he was bellyaching about his boss. Said he'd cheated him out of his commission on some big sale.'

'Really?' I jotted down a few words in my notebook, glad to have another piece of information about Michael confirmed.

'And then Michael said he was going to teach him a lesson.'

That was more interesting. 'Could I talk to this friend?'

'Fraid not. He's gone to Dubai and I don't have any contact details.'

Billy had nothing else to tell me about recent events, though he had remembered more about Michael's school-days. 'He was clever; I remember that. One year – year eight,

I think – he won the prize for the best student in his year. Afterwards someone found him crying in the bogs because no one from his family came to the prize-giving.' His brown eyes filled with sympathy and I asked myself why I never went for good, kind-hearted men like him. 'And after that, he started skipping school. He'd be there for a few days and then go AWOL for a week.'

He talked a little more about Michael's time at school – about how he kept himself to himself, and was often absent.

'Thanks so much for getting in touch and making the time to tell me all this.'

'My pleasure.'

I offered to buy him a drink, but Billy shook his head and insisted on getting me another glass of wine. I asked him about himself. 'What do you do? What's your work?'

He gave a little laugh. 'I'm the person everyone loves to hate: a traffic warden. But it pays the bills, and I've got two kids to support.' He gave me a yearning look that lingered just a bit too long. 'I'm separated from my wife. She's got herself a new boyfriend, and I'm footloose and fancy-free.'

I was just wondering how to get out of this in a diplomatic way, when his phone rang. One of his sons needed picking up from football practice. Phew. He drained his half pint of best bitter. We said goodbye, and I thanked him again.

I should have gone home after that, but gave into temptation, and decided to have another glass of wine. At the bar I tried again to get more information out of Wayne, the landlord, but he remained impervious to my charms. When I told him he was a dab hand behind the bar, he said he'd been at it for twenty years, and should know what he was doing by now. I asked him what Michael had been drinking on the night he disappeared, and he repeated what he'd told the police: that Michael was drinking shots of vodka in between glasses of wine.

'And did he usually do that?'

A swift shrug. 'Sometimes.'

'Only he didn't seem drunk to me.'

Silence.

'And what sort of mood was he in? Did he seem upset about anything?'

'He was his usual, smarmy self.' Hostile eyes the colour of treacle locked onto mine. 'And now, if you don't mind, I've got customers to serve.'

I gave up. Took the glass of Sauvignon to my regular corner table and picked up a local newspaper someone had left on a chair. After a pleasant half hour perusing the local news, (flower shows, charity events, petty crime, WI meetings – that sort of thing), I decided it really was time I went home and had something to eat.

Strolling through a balmy dusk, I decided that life was looking up. Granted, I hadn't yet solved the mystery of Michael's death, but I'd made progress and – incredibly – had made a small dent in my mountain of debt. I paused by a lilac just coming into flower, burying my nose in its perfumed blossom candles. The sound of revving engines and dodgy exhausts told me a couple of boy racers were out on the streets of Middleham: little bird-brains driven by hormones, of course – raging hormones.

Which reminded me: no word from Alaric. I shook my head in frustration: here I was, a feisty feminist and emancipated woman *still* waiting for some bloody man to call (or text, or email). Oh, fuck it. I was certain that Alaric would be back; we had unfinished business of the most pleasurable kind. From the corner of my eye I saw the boy racers in two battered cars (one red, one black) roaring round the junction near the market. As their throaty exhaust roars headed up the street in my direction I caught the faint scent of something citric, a lemony cologne, and through the happy fog of

Sauvignon I smiled: an early boyfriend had been a great fan of Brut and I still associated males drenched in scent with passionate kisses and fumbles in a Barnstaple bus shelter when I was a sixth-former.

But this fuzzy nostalgia was abruptly shattered. As I passed the shadowy entrance to the graveyard a strong hand shoved me into the path of the first boy racer's car.

It swerved to the right, but caught me on the edge of the bonnet. I flew up and over it, my body weightless and in those split seconds I thanked the goddess for the swift, youthful reactions of the driver. If the car had hit me head-on I'd be dead. I landed on the tarmac with a thump, as the second car swerved round me and screeched to halt. Warm blood spurted from my head and pooled round my ear. I smelled burning rubber, petrol; heard shouts and the distant bark of an excited dog.

I must have blacked out, because the next thing I knew a hand was holding mine, squeezing it gently, and a low voice was saying, 'Don't worry; you're all right, and the ambulance will be here soon.'

I squinted through blood to see Dad crouched down beside me. 'It's all right, love,' he said again. I felt no pain, but a whoozy wave washed over me every few seconds. Taking a deep breath, I rubbed the blood out of my eyes. 'Don't try to sit up. They need to check your neck is all right before you go moving around.'

How did he know that?

'I was a first-aider at work,' said Dad, who was obviously a mind reader – unless I'd got the words out without realising it. 'I was taking Napoleon out for an evening constitutional when I heard the crash.'

I was lying on my back, drenched in blood, in the middle

of King's Road. Perched on a low wall, a pale youth with a severe case of acne was sucking on a cigarette. His red car was half up on the pavement, with a broken headlight and a stonking dent in the left side of its bonnet. I made an effort to clear my throat. 'It wasn't his fault,' I croaked, then shut my mouth again, because I didn't want to scare Dad by telling him that someone had shoved me in front of a fast-moving car.

'Hush now.' Dad's hand stroked my hair.

A paramedic on a motorbike pulled up, apologising for the fact that she wasn't an ambulance. 'One'll be along soon, but I can take care of you now,' she said, pulling off her helmet to reveal a wicked crop of platinum hair. She laid a blanket over me, took my pulse, and ran her fingers gently down my limbs. 'I don't think anything's broken,' she pronounced, as she dabbed the wound on my head with antiseptic liquid. 'It looks worse than it is. You've got a cut on your temple, at the hair line. That sort of wound bleeds profusely, but it looks superficial. I think you landed on your side and not on your head – which is good news, believe me.'

'Thank you,' I said, aware of an ominous throb starting up in my right arm and leg.

At that moment a police car pulled up, and the pimply plod who'd been so unhelpful on the day Michael's body was found came over with another, older officer. The older man was gruff but courteous. He took down my account of what had happened. 'I'm sure someone pushed me into the path of the car,' I whispered, hoping Dad, standing a few feet away, couldn't hear. 'Someone wanted to kill me.'

'And did you see this person's face? Could you identify them?'

'No. I'm afraid not. But the car driver wasn't to blame. He had no time to stop.'

'And, in your opinion, was the driver exceeding the speed limit?'

'No.' Though I was pretty sure he was, I wasn't going to drop him in it.

At this point an ambulance screeched to halt, flashing blue lights. Two more paramedics clipped on a neck brace and strapped me to a stretcher, explaining that they needed to take me to King's Lynn Queen Elizabeth Hospital to check I hadn't sustained a spinal injury before they let me move my neck. Dad insisted on coming, too. 'You don't have to do that,' I said, brimming over with tears.

'Don't be daft. I'll follow in my car, so I can take you home afterwards. I'll just drop Napoleon at the house first.'

As the ambulance pulled away, a text pinged into my phone. I eased it out of my jeans pocket and held it above my head, where I could read it. It was from Alaric.

I'm on a survival course in The Lake District. Crap signal. Let's meet up when I'm back at the weekend.

No kisses. No 'love', but my shoulder stopped aching quite so badly.

Just been run over, I replied. *Tell you more when we meet.*

Despite my nonchalant text, I found myself shaking on the way to the hospital. The paramedic said it was shock and that it was normal to shake and shiver. She took my hand and held it as we travelled, which made me feel a bit better. Nonetheless my head, shoulder and back were throbbing with pain, and I realised I'd taken the skin off my right elbow. But worse than my physical pain was the knowledge that someone had tried to *kill* me. No one pushes you into the path of a speeding car hoping you'll sustain a few bruises. Iona's plaintive young voice came into my head: *He was murdered, wasn't he? I know he was.*

We were soon at the hospital, where I jumped to the head of the queue above those with sprains, cuts and alcohol-induced injuries. Dad arrived just as they wheeled me off for my scan. Afterwards, as we waited to talk to the registrar – a young man with freckles who looked about sixteen – I asked him about his date with Susie.

His cheeks went pink. 'It went all right.'

'So, what did you talk about?'

'All sorts. Turns out she's got a Labradoodle called Cocoa, so we're going to take the dogs for a walk together some time. She took a shine to Napoleon. Said he was a grand little chap.'

'And?'

'And what?'

'And did you find her attractive?'

'She was nice enough,' he said, blushing again.

They'd had a coffee in Fairham Market, then gone on to The Globe at Wells-next-the-Sea for an early supper. 'And she had steak and ale pie. That was a relief, after the lettuce leaf lady. We both had the sticky toffee pudding to finish.'

Before I could get more information out of him, the registrar returned with the good news that the scan showed no damage to my skull, brain or spine. Released from the neck brace, I sat up, wincing. I was ushered into another cubicle where a no-nonsense Irish nurse stuck the cut on my head together with clever tape (it didn't need to be stitched up with a needle, thank heavens) and dressed the graze on my elbow. 'That'll be painful,' she said. 'Do you have plenty of paracetamol at home?' I said that I did.

Dad was subdued on the drive home under a Milky Way showing off its sparkly tail. I was glad that he resisted the urge to say, 'I told you so,' though he had, hadn't he? He'd warned me. It wasn't until we got into the house that he spoke his mind. 'I heard what you said to the police officer. Someone pushed you under that car. I know I can't stop you doing what you want to do, but you must promise me you won't go out on your own at night, like you did this evening. And I want you to go to the police station tomorrow and get them to investigate what happened to you.'

Chastened, I agreed to everything he said.

23

Rags

DI Chloe Cooper was marginally more sympathetic this time, probably because I was beginning to develop a spectacular black eye. 'Are you sure you were pushed? Perhaps you stumbled. I gather you'd been drinking.'

I sighed; no point in denying it. 'Yes, but not enough to make me throw myself under a speeding car.' I wanted to add that three glasses of white wine didn't make a huge dent in my ability to walk in a straight line, but thought better of it. 'Don't you believe me?'

After a long pause, Chloe Cooper said, 'You might be right. But there's not much we can do if you didn't see anyone or anything suspicious.'

'What about the drivers of the two cars?' I asked. 'Did they see anyone?'

A shake of the head. 'But the driver of the car that hit you said you came out of nowhere. Think hard. Can you remember anything – anything at all? Perhaps an unusual sound or smell?'

Then it came to me. 'Cologne. Someone smelling delicious came up behind me.'

Chloe Cooper made a little sound of exasperation. 'Cologne. Any idea what brand?'

'No. But it was one of those that both women and men wear – something really classy – lemony.'

Looking terminally bored, she made a note on her pad. I fumbled in my bag and pulled out a summary of the report I'd written for Shell, listing the main points. 'Look, I know you think I've got an over-active imagination, but please, please read this. There are a number of suspicious circumstances around Michael's Cleverly's disappearance and death, and I think I've been attacked because I've been digging around.'

She frowned. 'We never encourage members of the public to try to do the work of the police. They can interfere with an investigation, and,' she said, leaning forward, 'they can get hurt.'

'Please. Just take a look.'

After a pause she took it. 'OK. I'll read it and see whether I can persuade the DCI to allocate some hours to looking again at Michael Cleverly's death. But I can't promise anything. The post-mortem report was clear that he was extremely drunk.'

Back at Dad's house I lay on my bed and popped a couple more paracetamol. Dad was working on his online course downstairs and I was – well, I was *thinking*. Thinking hard. Did I want to carry on? I could have been killed. I lay there for a bit, waiting for the paracetamol to kick in, then propped myself up on a couple of pillows and reached for my phone.

I was buggered if I was going to give up.

I called Shell, now in Antibes, and told her about what had happened. 'I'm sorry you were harmed,' said Shell, airily ignoring the injuries I'd described in colourful detail, 'but it shows that I'm right, doesn't it? You are getting closer to the truth.' Then she hung up, saying she had to get back to an important meeting.

My phone rang: Carola.

'What's happened? I got your messages, but it's been frantic at this bloody conference.'

'Oh, nothing much except ...' I let the dramatic pause stretch out: it wasn't every day you got to deliver this sort of news. 'Except I got knocked down by a car.'

'No!'

'Yes. But don't worry: I'm not seriously hurt. Just bruised to buggery and with a lovely black eye.'

'Oh, sweetheart! That's terrible.'

'And I'm sure I was shoved into the road.'

Silence. 'Are you serious?'

'Yes.'

'Shit. Any idea who did it?'

'No, but I'm pretty certain it's connected to my investigation of what happened to Michael Cleverly. It wasn't a random attack. Can I run some things past you? I really need to talk it all over with someone.'

'Course you can.'

So I did. When I'd finished Carola gave a long whistle. 'Wow. For what it's worth, I think your instincts are spot-on. Someone did want to get rid of Michael Cleverly. The only question is who and how they did it: there seems to be a long list of people who couldn't stand him. But I'm more worried about what's happened to you. You could be *dead*, Rags, and I don't want to have the hassle of finding another best friend.'

'I know. I'm not delighted about it, I can tell you. I was enjoying drifting around feeling safe as houses. It's ironic that I get attacked in a town where violent crime is practically zero.'

'You need a bodyguard.'

I was quiet for a moment, thinking of Alaric, of his fit body and dark curls. Oh, wouldn't it be good not to do everything on my own? But I soon filed that thought under *complete fantasy*. Alaric had a job, for heaven's sake. He couldn't hang around looking after me twenty-four hours a day.

'I need to find out who's behind the murder of Michael Cleverly,' I said. 'I won't feel safe until I've done that.'

That evening Dad made tea for us both: shepherd's pie, (Waitrose's best), frozen peas and broad beans, with ice cream and mandarin oranges to follow. Perfect. A proper Dad tea – the sort he gave me when I was a child, though back then we had Fray Bentos steak and kidney pie.

I was in bed by nine, and despite my bruises I slept soundly.

24

Rags

I woke up at eight to a sky decorated with a few fluffy white clouds, feeling miraculously happy. I felt less shocked and shaken up, and having a brush with death had reminded me how much I loved living. Wincing, I got out of bed and hobbled to the window: Dad and Napoleon were in the back garden. Dad was weeding, and Napoleon was flopped under the bench chewing a bone-shaped dog toy. I watched them for a few minutes thanking the universe for life, sweet life.

Then I got going. I needed to talk to Patsy. I fired up the computer, and searched for private clinics in North Norfolk. Tall Trees, a couple of miles from the village of Docking, was the only one listed in the area. This must be where Patsy was drying out while her hideous daddy topped up his tan in Cyprus with his bit of stuff. I rang the clinic, pretending to be an aunt who wanted to visit Patsy, and enquiring about the best time to come. The clinic confirmed that she was being treated there, but said I couldn't speak to her or visit, since clients were not allowed any contact with the outside world for the first four weeks of their treatment.

I wasn't going to let a little thing like that put me off.

But when I googled bus services to the clinic I came up with a hitch. I had to get a bus to King's Lynn and then another to Docking. And there was only one through service a day. I could get there but not get back. I could have got a taxi, but it would be much easier to drive. And Dad had that adorable car. Would he let me borrow it? I was a good driver, a safe driver, who'd never been involved in a collision, apart from an argument with a low brick wall in an IKEA car park. Plus, we were getting on so much better, weren't we?

I threw on some loose linen trousers and a baggy cotton shirt, and limped downstairs. Dad had come in from the garden and was at work on his computer, with a couple of books from the library open beside him. Not for the first time, I felt a swell of pride. He looked up.

'Oh, there you are. How are you feeling today?'

'Much better, thanks.' I paused. 'Dad? I've found out where Patsy is, and I'm thinking of visiting her today.'

Dad harrumphed. 'You won't get much sense out of her: she's blotto half the time.'

'But she's in a clinic, drying out, so she'll be sober now. I can ask her about Michael – the sort of person he was, and whether he had enemies we don't yet know about.'

Dad raised his eyebrows. 'I wouldn't bank on getting anything out of her.'

I bit my lip to stop myself snapping at him. Here he was, doing his glass-half-empty routine again.

Then Dad surprised me. 'I've been thinking. When you see her, why don't you get her to request a copy of the post-mortem report? As his widow, she can do that. And she could get it sent to this address.'

'Hey, that's a really good idea, Dad. You're not just a pretty face.' I held my breath for a second, because asking for help doesn't come easily to me. 'And I have huge favour to ask. Could I borrow your car?'

'No you cannot!' Dad barked.

'But ...'

'I'll drive you there.'

I blinked. 'Will you really?'

'Of course I will. I'm not letting you go roaming round on your own,' said Dad, sounding like he did when I was seven and wanted to run out to play in the dark. 'Not after what's happened. Me and Napoleon are coming with you.'

I coughed to hide the tears welling up in my eyes. 'Thank you.'

'Shall we have a little walk at Burnham Overy Staithe first? Some sea air would do you good, and Napoleon would love it.'

'Sounds great.'

'That's settled then.' Dad pulled a royal blue dog blanket decorated with bones out of the bottom drawer of the little chest by the dining-room window. 'We'll take this in case we have to leave him in the car while we go looking for Patsy. He'll have a snooze on it and be perfectly happy.'

'Thanks so much, Dad. I really appreciate your help.'

He pulled his specs back down and waved me away. 'Now go and sort yourself out and let me get on with my coursework.'

I scooted back upstairs and produced a letter to the coroner for Patsy to sign, which Dad printed out for me. Then I had a couple of slices of toast and butter while Dad packed up a little bag for Napoleon which included the blue dog blanket, a towel, a plastic dog bowl and a bottle of water. At the last minute he added a chew 'in case he gets bored waiting for us.'

Just after nine we set off for the coast, with Napoleon in his usual position with his front paws on the dashboard so he could see where we were going. It was another perfect day, with the sun beaming on hedgerows thick with sparrows. As we drove, I filled Dad in on what I knew about Tall Trees. 'She's not allowed to have any visitors for the first four weeks, but I'm sure we'll find a way to talk to her,' I said, sounding more confident than I felt. Normally something like this would be a piece of cake for me, but my energy had dipped since my accident.

Dad drummed his fingers on the steering wheel then said, 'I know. We'll ask for a guided tour of the place. Say we want to see if it's suitable for a young relative who has a serious drink problem.'

I gave a whoop. 'Good one, Dad. We could work it so you keep them talking while I go looking for Patsy. The place is small and I should be able to find her. Hopefully I'll be able to speak to her before they rugby-tackle me and drag me away.'

'Done.'

First, we had a walk to take. We parked the car on the sands at Burnham Overy Staithe, where Dad assured me that it wouldn't get washed away. Then we climbed up onto the bank that led out to the sea. In the channel beside us a small boat chugged towards the coast, with a handsome golden Labrador standing at its prow. Napoleon dived into the tall grass, scenting rabbits or water voles. Mallard ducks and coots waggled their tails in the drainage ditch, ignoring his cheerful barks and knowing he wasn't going to plunge into deep water after them.

As I walked, I breathed in the perfume of the sea lavender, and let the warmth of the sunlight soothe my bruises. Having Dad with me made me feel safe, and I was pretty sure that an attack in broad daylight was not the *modus operandi* of the person who'd shoved me in front of that car. In any case, there were other people on the path: birdwatchers, dog walkers, lovers strolling hand-in-hand who'd perhaps booked into The Hero for a romantic break. We made it to a wooden bench placed at the point where the path curves sharply to the right, and sat there letting the sun sink into our faces for a while before strolling back at a leisurely pace. When we got back to the car, it was indeed still way above the tide line. 'Told you,' said Dad, as he cleaned Napoleon's feet with his blanket.

Refreshed, the three of us set off towards Docking in his Mini.

Tall Trees was situated up a winding road bordered by fields of barley. A sign at the entrance to the car park announced that it offered 'Healthcare for the Discerning'. Dad did another of his harrumphs. 'Healthcare for the wealthy, more like.'

After seeing Napoleon happily settled on his blanket with a dog chew, we made our way to the main entrance. The reception area was not quite as I'd expected. I'd thought it might be like a boutique hotel, with pale furniture, tall jugs of flowers and squashy sofas. Instead it reminded me of the prep schools I'd visited while working the Yorkshire beat and investigating private education in the county. Two large, well worn rugs partially covered the parquet floor of what must once have been an impressive entrance hall, now truncated by a partition wall. The receptionist sitting at the desk was smartly dressed in a blue uniform, her tawny hair cut into an elfin cap. As we came in she looked up and smiled. 'How can I be of assistance?'

Dad stepped forward, his face solemn. 'It's all a bit sensitive. I'm looking for help for a young relative. He's got himself into a bad way – only twenty-two and he's getting through a bottle of vodka a day, and his family can't take it any more. They're at their wits' end.'

The receptionist's face became sympathetic. 'Oh, I am sorry. Please take a seat.'

'And look what he's done to my daughter,' said Dad, gesturing at my black eye, which was starting to bloom into tones of purple and blue. 'She was trying to help him, you see, and he wasn't having any of it.'

'It was frightening,' I said, looking suitably distressed. 'And he urgently needs to go into rehab. And because there's a waiting list on the NHS, we're looking into private provision.'

'Well, we are a highly regarded alcohol rehab clinic. And because we only treat those with an alcohol addiction, we can focus our energies to provide optimum care at a competitive price.'

Dad nodded. 'Ideally, we'd like to find somewhere that combines detox with counselling.'

'Of course. And that's just what we offer. Most clients come for six weeks, and then there are follow-up groups which we strongly encourage them to attend.'

Dad and I exchanged a look. 'Well – that sounds like the sort of thing we're looking for,' he said, 'but we'd want to take a look at your facilities before we go any further.'

'Of course.' The receptionist handed over a couple of glossy brochures. 'If you'd like to take a look at our literature, I'll arrange for someone to show you round.'

She murmured into the phone and returned to her computer while Dad and I leafed through the pages. It all looked above board. The unit accommodated up to twelve clients at one time. The prices for treatment were high but not astronomical: detox followed by counselling and group therapy came in at just under £3,000 a week. So if Patsy's father had coughed up for the six-week programme he'd be shelling out eighteen grand. Perhaps he wasn't a complete monster. Ah, but then I came to a name listed in the small print on the last page.

Associate Director: Major Harvey Macdonald.

I'd bet my last pair of Ugg boots he'd got her in here at a cut-price rate.

Before I could whisper this to Dad, the door opened and a grey-haired doctor in a sober, black suit came towards us, holding out his hand for us to shake. His grip was warm and firm. 'My name is Dr Anand. I'm the medical director of the clinic. I hear you'd like to take a look around. Please follow me.'

Behind the partition wall Tall Trees was a bit more scruffy, but it had a homely feel I liked. Dr Anand showed us the clients' lounge (empty, but comfortable, with sofas and a big widescreen TV), and the therapy room (painted green and blue, with a circle of chairs, looking out on a terrace and a long lawn).

'We've finished our morning sessions, so people are in their rooms or taking a stroll round the grounds,' said Dr Anand. 'Perhaps you'd like to take a look outside?'

'Yes, please,' said Dad.

Dr Anand pushed open double doors to let in the verdant smell of recently cut grass. The garden was laid mainly to lawn, and stretched to a wooded area. In the distance I could see a high brick wall, but clients clearly stayed here of their own volition, as any of them could have high-tailed it out of the main gate. Dad asked Dr Anand if he could show him round the grounds, 'Because I want to be absolutely sure that my nephew is in a natural, healing environment.'

'With pleasure,' said the doctor, starting down a path leading to the wooded area. As they strolled off, with Dad keeping up a stream of questions, I lagged behind, then turned round and bobbed back inside the building. I passed through the therapy room and went swiftly up the wide staircase. A landing stretched off to the right and the left. I went to the left. Each bedroom door had a name slotted into a neat plastic rectangle, but none of them were Patsy's.

I doubled back and scooted down the right-hand side of the landing. Result: the last room was hers. I tapped on the door. A voice called from inside, 'Who is it?'

'Rags. We met on the morning you found Michael had gone missing. I urgently need to talk to you.'

When Patsy opened the door, I hurried into the room, closing the door quietly behind us.

'What are you *doing* here?' she hissed. 'I'm not allowed any visitors until week five.' She paused, registering my criss-cross paper stitches and black eye. 'What's happened to your face?'

'Just a little accident. Look, I need your help. Do you want to know what really happened to Michael?'

'I know what happened.' Patsy's voice was flat, but her breath was coming in short gasps. She was thinner in the face, her brown eyes clear – a different person now she wasn't bloated by booze. On her bed lay an open copy of *My Family and Other Animals*. Suddenly her face screwed up and tears started to run down her face. 'The police found me and told me he was dead.'

I took hold of Patsy's hands and gave them a gentle squeeze. 'Now listen to me. The police think Michael's death was accidental, but there are things that don't add up, and I need your help. Can you answer a few questions?'

She nodded.

'Did you see him on the Friday he disappeared?'

'I saw him that morning, but he didn't come home after work. That was normal for a Friday, because he always went to the pub to unwind. And I – I had a few drinks and fell asleep on the sofa.' She frowned. 'And I think I heard voices out the back – arguing – but I can't be sure.' She hung her head. 'Sorry. Sorry. I can't remember much after that.'

'Were the voices male or female?'

She blinked back tears. 'I don't know. Sorry.'

'Never mind. Tell me: was Michael a big drinker? Did he sometimes get completely out of it?'

She shook her head vehemently. 'No. Michael liked to be in control. I never saw him drunk.'

'And how was his property business doing? Was it successful?'

'I don't really know. He hadn't talked about it for a while. He wanted Daddy to invest in it, but Daddy said no.' Her lip trembled. 'Daddy likes to say no.'

'And did Michael have any enemies? Anyone who might have wanted to harm him?'

She shrugged. 'Lots of people were jealous of him, but he never told me about any enemies. I mean, he wasn't frightened of anyone. He wasn't even frightened of Daddy.'

I dug in my bag and pulled out the letter for the coroner. 'Can you do something for me? Sign this letter, which requests a copy of the post-mortem report. It can only be released to members of the family. It'll give us more detailed information about how and when he died. The report'll come to my house, but I promise I'll let you see it as soon as possible.' A silence filled the room. 'Please. If his death wasn't accidental, we've got to get justice for him.'

Patsy's eyes spilled over with tears that ran down her cheeks. She rubbed them away with a hand, speaking rapidly, jerkily. 'Suppose ... suppose I had something to do with his death. I have black-outs, you see. I can't always remember things after I've been drinking. And I think I picked up a heavy frying pan when I heard noises from outside.' Her eyes drilled into mine. 'Maybe I hit him, maybe I hurt him. Maybe he was stunned and that's why he fell in the river.'

I took her hands again. 'Listen to me. You did *not* hit him over the head. I was at the inquest, and there was nothing like that in the autopsy report.'

'Are you sure?'

'Yes. He had some superficial wounds, but he hadn't been brained with a frying pan.'

She released a little sound of relief. 'Thank you. Thank you.' She took the letter and signed it quickly. 'Don't tell my father, will you?'

'I promise I won't.'

'I still love Michael, you know, even though he's dead. I'll always love him.'

And that made me feel like a complete heel, given that I was being bankrolled by Shell.

I was rescued by Dad's voice calling up the stairs. 'Rags? Are you all right?'

I grabbed the letter and stuffed it in my bag. 'Thanks for this. I promise I'll keep you informed. Are you allowed letters?'

'Not for another fortnight, but ...'

'I'll update you as soon as I can.' On impulse I pulled Patsy towards me and kissed her on the cheek. 'Come and see me when you're out.'

I hurried downstairs. 'You're not allowed up there!' barked Dr Anand. 'Those are the clients' private rooms.'

'I'm so sorry. I was looking for the Ladies.'

'Over there.' Dr Anand pointed sternly at a door clearly marked with the kitsch female sign of a girl in a dress – a sign I've always hated. I slipped in there for a few minutes, and then came out again to find Dad giving Dr Anand some flannel about me being traumatised and confused after I was attacked. I had to admit, he was taking to this like a duck to water.

Dr Anand shooed us back into the reception area, and we left after thanking him for the tour.

I filled Dad in on my brief conversation with Patsy as we drove home.

'Patsy confirmed that Michael wasn't a big drinker, and I know Michael didn't drink any vodka while I was talking to him. That means Wayne, the landlord, was lying about that.'

'But why? Why would he lie?'

I still had no answer.

25

Rags

By the time we got home from the clinic I was feeling knackered, so I took myself off to bed with *Pompeii*, by Robert Harris – a recommendation from Dad. After a couple of chapters I dozed off, only to be woken by the sound of a text arriving. *Sorry to hear about your accident. I get back this evening and will call round at 7 to cheer you up. A*

Still no kisses, but I couldn't stop myself from grinning.

I'd been told not to get my wounded elbow wet, so I took a shower with my arm in a plastic carrier bag firmly sealed with rubber bands. I even managed to wash my hair, using an ingenious method that involved a huge waterproof plaster stuck over the cut on my temple. Squeaky clean, I sat on the garden bench throwing the ball for Napoleon while my hair dried in the sun. The scent of the lilac in Doll and Freddy's garden drifted over. Shading my eyes with my hand, I looked towards the backs of the houses of The Terrace. Tim and Tracey's door was open, and Damon was vrooming a tractor round the yard, his hair bright in the sunlight. Tracey appeared in the kitchen doorway and shepherded him towards the back door.

'Hello!' I called, mainly to wind her up. 'Lovely evening, isn't it? Did you hear about my accident? Someone shoved me in front of a car.'

Tracey ignored me, bundling Damon inside before slamming the door.

'And sod off to you, too,' I muttered, wondering whether Tracey had been the one who pushed me into the road. Unlikely: she didn't smell delicious. As far as I could recall, Tracey smelled of sweat and the remnants of some heavy, spicy perfume.

The back door to number three opened, and Doll appeared, with a huge bunch of garden flowers. She made her way to Dad's garden and approached me, holding the flowers in front of her. 'Here,' she said. 'I was so sorry to hear of your accident.'

'Oh, thank you.' I buried my nose in the profusion of pink and white roses, delphiniums, stocks and Canterbury bells. 'That's so kind of you. They're gorgeous.'

'I hope you weren't seriously hurt.'

'I was very lucky: cuts and bruises, but nothing worse.'

'Could I join you for a minute?'

I patted the bench beside me. 'Of course. Take a seat,' I said, curious to find out what had prompted Doll's sudden friendliness.

'Is it true that someone pushed you in front of a car?'

'Yes,' I said firmly.

'Dreadful.' She tutted and shook her head. 'I hope it's nothing to do with what happened to Michael.' She paused then continued, looking intently at me, 'You see I think he'd got mixed up with some undesirables.'

'Really? What makes you think that?'

'Well, I overheard something peculiar in the market square. Two men I hadn't seen before – rough-looking types – were smoking outside the bookie's and, as I passed, I *think* I heard them say that whoever was poking their nose into what happened to Michael had better back off, or they might get hurt.'

My bullshit alarm was ringing, but I kept a straight face and asked, 'When was this?'

'On the day you had your accident.'

'Can you describe them?'

She paused to think. 'They both had shaved heads and gold earrings and were wearing baggy jeans and grubby tee-shirts. Oh, and they sounded like Londoners: they certainly weren't from round here.' She moved a little closer, her eyes locked into mine. 'And I know I'm going to sound like I'm interfering, but I think it might be dangerous for you to continue with your investigation. I mean, you've already been attacked, and the next time you might not be so lucky.'

'Thank you for your concern,' I said, in my coolest voice. 'Perhaps you should go and talk to the police.'

Doll gave me a patronising smile and patted my leg. 'They'll probably just think I'm a daft old woman, but I'm glad I've told you. Anyway, I'd better be going. Freddy's under the weather.'

'So she's back. I thought you said she'd be away for a week.'

'She came back a couple of days early,' said Doll, untroubled by my sharp tone. 'I think she's picked up a bug.'

'And did she enjoy her retreat?'

'Very much. She was sorry to leave early.'

As Doll stood up, the breeze blew a breath of her perfume into my nose: it was something classy – not an old lady's brand at all – with a hint of sherbet and rose. Could Doll shove someone under a car? She looked more like a teddy bear than an Amazon, in her cream blouse and comfortable cotton skirt, but I'd seen her digging, weeding, and humping bags of compost around. And the story about the 'undesirables'? I was going to suspend judgement on that one. It was possible that Michael had got involved in criminal activity: how else had he got the money necessary for the Antibes development? But those two thugs sounded like Doll had picked them out of a casting call.

The big question was why Doll was trying to stop me going on with my investigation.

I went inside to finish drying my hair, using a heated brush which smoothed it into long, sensuous waves. And I wanted long and sensuous for when I hooked up with Alaric that evening. I slipped on a loose Jigsaw skirt and blouse, both purple with a tiny flower print, as these were easy to get into with my aches and bruises and stiff limbs. It crossed my mind that they'd be easy to get out of, too, then told myself not to get my hopes up. Alaric was involved with someone else, wasn't he?

Coming downstairs, I heard Dad on the phone. 'I'm not sure about tonight. My daughter's had an accident and I think I should stay in with her.'

I waved my arms around and mouthed, 'I'm seeing Alaric tonight. Go out if you want.'

'Oh, it seems she's going to have someone sitting with her, so perhaps we could meet up. Let me ring you back in a few minutes. Goodbye then.' With distinctly pink cheeks, Dad put the phone down.

'Was that Susie?'

'Yes. She's got a piece of rump steak that wants eating up and she wondered if I could help her out. She's asked me round to her house in Holt.'

'That's brilliant, Dad. Go for it.'

'Are you sure?'

'Yes.'

'What time are you meeting Alaric?'

'Seven.'

'All right, then. But I'll wait until he arrives before I go out.'

Alaric appeared at the back door, lean and tanned from his survival course, wearing a faded denim shirt and jeans. He smelled good, too, of pine-scented soap and shampoo.

'Hello, you,' he said, leaning on the door jamb.

'Hello, you.'

As if linked by telepathy we moved forward and kissed, gently at first, and then harder. Hearing Dad's footsteps we pulled apart. 'Look at that eye,' called Dad, coming into the kitchen. 'I've never seen such a shiner.'

Alaric raised his hand and touched my face softly. 'I'm just glad she wasn't badly hurt.'

'So am I,' I said, taking his hand and squeezing it.

Dad cleared his throat. 'Well, I'll be off now.' Napoleon gave a short bark as Dad reached for his best, tartan lead. 'I'm taking the boy with me so he can play with Susie's Labradoodle.'

'I might be round at Alaric's when you get in, so don't panic if I'm not here.'

After waving Dad goodbye, we moved into the lounge. I felt cripplingly shy – which was daft, because I was in my forties and had slept with at least 20 people (I'd counted them up a couple of years back, during an evening spent with Carola blobbing in front of old episodes of *Sex and the City*). We talked. I told Alaric about the progress of the investigation, and about my accident. He listened carefully, drinking now and then from the bottle of Black Sheep beer I'd bought for him.

'And are you going to carry on?'

'Being shoved under that car shook me up, but I'm not going to give up on it – no way – not until I know the truth.'

'Let me know if you decide to go to the pub again, and I'll be your bodyguard. Did I tell you I used to be a martial arts fanatic?'

'No.' The tingle at the base of my belly started up again. 'But I'm impressed.'

'Don't get too excited. I haven't done it for years, but I got to be a brown belt in Tae Kwon Do before I gave it up.' He gave me a rueful smile. 'I was a weedy kid at school – didn't like kicking a sodden football round a pitch. I was the type who collected beetles and moths and kept them in jam jars and cardboard boxes while I found out what they were. What sort of a kid were you?'

'Me? A complete swot. I'd like to say I was a rebel, but I saved all that for my twenties. The worst thing I did was snog my boyfriend in the bus shelter and drink too much Diamond White cider in the park after my exams. I wanted to get out – to get to university. I was living in Devon, near Barnstaple, with my mum and stepdad. Beautiful but pretty staid. I wanted something more exciting. And I got it.'

He looked at me for so long that I felt a blush rise into my cheeks. 'I've called it off with Jenny,' he said eventually. 'It was time.'

'Oh.'

'It's all right. She was cool about it.' His gaze held mine. 'Do you want to come back to my place?'

It's not every day that you first make love with a man when you're black and blue. My injuries meant that there was no question of athletics on the hearth rug or the kitchen table. Alaric led me up to his bedroom (clean, white sheets; Mark Rothko prints on the walls) and with winces and groans I lay down on my back. Slowly, slowly, he kissed my mouth and neck. Slowly, slowly he eased up my blouse, undid my bra, stroked my breasts. Slowly, slowly he inched his fingers up my bare legs to the lace of my knickers. Slowly, slowly he touched me until I was on the brink of orgasm. Then he eased himself inside me.

I came within seconds – of course I did – and embarrassed myself by bursting into tears and then laughing. Afterwards he kissed me long and sweet and slow.

We lay chatting for hours, the way you do, swapping tales of past loves and relationships as the light drained from the sky. I was careful about what I revealed, deciding to wait before I told him about the intense lesbian affairs I'd had at college. Those relationships had taught me more about my body and how to give pleasure to someone else than all the fuck-by-numbers films and advice out there on the internet, but men sometimes became curious – too curious – in a way that bordered on creepy.

He told me about the partner he'd been with before he met Jenny. Like me he'd been with someone, another ecologist, for almost a decade. And, like me, his ex-partner was now married with two small children. 'Sasha's an environmental activist. In fact she's just taken a job in India, in the Tamil Nadu biosphere. Her family are going with her.'

'She sounds admirable.'

'She is.' He burrowed beneath my hair and kissed my neck. 'But not as fuckable as you,' he said, voice muffled.

Oh sex, beautiful sex. Right at that moment I didn't give a stuff about Michael Cleverly or who killed him. I didn't give a stuff about my debts. I was perfectly happy bobbing along on a sea of post-orgasmic pleasure.

Until the phone rang.

Alaric was going to ignore it, but it rang again. And again.

'Shit! Must be work. Now and then we get idiots

trespassing on the reserve late at night. Sorry about this.' He picked it up. Listened. His face became grave. 'Where? And have you called the police? I'll be right over.'

'What? What's happened?'

'They've found another body.'

26

Rags

I insisted on going with Alaric, though he tried to get me to stay in his bed.

'Look at the state of you: you need to rest up. And it's probably nothing to do with that fuckwit Michael Cleverly.'

'Two bodies in two weeks, in an area where there have been no suspicious deaths in thirty years? Of course it's got something to do with his murder.'

Buttoning his jeans, he glared at me. 'You've got a one-track mind, haven't you?'

I took a sharp breath. 'What's got into you?'

'Nothing,' said Alaric, pulling on a tee-shirt and jumper and turning away.

With difficulty, I climbed out of the warm bed and winced my way towards my clothes, strewn on the floor. 'Something's up, isn't it? Something you're not telling me. Alaric, please: it's not fair to pull all my defences down and then shut yourself off.'

He stopped fiddling with his clothes and faced me. 'I'm sorry, but I can't be all lovey-dovey when I've just heard that they've found a dead body in a ditch on the Nature Reserve.'

With a lump in my throat, I struggled into my clothes: I was damned if I was going to be sidelined by him. Who was *he* to tell me what to do?

He threw a heavy-duty Aran sweater across the room at me. 'Here. If you insist on coming with me, you need to keep warm.' It smelled of his soap, and of *him* – his lean, sexy body. I limped downstairs after him and into a night sprinkled with bright stars. As I walked through the garden to his van, I noticed his bike propped up against the shed.

And it came to me, with a jolt. Oh, shit.

I waited until we were in the van. 'It was you, wasn't it?'

'What do you mean?' He turned the key in the ignition.

'You cycled past Michael and shoved him over on the night he went missing. Iona saw what happened, but didn't know who did it.'

Alaric switched off the ignition, but didn't look at me. Starlight lit up the tense contours of his face – a face I'd been kissing ten minutes before. 'Yes. It was me. Satisfied?'

'But why didn't you tell me?'

He gave one of his short, bitter laughs. 'I thought you might go off me if you found I was a psychopath.'

'Alaric.' I touched his arm but he jerked it away. 'I know you're not a psychopath. Believe me: I've met a few. You were pissed off with Michael, and you gave him a shove. He fell over, yes, but the only thing hurt was his cool. Iona saw him get up and walk away.'

Alaric's hands tightened on the steering wheel. 'Are you sure?'

'Yes, I'm sure,' I said firmly. 'I was at the inquest. You had nothing to do with his death.'

Letting out a long breath, Alaric turned to look at me. 'I'm sorry. I've been going over and over this ever since we met, wanting to tell you, but not finding the right time. And, yes,' his face relaxed a little,' I know I'm a moody sod and I know I have a temper. I just felt so bloody ashamed. I mean, what sort of person knocks someone over?'

'Someone who's very angry.'

Alaric's hand moved slowly towards me; he stroked a strand of hair back from my forehead. 'So you forgive me?'

'There's nothing to forgive, you stupid arse! Look: we've all done things in the heat of the moment and regretted them later. When Matt told me he was leaving me for his fluffy secretary I threw a pint of beer over him.'

'Did you?' Alaric's face softened into a smile.

'Yes. And I gave him a shove when he was carting his stuff out of the door – the stuff we'd bought together over the decade we'd lived together. And, yes, he fell over, too, though he fell onto a duvet in a black bag, so it was a soft landing. I felt ashamed, too, but I'm not a psychopath, and neither are you.'

Leaning over, Alaric gave me a brief, gentle kiss. 'Thank you,' he said, and turned the key in the ignition again.

The body had been found in a drainage ditch in a part of the reserve about three hundred metres from the sand dunes. I pulled Alaric's sweater tightly round me, crossing my arms to keep my teeth from chattering. Despite our melancholy reason for being here, the landscape was beautiful in a ghostly sort of way. A fat cloud had sailed in front of the crescent moon, and the reeds were gossiping in the breeze. To begin with I hung back, leaning on the van door, watching. Two police vans and an ambulance had parked on the muddy track, their headlights pointing towards the ditch. A small silver car sat in the shadow of a solitary tree a little further up the track. I took a deep breath and moved quietly forward. There was no sign of the body – it must have been put in the ambulance – and DI Chloe Cooper was talking to Alaric beside the strips of yellow tape put up to protect the crime scene.

'So this is not an area open to the public?'

'No. I come down here regularly to check on the wildlife: the marsh harriers often nest in the bushes in that field. There's a clear sign stating that the public are not allowed – not that it stopped those idiots.' He pointed towards the silver car. Two dark figures were huddled together on the front seat. 'What were they doing, in any case? The usual, I suppose.'

I heard Chloe Cooper sigh at Alaric's judgmental tone. 'Believe it or not, they'd come down here to watch owls, and take photographs. So, not the usual.'

'Oh. Well, they still shouldn't have been here. It disturbs the birds.'

'They saw the body of a woman floating in the ditch, rang 999 at 11.12 pm, and we got here at about 11.35. How long is it since you drove down here?'

'Let me think. A few days – Monday, probably.'

'Hmmm. There are only two sets of tyre tracks. One of those was clearly from the birdwatchers' car. The second track is older, and probably from your van.'

'So how did she get here?'

'We think she walked.'

My heart skipped a beat. Michael had last been seen walking towards his house; I'd been walking when I was shoved under a car. This woman had been walking and then – what? Had she been shoved into the ditch?

'Are you prepared to look at the body? I'd like to know whether you recognise her as a regular visitor to the reserve.'

I followed them towards the ambulance. 'Please can I come with you? I might know her.'

The tired eyes of Chloe Cooper flicked over me. 'That's unlikely. You're a newcomer.'

'I promise I won't pass on any information. Please.'

The detective shrugged her shoulders. 'Oh, all right. But don't you dare breathe a word about any of this until we've released information to the media. Same goes for you, Mr Veil.'

When we got into the ambulance the paramedic unzipped the body bag to reveal a slight, bony woman with straggly brown hair, clearly dyed and white at the roots. She had a beaky nose, thin lips. Bad teeth, with a couple missing from the lower jaw. She smelled noticeably of alcohol – whiskey, I thought – and was wearing a tatty black polo-neck jumper with a frayed neck. I felt a lump in my throat: she looked unloved, uncared for.

Neither I nor Alaric had seen her before.

'We think she's not been dead long, though the PM will give us a more accurate idea.'

'And I suppose you think the death is accidental,' I said.

Chloe Cooper shrugged. 'There are skid marks from her boots on the bank where she went into the ditch, but it's hard to distinguish particular foot prints on the muddy path.'

'And plenty of people walk here, even though they're not supposed to,' said Alaric, his voice still tinged with disapproval.

'Precisely.'

We were quiet in the van on the way back until we reached the outskirts of Middleham.

'I'm sorry that happened on the reserve.'

'So am I,' said Alaric. Then, after a pause, 'poor cow.'

'Did you notice the smell of booze?'

'Yes.'

'And she had the face of a heavy drinker.'

'Perhaps it was an accident. Perhaps she went into the reserve to meet someone – a romantic assignation, perhaps – and fell in the ditch.'

I made a scoffing sound.

'OK. Perhaps not a romantic assignment. But she had to have some reason for wandering into the reserve.'

'Agreed. Perhaps she was scoring some drugs.' Even as I spoke, I didn't feel convinced. The woman had the look of a heavy boozer, and why on earth would someone be selling drugs in the middle of a nature reserve?

We passed the rest of the drive home in silence and parted with a chaste kiss, both needing to rest in our own beds. Alaric was tied up at the weekend with open days on Saturday and Sunday, giving illustrated talks on his beloved marsh harriers in the evenings. 'But I want to see you again,' he said, cupping my face in his hands. 'I'll have some days off next week.'

'I want to see you, too,' I said, breathing an inner sigh of relief.

The next morning I woke up just as Dad was coming back into the house after taking Napoleon for his morning walk. Despite the discovery of the body the night before I'd spent the night in a deep, satisfying sleep. Probably because of all that lovely sex, I thought, making a mental note that the health benefits of fantastic sex might be a good topic for a Bee Cool piece. Yawning, I looked out of my bedroom window. Alaric was coming out of his backyard, wearing a funky green tee-shirt, his dark curls loose and glossy in the early sun. My stomach gave a lurch. Oh-oh: I hoped I wasn't falling in love with him. I didn't fancy another dose of heart-ache, thank you very much. Alaric rolled his shoulders then pulled his hair back into a ponytail as he headed through his garden towards his van. My stomach gave that lurch again: I was a sucker for men who let their hair down when they got into bed. The contrast between loose hair and a trim ponytail was a definite turn-on.

As I got dressed, I heard the sound of the letter box. I went down to see an envelope on the mat and picked it up. It was addressed to me. I took a sharp breath: perhaps it contained some information about Michael's disappearance. I ripped open the envelope.

Fuck off you sex mad bitch. We don't want you here.

27

Rags

Great. So now I was receiving poison pen letters as well as being shoved under cars. The letter was printed in Arial, 14 point. (I notice things like that) on cheap paper. I stood in the hall, with my heart beating loudly in my ears. From the kitchen I could hear Dad singing along to *Bad Moon Rising*. He had a good, tuneful voice, and sounded happy. Part of me wanted to run to him and ask for help, but I didn't want to spoil his day. So I took the letter upstairs and put it in a drawer. I'd talk to him about it when the time was right. As it was, I wasn't looking forward to telling him I'd been out on the nature reserve in the middle of the night looking at another dead body.

I bobbed into the kitchen to make a cup of coffee, then sat at my desk and began to draft Bee Cool's piece on bondage (*Sweet Surrender*), thinking wistfully back to the days when bondage, S and M and vibrators had been transgressive. Now it seemed that every reader of mags like *All for You* wanted to be trussed up, spanked, or prodded with naff plastic devices. 'Must be getting old,' I muttered, thinking of the delicious sex I'd enjoyed with Alaric. I wrote a cheque for the £200 I owed Carola, and popped it into an envelope to her with a postcard of Cley windmill. That felt good. It was a drop in the Atlantic Ocean of my debts, but the others could wait.

At around half eleven I strolled into town to buy a few groceries – bread, milk, a couple of chews for Napoleon – and, on my way back, saw Freddy walking ahead of me with a bag of vegetables. I broke into a jog-trot to catch up with her.

'Morning!' I said, with a bright smile.

'Thought it was afternoon.'

'And how are you feeling? Doll said you were under the weather.'

'Fine.' Two suspicious eyes flicked towards me, then opened wide as they took in my purple and blue black bruises.

'Well I'm not so good,' I said, pointedly. 'Someone pushed me in front of a car. I'm lucky to be alive.'

She stumped along for a few moments then offered, 'you sure it wasn't an accident? Nothing like that ever happens round here.'

'Something happened to Michael Cleverly,' I said, all smiles gone.

Freddy took in a sharp breath. 'Well, everything was all right until *you* turned up.'

'What are you saying? That I drowned Michael Cleverly and threw myself under a car?' No answer to this – which got me riled. 'Look: why are you so bloody hostile? I haven't done anything to you. I'm just trying to find justice for someone whom I believe was murdered.'

Freddy stopped dead and whirled round to wag a finger at me. 'You're a troublemaker, you are. People like you think they own the place. You've only been here five minutes, and you go round stirring up a load of stuff that should be left alone.'

'What sort of stuff?'

But as I spoke, the hairs on the back of my neck stood on end. Freddy's perfume: it was the one I'd smelled just before I was pushed under that car. And Doll had told me that Freddy had got back on the day of the accident, so she could have done it. With my pulse uncomfortably loud in my ears I hurried ahead of her. My mind was whirling as I dashed into the house and put away the groceries. If it was Freddy who'd given me that shove, was it because she wanted to stop me 'stirring up a load of stuff', or because she'd killed Michael? I needed more information, and so rang Paddy McKee for the third time, and asked him to find out if a woman called Susan Fredericks had a criminal record or any history with the police.

'She's living in Middleham now, but from her accent I'd say she was originally from Yorkshire.'

'Will do, babes.'

Sitting at my computer, unable to concentrate on Bee Cool's article, I opened my Michael Cleverly folder, and noted down the evidence against Freddy.

1. I saw her cleaning her garden wall on the morning after Michael disappeared, using bleach. Were there traces of Michael's blood on the wall? Perhaps she fought with him, stunned him, then poured a bottle of vodka down him before dumping him in the river. That would increase his blood alcohol limit, and make it look as if he fell in the river by accident.

2. Her perfume is the same as the one worn by the person who pushed me under the car.

3. She's been jumpy, aggressive, suspicious, ever since I started asking questions.

Finding I couldn't settle to anything, I headed off to the police station yet again and asked to speak to DI Chloe

Cooper. But DI Cooper wasn't there; she was being filmed up at the Nature Reserve. After leaving a message for her to ring me as soon as she could, I made my way home. As I came in the door, Dad called me into the front room, where the local news was blaring out of the television. I rushed through: Chloe Cooper was giving a statement. Behind her I could see the path and ditch where the dead woman had been found.

'An unidentified woman was found dead on the Coastal Reserve last night. Enquiries into her death are continuing, but meanwhile we'd like anyone who recognises the woman to come forward. We believe she's from the Eastern European community.'

A photograph of the woman appeared on the screen. They'd tidied her up but she still looked rough, her cheeks sunken, her hair in coarse straggles. Dad gripped the arms of his chair with his hands. 'Blimey. I know that woman. I sometimes meet my friend Greg at the Waggon and Horses down by the coast, and she's always in there. A complete lush.' He looked over at me. 'Should I ring the police?'

'Yes. The sooner they know who she is, the better.'

Dad went next door to phone. I turned off the TV and sat quietly, trying to think it all through. Last night I'd felt certain that this death was linked to the death of Michael Cleverly, but if Freddy had killed him, perhaps this woman had just wandered into the reserve when she was totally out of her head, slipped into the ditch and drowned. It did happen.

Dad's head popped round the door. 'Phone line's engaged. I expect lots of other people are ringing in. Do you fancy some lunch?'

I did: my stomach was rumbling. He heated up a tin of Heinz tomato soup (his favourite), cut some thick slices of granary bread and laid out butter and strong Cheddar cheese on the table. When we'd sat down he asked, tactfully, how things had gone with Alaric the night before.

Feeling about twelve years old, I went bright red and mumbled that we'd had a lovely evening.

'He'll be upset about the body on the reserve, won't he?'

'Yes.' I paused, then forged on. 'Dad: there's something I need to tell you. The police rang Alaric when the body was found, and I went down there with him. I didn't tell you because they asked us to keep quiet about it until after the news was released to the media.'

Dad almost choked on his bread and butter. 'What the bloody hell did you do that for? You're supposed to be resting. And you told me you'd be careful. I don't want you gallivanting around in the middle of the night.'

'I know, but Alaric was with me the whole time, and I hope my investigation will soon be wrapped up. I'm looking into a definite lead.'

Dad's face became stern. 'Well I certainly hope so. I don't want you putting yourself into any more danger.'

'I promise I'm being careful, Dad.' I reached out to squeeze his arm. 'Now: tell me how things are going with Susie.'

The call from Paddy came through at three o'clock, while I was ploughing my way through a second draft of *Sweet Surrender*. He sounded excited.

'You're going to love this, babes. Susan Fredericks killed her uncle when she was sweet sixteen.'

'*What?*'

'She thumped him, and he fell and cracked his skull open, but it was clearly self defence because he was assaulting her at the time. Reading between the lines, he'd been sexually abusing her for some years. She swore it was an accident, and wasn't charged with any offence.'

Yes! I rang the police station again, and got through to Chloe Cooper this time. She heard me out with a distinct lack of enthusiasm. 'Nothing you've told me can be used to build a case against Susan Fredericks for the attack on you, or on Michael Cleverly. For a start, you can't prove that the person who attacked you (*if* you were, in fact, attacked) was wearing the same perfume as her. Regarding the death of her uncle, even if what you say is true, she's never been charged with any crime, and it's not relevant to this investigation. And, by the way, how did you come across this information?'

'I can't reveal my sources.'

Chloe made a dismissive sound. 'Precisely.'

'But what about all that cleaning and bleaching?'

'Is their yard usually spotless?'

'Yes.'

'And does Susan Fredericks clean it regularly?'

I sighed. 'Yes.' Freddy had been out there again with the bucket yesterday. 'But not the way I saw her go at it on that first Saturday.' My case sounded feeble, even to me.

'I couldn't get the DCI to approve further investigation of Susan Fredericks on the flimsy evidence you've given me. And, in any case, Michael Cleverly was found in the river, a couple of miles away.'

'She could have carried him there in her car.' But even as I said it, I admitted to myself that Freddy's scarlet MG Midget – which I'd looked at with considerable envy – would not be ideal for the transportation of a comatose, full-sized man.

Chloe Cooper gave another of her impatient sighs. 'Look, I'll make a note of our conversation, but I can do nothing more until you come up with some hard evidence.'

I was in a strop when I hung up. OK, so the evidence wasn't watertight, but it was obvious that Freddy had had some sort of barney with Michael when he was drunk, got him down to the river and shoved him in. *And* she'd pushed me in front of the car. I'd practically solved the case, bar a few loose ends, but Chloe Bloody Cooper still wouldn't take any action!

I decided I needed some low-grade retail therapy and hit the charity shops. The Salvation Army shop was a humdinger; I emerged after about twenty minutes with two cream lacy tops and a pair of plum pumps, all bought for a fiver. As often, I thanked my lucky stars that my feet were only a size four. My female friends with normal size feet (seven and above) were left with the clumpy, frumpy big girls' shoes on sale after all the tasty footwear had sold out.

This little spell of retail activity improved my mood, but when I arrived home, and called out a cheerful greeting, Dad didn't answer. I found him in the dining room staring at a piece of paper.

'Look what's come through the door,' he said, handing it to me.

Get rid of that sex mad bitch your daughter or you'll be sorry.

I read it with cheeks burning. 'I'm so sorry, Dad. I never wanted you to get dragged into any of this.'

'I didn't know we had such nasty people in this town.'

'I got one too, a couple of days ago.' I ran upstairs and brought down the poison pen letter addressed to me. We laid them side by side on the table and agreed the paper and font looked the same. 'I didn't tell you about mine because I didn't want to worry you.'

'I'm your father, and I'm *supposed* to worry about you,' said Dad, cross. 'Will you stop trying to protect me? It doesn't help.'

'All right,' I said, chastened. 'It's just that I'm used to doing everything on my own.'

'Well you can just get unused to it.' Then, after a pause:

'Do you think they've got anything to do with Michael Cleverly?'

'I don't know. I've been meaning to find out if other people have received them, but I haven't got round to it because of everything else that's been going on.' I shut my eyes for a moment, thinking. Could Freddy have sent the letters? Just that morning she'd told me in no uncertain terms to stop poking around in things that were none of my business. I decided I had to bring Dad in on this. 'Dad?' I said. 'I think it was Freddy who attacked me, and I think she's implicated in Michael Cleverly's murder. Perhaps she's sending the letters, too.'

'Freddy? Don't be daft. The woman's nearly seventy. Anyway, I've been her neighbour for the past two years, and I think I'd know if she was a murderer.'

'I know it seems unlikely, but I've found out a few things about her, and there are a number of suspicious circumstances.'

I filled Dad in on Freddy's history. He listened thoughtfully, and when I'd finished said, 'but that business with her uncle was a long time ago. And as for all that cleaning, she goes at it every weekend – has done since I moved in.'

'But, Dad, what about the perfume? I swear I smelled that same scent when I was shoved in front of the car.'

'That couldn't have been her, love.'

'Why not? Just because she's a woman and knocking seventy doesn't mean she's a sweet old lady.'

'Get down off your high horse, will you? She couldn't have pushed you in front of the car because I saw her in The Terrace, with Doll, shortly before it happened.'

'*What?*'

'I was taking Napoleon for his evening constitutional and they were on their way home from a meal at the Middleham Tandoori. I spoke to them both. They told me they'd been out to celebrate Freddy's homecoming. I heard the crash just as they were going into their house.'

And then, to my mortification, I burst into tears.

'There, there,' said Dad, coming round the table to pat me awkwardly on my good arm. 'You're still in shock from your accident. Why don't you take it easy for a day or two? I know you won't give up, but you need to rest and get better, too.'

I clung to his striped sweatshirt and sobbed until I was all sobbed out. 'Thank you,' I said, through a blocked-up nose, when I finally stopped. 'I think I needed that.'

Dad returned to his seat on the other side of the table as I blew my nose on a man-size tissue. 'Now,' he said, 'that's settled, then. I'm not having you doing this all on your own. From now on you're going to tell me everything, and we're going to tackle this together.'

28

Graham Whistledown

That afternoon, while Rags, on his orders, was taking a nap, Graham sat in the garden throwing the ball for Napoleon and wondered what the hell had got into him. 'Am I nuts, Napoleon?' he asked, reaching down to pat the dog's silky ears. Napoleon replied with a soft bark and, as often, the answer came to Graham. No, he wasn't nuts: he was furious with whoever had attacked Rags, furious with the nincompoop who was sending poison pen letters, and he was buggered if they were going to get away with it. He had to admit that he now believed Rags when she said that the attack on her was linked to Michael's death. The man had been a nasty piece of work, but if he had been killed by someone, they should be called to account. Oh, heck, he was stubborn as she was! Neither of them wanted to slink away and pretend nothing bad was happening.

As he threw the ball and Napoleon ran after it, returning with his tail wagging, Graham let himself admit something he'd kept locked away for a long time: he hadn't been the best father to Rags when she was a baby. He'd been jealous of her from the moment she was conceived. He'd wanted

Gwendolyn all to himself, wanted to bury his nose in her river of blonde hair, stroke her satiny skin, make love to her as they had in the sand dunes the night they first met. Instead he was shoved away because she was nauseous or had piles or indigestion. Then, when Rags arrived, Gwendolyn descended into an apathy that took years to lift. These days it would be recognised as post-natal depression and he might have been more sympathetic, but back then he'd simmered with resentment against the baby with a head of chestnut curls who'd stolen Gwendolyn from him.

'Dear, dear,' he said to himself now, thinking ruefully that you spend your whole life growing up. Here he was, sixty-seven years old, and still learning how to have a relationship with his own daughter. Well, he may have let Rags down when she was little, but he was going to make up for it now.

They agreed that he'd investigate the poison pen letters. Rags had ruffled a few people's feathers, but he could play the harmless-old-git card. No one was going to slam the door on him. He started at Gerry and Hector's house: he'd seen Gerry jog along the path to her back gate earlier, her runner's vest wet with sweat, so knew she'd be in. As he came in the back gate he noted that the curtains of Iona's bedroom were closed: the poor girl had hardly been seen since Michael Cleverly's body was found. Rags had told him about her outpouring in the graveyard, but he'd dismissed most of it as the result of raging teenage hormones. Now he wasn't so sure. He made a mental note to ask Rags for her record of that conversation. From inside the house he could hear chirpy dance music and the sound of someone jumping around; Gerry was at it again, doing aerobics, or whatever they called it these days. Passing the neat pots in the yard, he came to the back door and tapped on it. No response. He tried the handle and the door opened, so he went in, calling 'Hello!' in a voice loud enough to cut through the dance music. Gerry bounced into the kitchen, hopping from foot to foot, wearing one of those tight pink and orange outfits that leave nothing to the imagination.

'Oh, hang on a minute,' she said. 'I'll just turn off the music.'

In a minute she was back, with a large white towel wrapped round her. 'Now, what can I do you for?' she said, grinning through a fog of endorphins.

Graham arranged his face so he looked pathetic. 'This is a bit embarrassing. I do hope you don't mind me interrupting your exercise session, but something rather upsetting has happened, and I wanted to talk to you about it.'

The manic grin was replaced by concern and Graham was reminded that under her sweat soaked gym clothes, Gerry was a kind, caring person. 'Of course. Sit down. Can I make you a cuppa?'

'No thanks. I've just had one. Look, I'll come straight to the point.' He pulled his poison pen letter out of his jeans pocket. 'I've been in a complete state since I received this, and I'm trying to find out whether other people have got one, too. I don't want to feel I'm being singled out, you see.'

Gerry leaned forward to look at the letter then recoiled as if she'd been stung. When she looked up her green eyes were bright with hurt. 'Yes, I have. Come into the lounge and we can have a chat about it.' Then, in a whisper, 'Iona won't be able to hear us in there.'

He followed her into the lounge, where they sank down onto the black leather sofa. Gerry moved close to him, delivering a whiff of halitosis that took Graham by surprise. 'I got one a few weeks ago. I've thrown it away now. Didn't want to have it in the house.'

'And what did it say, if you don't mind me asking?'

Gerry sighed, sending another blast of stale huff Graham's way. 'It made nasty accusations about the state of my marriage.'

'Ah. I see.'

'Ridiculous things, suggesting that Hector was ...' As she moved closer Graham held his breath. ' ... having an affair.' She straightened up, her nose and cheeks flaring red. 'Absolute nonsense. I showed the letter to Hector and he just laughed his head off. Said it was total rubbish.'

'That's the way to deal with it,' said Graham. 'And you say this was a few weeks ago?'

'Yes. I remember that it was before half-term, so it must have been in the third week of May.'

'Well, you've put my mind at rest. At least I know I'm not being singled out. Do you have any idea of who could be sending them?'

Gerry thought for a moment then shook her head. 'No. Unless it was Patsy, when she was blind drunk. We'd had a few cross words, you see, before I got my letter.'

'What about?'

'Silly things. She'd forgotten to put her recycling out and there were bottles scattered round her yard. I suggested she tidy them up. Another time I invited her to come to the gym with me, and she took offence. That sort of thing.'

'Oh dear. She could be like that, couldn't she?'

'Yes. She wasn't the easiest person to have as a neighbour.'

Graham struggled to his feet from the shiny leather sofa. 'Well, I'd better be getting along. Thanks for confiding in me.'

Graham said his goodbyes and made his way to Freddy and Doll's house, where he found them sitting in the garden sipping gin and tonics. 'Hello there!' called Doll, when he made his way in the gate. 'Come and join us.' Freddy nodded a greeting, but didn't smile. Graham nodded back, thinking that Rags was right about one thing: something was up with Freddy. She'd never been a bundle of fun, but now she looked like she was at the head of a funeral procession. 'Don't mind Freddy,' said Doll. 'She's a bit off-colour, aren't you, love?'

To which Freddy grunted.

'I won't keep you long,' said Graham, and launched into the same routine as he'd used with Gerry.

Doll pulled a face as she read the letter. 'Oh, how awful for you! No, we haven't had anything like that, have we, Freddy? But I can see why you were so upset. Why do people *do* these things? Do you know, we had a spate of letters like these at the school where I worked. Some people were so upset they had to take time off. I didn't get one, but …'

As she prattled on, Graham zoned out. When he'd brought out the letter, Freddy's stony face had flinched. She'd looked at the letter with wide eyes that he'd swear were bright with fear.

His last port of call was at number one. Tim was at work, but Tracey was puffing into the garden with a huge basket of washing clasped in her arms.

'Can I help you with that?' he called. When she didn't protest, he helped her hang out sheets and duvet covers decorated with tank engines and motor cars. How to peg out washing was one of many things he'd learned when Rags was young and Gwendolyn had spent the whole time flopped on the sofa.

'Thanks,' said Tracey, with a hint of a smile. 'Damon's been wetting the bed recently, and it makes for a heck of a lot of washing.'

'I know,' said Graham, though Rags had never had a problem in that department.

'Actually I came to ask you something,' said Graham, when the washing was safely on the line.

Tracey listened to him with an impassive expression. When he showed her the letter, she wrinkled her nose as if he'd wafted a bad smell under her nose. 'Probably kids, isn't it? They get up to all sorts these days. Their parents don't discipline them properly. It could even be that Iona, from number five. She hangs around in the park all the time.'

'If you don't mind me asking, have you had one?'

Tracey opened her mouth then shut it again. Her eyes hardened. 'Yes, I have. Some rubbish about my kids making too much noise. And, before you ask, I threw it away.'

'And would you be prepared to talk to the police about it?'

'The police? No way. And now I've got to get a move on.'

Shoving past Graham, she waddled off towards the house, slamming the gate behind her.

Over a dinner of haddock and chips, mushy peas, and a glass of ruby-red Barolo, Graham summed up his findings.

'The letters started a few weeks before you got here. Gerry received one. Freddy and Doll received one but are pretending they didn't. And I've got a hunch about who's been sending them.'

* * *

Doll Perkins

Doll came into the kitchen to find some painkillers, leaving Freddy dozing in front of the TV. Her left hip was becoming a bloody nuisance. She'd had the other one done four years before, and until recently had enjoyed being free of pain. Oh, she'd had a bout of sciatica last year, but that had been nothing compared to this bloody hip. And it got worse after she'd been gardening. The doctor at the local surgery had been sympathetic: he'd given her a cortisone injection a few weeks ago and that had helped, but the effect was wearing off now, and he'd told her he couldn't keep doing that indefinitely. What's more, he'd hinted that it would have to get worse before she could go on the waiting list for a second hip replacement.

Bah. She felt like banging a few cupboard doors and smashing a cup or two, but of course *nice* Doll, *docile* Doll didn't do that sort of thing, did she?

But then *nice, docile* Doll would have rung for the ambulance as soon as her sadistic husband started having his heart attack, instead of fussing over him and getting him a cup of tea, telling him it was just a spot of indigestion as his face went purple then faded to a sickly grey. She'd taken a first aid course and had a pretty good idea of what was happening to him. She might have reached for the phone if he hadn't started ordering her around. *Get a fucking move on, you dozy cow. Get me a bucket or something. I'm going to throw up.*

Standing there, in her kitchen, with the sun pouring over the pots of lobelias and alyssum on the windowsill, Doll gave her head a vigorous shake. What was the matter with her? That was all done and dusted. She had it all – a loving relationship, a gorgeous home. Her tiresome daughter Beth had found Jesus. Her son was established in Boston as an attorney, married to a stick-thin woman who did something in marketing. Doll suspected they were both closet cases, but she wasn't going to say anything. *Nice, docile* Doll would never ruffle the waters.

And she had Freddy – silly Freddy, getting herself all worked up over nothing. Thank goodness she'd got Freddy to tell her what she'd had on her mind for the past couple of weeks. They'd talked about it and Doll hoped she'd made Freddy see sense. For a moment Doll's face clouded: Freddy was still touchy, still jumpy. She kept grumbling about Rags, even though Doll had told her she had nothing to worry about. Just now and then Doll wished that Freddy was a bit less sensitive.

Another dart of pain shot through her hip. Wincing, Doll poured herself a glass of Evian from the bottle in the fridge and opened the drawer where they kept all the bits and bobs – rubber bands, plastic teaspoons, wine bottle stoppers, bus timetables, programmes for local theatres – looking for some painkillers. Her fingers found a bubble pack of paracetamol. But as she pulled it out, her fingers snagged on a crumpled letter – a letter addressed to her and Freddy, from their bank. Her fingers froze for a moment. What was it doing in here? They had a drawer in the living room for bank statements and financial gubbins. She opened the letter. It was about their joint savings account. Put it down.

Picked it up again, unable to believe what she was reading.

29

Rags

'Looking good.'

It was eight in the morning, and I was talking to my reflection while studying my black eye in the mirror. Its glorious purple had taken on an olive-green tinge, enhanced by a sooty ring smudged round the bone of the eye socket. I took a selfie on my phone, as I had every day since my accident/assault, to record its progress, and had enjoyed watching the colours bloom then decay. The human body was always interesting – its capacity for pleasure, and its skill in repairing itself. Leaning closer to the mirror, I lifted the hair on my right temple to find that the scab had deepened to a blackberryish purple, with a bobbly crust. Gross. But, on the bright side, it was healing well. The tape used to hold the edges of the wound together looked grubby, though I wasn't going to peel it off. Not yet. I looked more closely at my hair and tutted. Oh, I wasn't going grey – not really – but a few white strands had crept into the brown, and the chestnut glow that had caught the rays of the sun when I was younger had been livened up by hair colour for the last ten years. Not that there was anything wrong with that. *Everyone* coloured their hair, didn't they? Even kids of fourteen who, lord knows, didn't need to. For years I'd swanned off to Toni and Guy for a tint and a trim once a month. Ha. That had gone out the window since I lost my job, though I had to admit that my hair looked almost as good when I coloured it at home.

Over a late breakfast Dad and I planned our next moves. 'We're not back to square one, you know,' said Dad. 'At least we can be sure that Freddy didn't attack you.'

I groaned. 'I feel a complete idiot for going down to the police station and insisting that it was her.'

'You were absolutely right to tell them what you knew. And there *is* something funny going on with her and Doll. We've just got to find out what it is.'

'I suppose you're right.'

'Yes, I am,' said Dad, who'd never been one to waver in his opinions. 'And we've now got a good idea of what's happening with the letters. Let's start with them, and they might give us a lead on what happened to Michael, and who attacked you.'

'Sounds good.'

'I'll bet my pension pot that Tracey's sent them. I mean, think about it. She's got a chip on her shoulder the size of the Houses of Parliament; she's an intelligent woman stuck at home with two difficult children; she's fallen out with just about everyone on the street. And her reaction when I asked her if she'd received a letter was peculiar. No, she's sending them all right, just to be spiteful. The one to Gerry was sent weeks before you arrived.'

'But the nasty letters *we* got were warning us off, which suggests Tim might be somehow implicated in Michael's death. Tracey's trying to get rid of me.'

Dad sighed. 'I hate to say this, but you might be right. We need to talk to them both again.'

'Tracey's a tough nut to crack. I got nowhere with her.'

'Ah but Tim's a different kettle of fish, isn't he? Come on, Rags. What would you do if you wanted to get a quote out of him for a news story?'

'I'd doorstep him. Pester him until he said something – gave something away.'

'There you go then. We'll do that, but not at his home where the warrior queen will pour boiling tar all over us. Let's pay him a visit at the salon.'

We gave each other high fives with both hands. I found myself grinning from ear to ear. This was more like it! I'd been lonely, I realised – living on my own, working on my own, writing piffle. OK, so some maniac had tried to kill me and I was living in the Back of bloody Beyond, but I wasn't on my own.

We decided to head off to Wells-next-the-Sea for a walk, since there was nothing more we could do on a Sunday, and Dad was adamant that I needed to relax and get some fresh air.

The day was overcast but warm, and we were soon cruising down the dry road, with Napoleon standing on my knees. As we passed the easterly edge of the Holkham estate the scent of brine crept through the open windows. In the distance a strip of sea shone like a streak of pale blue paint on the horizon, merging with the sky. I could get used to this, I thought, realising that I hadn't spent a single second of the day missing my London world. Or perhaps I could live in both places, if Dad would let me visit whenever I wanted. That's what rich people did.

But even as I built this castle in the air, the figure of

£11,000 popped into my head – the amount I still owed in back rent, credit and store cards. Oh, and I had an overdraft of two grand. When was I ever going to be able to scrape together the deposit to rent a London flat?

'Penny for them,' said Dad, slowing down as we came into the town and turned right to drive into the little town.

'Just thinking about London.'

'You'll soon be back there, love.'

I wasn't so sure.

We found a parking space close to the post office on Station Road (though sadly the station was long gone), and strolled down through the back streets towards the sea, past gardens bursting with the colours of mallows and roses, delphiniums and lupins. Napoleon gave a couple of barks of appreciation as we crossed the road to the quay. We turned right, away from the crowds eating fish and chips or crabbing in the harbour, to walk along the East Quay, past the handsome custom house (now a B and B) and the yacht club. The sun eased the ache in my shoulder as we strolled down the quiet road and along the track that passed the old whelk sheds. Dad let Napoleon off his long lead, so he could run ahead to the coast path.

'I'd forgotten it was so beautiful,' I said, thinking of a long-ago outing with Dad when I was a stroppy teenager on my summer visit to the house in King's Lynn.

'What? These scruffy old sheds?' said Dad, laughing as he pointed at one of the sheds piled with crab baskets, plastic crates and other fishermen's bits and pieces.

I gave him a gentle dig in the ribs. 'You know what I mean. And I like the fact that this is still a fishing town.'

'I was just teasing you.' He gave his head a small shake. 'I don't know why it took me so long to move out of Lynn.

I suppose I got stuck – in my job, and in that house.' He sighed.

And in the past, I thought.

'Ah well. I got here in the end.' He pushed open the gate to the footpath that wound its way along the raised bank separating salt marsh from farmland. 'Come on. Napoleon's waiting.'

We walked up the small slope and onto the bank of the coastal path, admiring the sheen of the salt marsh mud stitched with the footprints of waders and gulls. Napoleon tore down into the meadows that opened up on the land-ward side of the bank. Dad and I strolled, stopping now and then to look at birds.

'Look: egrets!' He passed over his binoculars.

Two stately birds, white as frost, were wading through a shallow stream, darting black beaks into the water in search of fish.

We watched them for a while then walked on. 'I like it here,' he said. 'You get to watch a whole world that's free of human interference.'

I agreed. I was sick of human interference of the malev-olent kind.

After about forty minutes we turned back. Before we left the coast path to return to the town we sat on one of the benches in front of the boat yard, closing our eyes to catch the sun on our faces. Napoleon was flopped at our feet. Behind us, the masts sang in the breeze. Tall Alexander plants, (imported by the Romans, Dad informed me), perfumed the air with their scent of mead. Dad spotted a curlew and handed over the binoculars so I could watch its long, curved beak dipping in and out of the estuary mud.

'My mum and I used to come down to the coast to pick

samphire when I was little,' said Dad, surprising me, as he seldom talked about his family. 'She'd boil it up for supper and serve it with a dab of butter, salt and pepper.'

'I'm sorry I never met her.'

'So am I. You look a bit like her, you know.'

'Do I? What was she like?'

'Well, her hair was the same colour as yours, and she had the same, determined look about her.'

'Really?'

'Yes. She was the youngest of six, and *her* dad worked on the fishing boats. But the family moved into Lynn after the war because the fishing work was drying up in Wells even then. When she was fifteen she started work in a canning factory, and that's where she met my father.' He paused for moment, looking down at his hands. 'They died within a few months of each other, in 1959. They both smoked, you see. Woodbines. The whole family did. I was brought up by Aunty Molly – my father's sister – from when I was twelve. You remember her, don't you?'

'Yes.' I remembered regular visits to Great-Aunt Molly's tiny, over-heated terraced house on the Gayton side of Lynn, where she lived with her poodle, Peppy. The place had smelled of woodsmoke and pots of plum and blackberry jam which Molly made and sold at WI meetings and stalls. Fat, wheezy, wreathed in cardigans, she'd plied me with cough sweets and jam tarts whenever we visited. I know so little about Dad, I thought, glancing at his clean-shaven, sensible face, hoping he'd say more. Avoiding my gaze, he reached down and stroked Napoleon's silky ears, signalling the end of the conversation for the time being.

I rubbed my neck and shoulders to tease out a few more knots left by my collision with the tarmac, and, as I did so, became aware of a young woman in shorts and a baggy, white jumper sitting, hunched, on the bench beside ours.

Blonde hair so pale it was almost silver spilled round her face and shoulders. Then I realised she was crying. Napoleon gave a quiet whine. He doesn't like people crying; Dad says it upsets him.

'Are you all right?' I called, softly. The girl replied with a fresh torrent of sobs, caught in a tatty tissue that looked soaked through.

'Here.' Dad went over to her bench and held out a proper cotton handkerchief. She waved her hand and shook her head, but he insisted. 'Go on. That tissue's not going to last long.'

'Thank you,' she gasped, and buried her face in the clean cotton.

'We'll just sit down over there,' said Dad, coming back to sit beside me. 'Don't mind us.'

The sobs from the other bench subsided. 'I'm sorry to disturb your peace and quiet,' called the young woman, in an accent I couldn't quite place.

'You haven't disturbed us at all,' I said. 'Here. Do you want to take a look at the curlew? Over there.' I held the binoculars out and, after a short hesitation, the woman joined us on our bench and took them.

'Thank you.' She watched for a couple of minutes then handed back the binoculars. 'You must think I'm crazy,' she said, the words tumbling out. 'But I have come here because I am sad – very sad – and I love this place. It is – how do you put it? – a consolation. You see, my friend has died – she was found on the reserve – and ...'

'I'm so sorry,' I said, exchanging swift glances with Dad: she might be able to tell us more about the dead woman. 'Is there anything we can do? Buy you a cup of coffee, perhaps?'

'No, no. I can't ask you to do that. I am not a child. I am a grown woman.' She blew her nose fiercely.

But we'd like to buy you a coffee, wouldn't we, Rags?'

chipped in Dad. 'Or an ice cream. That always makes things better, and I know where we can get good ones in Wells.'

The young woman gave Dad a smile which lit up her whole face – a striking face, with high, wide set cheekbones and pale blue eyes. 'OK. You are very kind. Perhaps an ice cream would be nice.'

Five minutes later we were sat on the wall beside the quay spooning ice cream into our mouths. I had vanilla – well, what other flavour comes close? – Dad had chocolate, and the young woman had strawberry. Right: it was now or never to find out more about the woman who'd been found dead on the reserve.

'I'm so sorry to hear that your friend died. What was her name?'

'Katerina. She came from my home town in Lithuania. I didn't know her well, but it was because of me she came here, and I feel responsible for her death. She was so unhappy, you see. She came with my cousin, Ramon. He's not a real cousin – he's my auntie's stepson but I call him my cousin – and he's not a nice man, not a nice man at all. He drinks and drinks, and she drinks and drinks and they pretend they're happy when they're not. But Ramon is ten years younger than her so he laughs at her and insults her and she gets upset.' Her words petered to a halt while she looked out over the salt marsh gilded by rays of sun. 'I thought it would be good for him to come here, but he is lazy. She is the one doing all the work – cleaning, cleaning, cleaning. When she is not drunk she is a good person.' She looked at me with eyes bright with tears. 'And I think that she killed herself. I think she threw herself into that ditch. She couldn't swim, you see, and I think she wanted to drown.'

'But that's not your fault.'

'It is,' said the young woman vehemently. 'It *is*. I told them to come while they could, to make money before

Brexit. I even got Ramon some work, doing odd jobs for my boss. And then ten days ago – *pouf!* – he goes back to Lithuania. Says he's had enough, and that he's finished with her. And he takes all her savings, so she's left with nothing. And I offer to lend her money but she says no because she's a proud woman.'

'But you're not responsible for whatever this Ramon has done,' said Dad. 'You sound like you were a good friend to them both.'

'Was I?'

'Yes, you were.'

She let out an audible sigh. 'Thank you,' she said, handing back Dad's handkerchief. 'You make me feel much better. You are good people.' She stood up. 'And now I should be going. I have to pack. I am going home to see my parents.'

'Do you think you'll come back?'

'I might, though people are not nice to me now that Britain is leaving the EU. They look at me like I'm a criminal.' She shrugged. 'In any case my boss has given me the sack. He says he needs a person who is better qualified. And because I am on a short-term contract he can get rid of me, just like that.'

'That doesn't sound fair.'

'It isn't.' Her face clouded over. 'He is so nice to me, so complimentary, and then he turns on me. One day he is charming, the next day he says I have to leave straightaway.' She released an angry breath then pulled her shoulders back. 'But you don't want to hear me moaning like this! I am strong. I will – how you say it? – bounce back.'

'I'm sure you will.'

The woman shook both our hands and set off towards the bus stop, giving us one final wave.

'Well, that's one mystery solved,' said Dad. 'It sounds like Katerina committed suicide. Sad story, though.'

'Yes.' The young woman's face was familiar, but I couldn't place where I'd seen her – perhaps at Middleham market, which attracted people from all the surrounding villages.

'And what a nasty thing to do – to sack her just like that,' said Dad. 'Some people are pond life, aren't they?'

I couldn't argue with that.

30

Rags

Since Tim's salon wasn't open on Monday, I spent the day lazing around, reading *Imperium*, another Robert Harris novel plundered from Dad's bookshelf, about the Roman orator Cicero. As before, I was blown away by his creation of the Roman world, and the depth of the characters. Totally gripped, I read it for most of the day, only stopping to share a pizza with Dad. By the evening I felt rested, recovered.

I woke early on Tuesday with anticipation singing like a lark in my head. Alaric was coming round later for a meal – a meal I sincerely hoped would be followed by a night of red-hot sex, during which I might be able to do more than just lie on my back. I hadn't seen him since our visit to the reserve in the middle of the night, and I was missing him.

But things were looking up on the investigation front; the chance meeting with the girl on Sunday had ignited a small glow of optimism in my heart. It seemed likely that Katerina had taken her own life (poor cow) and with her death explained, I could devote all my efforts to closing the Michael Cleverly enquiry. I'd had enough now, and wanted it to be over. Apart from anything else, I didn't fancy being killed or maimed. If I could get rid of the psychopath who'd attacked me and killed Michael, I could get on with sorting out the rest of my life.

Over a breakfast of boiled eggs and granary toast Dad and I discussed how to deal with Tim. We wanted to lean on him, but agreed it would be best not to tackle him in the salon. So Dad would get him outside on some pretext, and then we'd both pounce.

We headed into town at half ten and found *Strands* empty of customers. I hid round the corner while Dad went in and asked Tim to come outside for a few moments as he wanted his help with 'something confidential'. When they turned the corner into the market square, I appeared and linked my arm through Tim's. Dad did the same with his other arm, and before he could protest, we steered him over to an unoccupied bench and sat him down.

'Right, let's stop pissing around,' I said. 'You know something about what happened to Michael Cleverly on the night he disappeared. Several people, including me, saw you sitting with him at the bar, yet you swore blind that you weren't in the pub that night.'

'I got confused. Anyone can get confused.'

He tried to stand up, but Dad pulled him firmly down onto the bench. 'Sit *down*.'

'And someone tried to kill me the other night, and I bet you know something about it.'

'I don't! I swear I don't!'

I leant closer, my voice a harsh whisper. 'And if you don't start talking, I'm going to tell the world and his wife how you ruined my hair with your appalling haircut. It wouldn't be hard: a few posts on Facebook, a couple of tweets.' As I spoke drops of sweat appeared on Tim's forehead but I quashed any feelings of guilt. 'I need some answers. *Now.*'

'Come on, son. You'll feel better if you just tell us what's going on,' said Dad, playing the good cop role to perfection.

We sat for a minute or two listening to Tim's panicky breaths. 'If I tell you, will you leave me alone?' he said at last.

'Of course.'

'And you won't say anything to Tracey?'

'Of course not.'

'It's embarrassing. You see Michael had found out that I was nicking flowers and vegetables from the allotments, and he was blackmailing me.'

Blackmail. The word sank into my stomach like a stone.

'Oh, he never got much money out of me,' continued Tim, voice raw with humiliation. 'He knew I was broke. But every time I ran into him in the pub he started hinting that he could make life difficult for me. And he went on and on until I bought him a glass of his poxy wine. It amused him: he thought it was funny to see me squirm.'

'But why didn't you tell me this before? Why did you say you weren't in the pub?'

Tim turned a hot, angry face towards me. 'Because I was ashamed. Because I thought it might come out that I'd been nicking things – and nicking from the *allotments*. If word got out about that I'd be finished! In a town like this stealing from the allotments is like – I don't know – being a paedophile, or something.'

Me and Dad exchanged looks.

'You won't tell anyone, will you?' said Tim, his voice tight with worry.

'Not unless it's absolutely necessary.'

'Now can I ...?'

'Sit *down!*' said Dad again. 'We've not finished with our questions, and you've already wasted my daughter's time by lying to her.'

'That night – the night I arrived in Middleham – did Michael seem drunk to you?'

Tim dropped his head to look at his trembling hands. 'A bit more than usual, yes. Wayne said he'd had a few vodkas as well as wine. Michael told me he was celebrating a stroke of good luck, though he was so full of bullshit I don't know if that was true or not. He was cruel, you know. He enjoyed having power over people. He was ... he was a fucking monster.'

'How long had this been going on? The blackmail, I mean.'

'About a year.'

'And was he blackmailing other people, too?'

A loose shrug. 'I know he was getting free drinks out of Wayne. He was probably tapping him for cash, too.'

'The landlord?'

'Yes. Wayne told me about it one night, after the pub had closed. I don't want to say what Michael had on him, but let's just say that Wayne's wife wouldn't be too pleased if she found out. He knew we were both in the same boat, so sometimes, if I was really short, he'd not take money off me for Michael's drinks.'

'And you don't know about anyone else he was black-mailing, apart from Wayne?'

'No!' Tim jerked his arm away from me. 'And I've got a perm coming in at 10.45 so I need to get back to the salon.'

'Are you sure there's nothing else you can tell us?'

'No.'

I wasn't convinced. He still looked shifty, and I wanted to ask him about the poison pen letters, but he was struggling to get up and an elderly couple were watching the three of us and whispering to each other.

'Go on, then,' said Dad.

We watched him walk off, a slender figure with his hands stuffed into the pockets of his jeans, thin hair caught by the wind whistling round the town centre.

'I told you Michael Cleverly was a nasty piece of work,' said Dad, when Tim had disappeared round the corner.

'You were right.' And I was wrong, I added to myself.

I was subdued on the way home, busy tearing myself to pieces for not seeing the bleeding obvious in front of my nose. *Of course* Michael Cleverly had been a blackmailer! It was the perfect way to get hold of money without the hassle of dealing drugs or stealing. And he was expecting a payment (or payments) that weekend, to make up the dosh he needed to invest in the Antibes development.

Back at the house, over a cup of Earl Grey, we discussed whether to go to the police with what Tim had told us. 'It's an important lead,' said Dad. 'We should let them know.'

'You're right.' I picked up my phone and dialled the station, but Chloe Cooper was testifying at Norwich crown court in a major armed robbery case. I left a message saying I had something significant to tell her, and then Dad and I got out all the notes I'd made since I took on the investigation, and discussed the most likely candidates for blackmail.

'Well, Freddy is the obvious one,' I said. 'I bet he found out about her past and threatened to tell Doll.'

'Perhaps. But I wouldn't have thought she'd be able to lay her hands on much money.'

'I don't know about that. She used to be a teacher and would have received a sizable lump sum as well as a good pension.'

'But we know she didn't attack you.'

'She could have paid someone else to do that.'

Dad pulled a face. 'Maybe. I'm not convinced, though. What about Gerry and Hector?'

'I just can't see it. All right, she's a gym bunny and a bundle of nerves, but that's not blackmail fodder, is it?'

'And Hector?'

'Does he look like a man who's being blackmailed?' I said, thinking of his easy demeanour and open smile. Of all the people I'd met, he seemed the least uptight. 'Have you heard any rumours about him?'

Dad shook his head. 'Only rumours about what an excellent dentist he is.' He thought for a moment. 'I suppose Wayne, the pub landlord, is a possibility.'

'Yes,' I said. 'In fact he's a *distinct* possibility. His behaviour has been suspicious right from the start. He's been downright obstructive. And as he runs a pub, he'd be able to lay his hands on a sizeable amount of cash. I wonder what Michael could have on him.'

'Probably some seedy love affair. He and his wife live in a house out near Holt, and I've heard she's the one with the money. If he's been playing away, he wouldn't want her to know about it.'

'I suppose we should look at Michael's family again, just in case I've missed something.' Together we went through the notes I'd made of my interviews with Michael's mother and sister, but agreed they were unlikely to be blackmail victims.

'They didn't have any spare cash, and without his money Leeanne's rehab is stuffed. Plus, as far as I could see, all their dirty laundry was hung on the washing line to dry. Everyone knew their business. You can only blackmail people who want to keep secrets.'

'What about the nephew?' said Dad. 'Could Michael have been extorting money from him?'

'Again, I can't see it. He's only recently got out of youth custody, and Michael was giving the family money to support him.'

'Well then, what about his work colleagues? He'd left on that Friday, hadn't he?'

'Yes. And he'd told Shell he was getting a big commission, which we know never came through.' I thought for a moment. 'Perhaps his boss was fiddling the books and Michael found out. I think I should dig a little deeper into the affairs of Gordon and Gordon.'

We sat in silence for a while, then Dad said, 'And what about Alaric?'

I sighed: the same question had crossed my mind. He'd been having it off with the boss's wife, hadn't he? Perhaps Michael had extracted money from him in return for keeping quiet about it. 'Let's talk to him when he comes round later.'

But we didn't get the chance to speak to Alaric. He rang me that afternoon, his voice tight, saying that his father had been rushed into hospital. 'He's had a heart attack – a major one – and I'm on my way to Sussex now, to see him. I'm sorry I can't make it tonight. You know I'd love to see you, but ...'

'I understand. I hope he's OK.'

'It's touch and go. I'll ring you later or tomorrow.'

As I put the phone down I felt shivers running up the back of my neck and sneezed five times. Great: now I was coming down with a cold. I went to bed early with a thumping headache, the last few chapters of *Imperium*, and a cup of cocoa.

31

Rags

I spent most of Wednesday in bed, snuffling and devouring books. I finished *Imperium* and moved onto a Henning Mankell novel. Its sodden, glum tone chimed with my mood. I felt like I was wading through porridge with the investigation. It didn't help that Shell rang just as I was dozing off while listening to the Radio 4 afternoon play.

'So: I am back in England, and I want to hear what progress you have made. Two weeks I've been waiting for a solution, and still you are feeding me crumbs.'

I raised my eyes to the ceiling. What did the bloody woman want? A miracle? 'You've received my reports, haven't you?'

'Reports, reports. All I get is reports. I want answers, not reports.'

'Actually, we've just found out something crucial to the investigation, Michael ...'

'*We*? Who is this *we*?'

'My father's been helping me out.'

A dismissive splutter burst out of the phone. 'Your *father*?

How old is he? If you want an assistant, you should find a young man, a *virile* man, who can protect you.'

'My dad is a perfectly healthy man, thank you very much. And he knows the town and all our neighbours. He's a great asset to the investigation.'

'Pffff.'

'Anyway, as I was saying, we've made an important discovery.' I braced myself. 'Michael was blackmailing people. That's how he was building up funds for the Antibes development.'

For once Shell was silent. When she did speak, her voice was icy. 'That's not possible. You have made a mistake. Michael was not a blackmailer.'

'Yes, he was!' I snapped. 'Someone told us that Michael was blackmailing him, and I believe him.'

'Who? Who has told you this? Is he the killer?'

'No. I don't think he's the killer. He doesn't have the balls or the brains.'

'Have you gone to the police?'

'Not yet, but ...'

'Then go *immediatement*. I am very disappointed in you. I think you can do this, but now I'm not so sure.'

'Oh put a sock in it,' I yelled. 'I've been working my arse off for you. Someone's tried to kill me. The police are doing fuck-all. And if you don't like what I'm doing you can find someone else.'

Oops. I hadn't meant to say that last bit. I held my breath, expecting the bank of Shell to dry up, leaving me to slide back into my financial sinkhole, but when Shell next spoke, she sounded a tad less imperious. 'That's better. I like to hear the fire in your belly.'

'Do you?' I said, feebly, deciding that I wouldn't comment on Shell's mixed metaphor – not while she was being conciliatory.

'And I want to assist now that I am in the UK. I don't want to just sit and wait for *reports*. What can I do?'

Phew. 'Could you look at the public documents relating to the inquest? They're online and available to the public. Search under Norwich Coroner's Court. You might see something that I've missed.'

'OK. I can do this.'

'And can you talk to his associates down in Diss to see if he could have been blackmailing any of them? Business associates? His old boss? We know he'd been cheating Michael out of commission on house sales.'

'So you think the killer might have come from Diss?'

'It's possible.' I took another big breath. 'And I'd like to authorise my expert to check out all the occupants of The Terrace, to find out if they were blackmail material. Is that OK?'

An audible sigh. 'Yes. But you could have done that before, instead of concentrating on this Freddy.'

'I know, but she looked like the most likely person to be the murderer.'

'It seems to me that you have been wasting time.'

I clenched my teeth, determined not to have another ding-dong. 'So I can go ahead? It might cost a few hundred quid.'

'Just do it.'

After we'd hung up, I dialled Paddy's number. This time I asked him to look into all the adults living in The Terrace and gave him a wider brief. 'I want anything – not just what's in police files. I want to know about anything that's been in the media – any sex scandal, marital blip, PR disaster, university prank. Anything.'

A long whistle came out of the phone. 'That might take a bit longer. And cost a bit more. A few ponies, in fact.'

'It can be a whole bloody herd, for all I care. She's said she'll pay.'

'Blimey: she sounds wonderful. Can you fix me a date with her?'

'She'd eat you for breakfast.'

'Sounds like my sort of girl.'

As we signed off, I found myself smiling. It was a shame Paddy looked like a bear with a broken nose and had a gambling habit. Apart from that, he was a real catch.

Early the next morning my sleep was broken by a hail of sharp, loud barks. 'Oh, shut up,' I mumbled, having suffered from a succession of barking, howling and yelping dogs in London. Then I realised it was Napoleon, making shrill sounds nothing like the joyful barks he produced when he was happy. With a racing heart I threw back the duvet and jumped out of bed. From my window I could see Dad lying on the garden path clutching his leg, groaning in pain. Throwing my kimono over my cotton pyjamas I dashed downstairs and out into a misty, drizzly morning. 'Dad! What's happened? Are you all right?'

'I've hurt my bloody knee. Jesus! And my ankle.'

'Did you slip over? What happened?'

Dad looked up at me with tears of pain in his eyes. 'No I didn't ruddy well slip over. Someone put a wire across the entrance to the garden to trip me up.'

'You've got to be kidding me!'

But he wasn't. A spiteful snake of thin wire – the sort you use to tack plants onto garden trellis – lay on the stone garden path. One end of it was still hammered to a gatepost; the other end had been dislodged when Dad tripped over it. Some sick bastard had hammered this piece of fencing wire about a foot from the ground so Dad would trip over it and break his leg or crack his head open. Suddenly I felt sick. They'll go after Napoleon next, I thought. They'll poison him, and we'll find him dead. In the middle of my ribcage I felt the stirring of a molten, incandescent fury. This was personal. Someone was after me and my dad and his dog and I was not going to let them succeed.

'Shall I call an ambulance?'

'No! I don't need a blooming ambulance. Nothing's broken.'

'You can't know that, Dad.'

'Yes, I can. Help me get back into the house and we'll take a look at the damage.'

His grumpiness gave me hope: this was the Dad I knew, the default Dad, if you like. He couldn't be that badly hurt. I dashed back inside and fetched a kitchen chair. 'Lean on me and on the chair, so we can get you on your feet without you putting too much weight on your damaged leg.' With a lot of tussling and groaning from us both, we got him upright, and he hopped into the house, leaning on me. Installed in the kitchen, he tried to roll up his jeans, but they wouldn't go far enough. He turned to me with a grunt of exasperation. 'I know you'll think I'm an old fool, but can you please fetch me a rug from the lounge? If you promise not to watch I'll take my jeans off, and put the rug over my legs.'

'OK.' Once I'd brought him the tartan rug thrown over the sofa, I looked out of the window at the mizzle as he winced and groaned his way out of his jeans.

'You can turn round now.'

Gingerly, we took a look at his injuries. His right knee was hatching a fat, red bruise. More worrying was his ankle, which was visibly swelling, and which he couldn't put any weight on. 'That needs looking at. Please let me take you to A and E.'

'There's no need. It's a twenty-mile drive, and we'd have to wait for hours.'

'Then we'll go to the doctor's surgery as soon as it opens.'

Dad opened his mouth to argue, but I silenced him by raising a finger, as you do to a disobedient child. 'And I'm not taking no for an answer.'

Dad let out a breath. 'Oh, all right. Can you find me some painkillers?'

'I've got some Co-codamol upstairs: a couple of those will take the edge off the pain until we can get to the surgery.'

'Napoleon needs to go for a walk.'

'No, he doesn't. He'd prefer to stay here with you.' Napoleon, alert and watching everything, gave a quiet whine. 'See?'

'But you'll take him out later?'

'Of course I will, when you're sorted out.'

After cups of sweet tea and four rounds of buttered toast, we pitched up to the surgery when it opened at 8 am. By what seemed like a miracle to me, used to the ordeal of waiting a week to see a doctor in Hackney unless you were dying of appendicitis, we got an emergency appointment straightaway with a young, red-haired doctor who examined the ankle with gentle fingers and pronounced it badly sprained but not broken. He sent Dad off to one of the nurses to have it bandaged, and we left with Dad leaning heavily on my shoulder. We'd been told we could pick up a stick from the hospital, but Dad said he had a couple of walking poles at home.

'Told you,' said Dad, as he manoeuvred himself into the car. 'Told you it wasn't broken.'

For once, he consented to go back to bed for a bit, saying the heavy-duty painkillers were making his head fuzzy. I rang the police station, to be told that Chloe Cooper hadn't come in yet and sat at the kitchen table, drinking a double espresso which did nothing to calm the thumping of my heart. After half an hour I was still seething: I couldn't just sit there doing nothing.

So I went next door to have it out with Freddy and Doll. I knew Freddy was hiding something from me: she knew something about Michael's disappearance, and I was going to get it out of her. I knocked quietly, then more loudly, on their back door. I knew they were in: there was steam on the windows, and the sound of a radio bubbling Radio 4's genteel tones somewhere in the house. No one came. I banged again. Got no response. I marched round to the front door and hammered on that, too, then yelled through the letter-box: 'If you don't let me in I'm going to make sure everyone in the Terrace knows about what you did, Freddy. *Everyone!* And after I've done that I'll put notices up around town. I'll make your life a nightmare.'

At last. Whispering voices and quiet footsteps. The door opened, but only as far as the security chain would allow. Doll's face appeared, pinched and pale. 'Stop making an exhibition of yourself.'

I stuck my foot in the door jamb so Doll couldn't shut the door. 'Stop fucking around and let me in! I know Freddy's been lying to me, and I'm not leaving until she starts telling the truth.'

'Go away!'

'I mean it. And if you don't let me in I'll tell everyone she's a killer.'

'Do you think we care? All that was a long time ago. Tell the world if you like! We've got each other and that's all that matters.'

That knocked the wind out of my sails. Time for plan B: an appeal to Doll's better nature. Lowering my voice, I went on, 'look: I need your help. I was attacked and now my dad has been targeted – my dad who's never harmed a soul.'

'I've told you before: we can't help you.'

'But ...' And then something weird happened. The foot I'd stuck in the door jamb was suddenly dowsed in warm liquid – not hot enough to burn my skin, but hot and wet enough to give me such a surprise that I withdrew my foot. The door slammed shut. I looked down at my trainers: the right one was steaming, and smell coming off it was the scent of Earl Grey tea. 'Oh, for fuck's sake!' My hand itched to pick up one of the rocks strewn on the unmade up road and chuck it through Freddy and Doll's front window, but I resisted. Instead I stood there like a lemon, shifting from foot to foot, feeling a fool for having been ousted by two women knocking seventy.

As I was walking back to Dad's house, a car drew up in front of Freddy and Doll's house. DI Chloe Cooper got out of the passenger side, pinning a stray lock of hair in place. A man with the shaved head beloved of most men over 30 in this part of the world got out of the driver's side. They nodded at each other before DI Cooper knocked firmly on Freddy's front door. Wounded pride and soggy sock forgotten, I scooted back to my house and ran in, calling up the stairs to Dad, 'You're not going to believe this, but the police have just turned up at Freddy and Doll's house.'

'I know. You were making such a racket I got up to see what was happening.'

I pulled off my shoes and ran up the stairs two at a time to meet Dad on the landing. 'They poured tea on my foot.'

Was I imagining it, or was Dad trying not to laugh?

'It's not funny, Dad.' But then I was laughing too, and once we started we couldn't stop. I had to go and fetch some tissues so we could wipe our eyes and blow our noses.

'You must admit it's unusual to be seen off by a mug of Earl Grey tea,' spluttered Dad, through hiccoughs of laughter.

As I washed my foot and changed my socks, I admitted

to myself that part of the laughter came from relief that the police were at last *doing* something.

32

Rags

Dad seemed to be refreshed by his short nap, so the two of us camped out in the lounge, peeping through the net curtains, waiting for DI Chloe Cooper to come out of Freddy and Doll's door so we could nab her. About twenty minutes later she emerged and I pounced, dashing into the street, calling, 'I need to talk to you. Someone set up a tripwire at the entrance to our garden. My father fell over and could have been seriously injured.'

But she was already walking towards our door. 'I was just about to knock. Can we come in?'

We perched on kitchen chairs as Dad told them about his fall, and showed them his bandaged ankle. 'It could have been very nasty – very nasty indeed. I was lucky I didn't break a limb.'

'And I'm still convinced Freddy – Susan Fredericks – is involved in all this,' I said.

Chloe looked up from her notebook and swapped glances with her companion, whom she'd introduced as DS Williams. 'OK. I think we'd better fill you in on the latest developments. Someone has come forward who saw Susan

Fredericks arguing with Michael Cleverly on the night that he went missing.'

'I knew it! I knew she had something to do with it.'

'Shh.' Dad put his finger to his lip. 'Let the police officer speak.'

'This person – a woman – got in touch with us yesterday. She's been away, and has only just returned and seen our appeal for information in the local paper, which is why we haven't heard from her before.'

At this point Chloe Cooper's mobile phone rang. She excused herself and went into the kitchen to take the call. Dad and I exchanged a look. He mouthed, 'Judith Wright, from number 7.'

A minute later, DI Cooper was back. 'Sorry about that. Where were we?' She flipped open her notebook. 'Oh, yes. This person witnessed an altercation between Michael Cleverly and Susan Fredericks on the night he disappeared. She saw Michael Cleverly walking along the path between the backyards and gardens of The Terrace, clearly swaying and unsteady on his feet. Outside number 3 he slipped and grabbed at the branch of a tree in Susan Fredericks' garden. Susan Fredericks came out of her house and they had a brief argument, during which he fell over. She then threw a bucket of water over him.'

'So she *did* attack him!' I burst out. 'I bet she shoved him over, and he banged his head and that's why she was going berserk with the bleach the following morning.'

'That's by no means certain. The person watching didn't have a clear view of what happened during the argument, though she did see the incident with the bucket of water.'

'So you're not going to arrest Freddy?'

'Susan Fredericks admits having an altercation with him. However, she's adamant that she didn't harm him. She says he fell over because he was blind drunk.'

'And you can't prove otherwise.'

'No. The evidence we have at present would never lead to a conviction.'

I closed my eyes and counted to three, then opened them again. 'And did Freddy tell you that she was being blackmailed by Michael?'

A short pause. 'What makes you say that?'

'My father and I found out yesterday that Michael had been blackmailing at least two other people – we were going to come and tell you about it today – and so I deduced that he'd found out that Freddy had killed her uncle when she was a teenager, and was extorting money from her, too.'

Chloe Cooper gave me a look that might have held a touch of admiration. From the corner of my eye I saw DS Williams give a miniscule nod. So I was right! 'I can't give you any further information,' said Chloe Cooper, with a touch of pomposity.

A penny – several of them – dropped in my head. 'And Freddy's finally told Doll about her homicidal past – and that was why Doll told me to piss off.'

'As I said before, I can't give you any further information.' She sighed. 'But I can confirm that Michael Cleverly was alive and well after she threw water over him. Our witness says that two men appeared and helped him to his feet after Susan Fredericks had gone back into her house.'

'She didn't recognise them?'

'No. But she heard them laughing together, and saw all three of them walking away through Michael's garden.'

'And are you going to look for them?'

'Of course. We're preparing a fresh appeal for information,' said Chloe Cooper in a don't-tell-me-how-to-do-my-job tone of voice. She stood up. 'Now: can you show me the tripwire?'

They went into the backyard, crossed the shared path,

and found the wire still curled into a lazy S on the concrete path. 'See? One end was pulled out of the gatepost when Dad tripped over it.'

Chloe Cooper crouched down. 'I see what you mean.' DS Williams pulled out his phone and took several photographs. They had a quiet conflab I couldn't quite hear then Chloe Cooper straightened up. 'Let's go inside.' We took our seats at the table again. 'I'm very sorry to hear about your father's fall, but I think you should know that we've had reports of two other similar incidents this morning.'

I felt my jaw drop. 'And have other people been injured?' I managed.

'No. But that's because they saw the wires and took them down. The houses were on King's Road and Lavender Terrace.'

'So you think it's just someone playing a prank?' I said, feeling the rage rising in me again.

'We just don't know. But we *do* know that your father wasn't singled out.'

'But can't you see that someone *targeted* my father? They know he goes out early in the morning and takes Napoleon into the garden.'

Chloe Cooper started putting her notebook and pen into her bag. 'As I say, I'm truly sorry that your father has been injured, but ...'

'And they put up the other tripwires to put you off the scent!'

' ... but his accident is probably unrelated to the Michael Cleverly investigation,' she continued, in a loud, shut-the-fuck-up voice. 'You can rest assured that we'll look into all the tripwire incidents and try to get to the bottom of it. A crime scene investigator will come round later today. Please don't touch the wire.' She stood up. 'And now I must get back to the station. Could you come in at some point and make a formal statement? I'm required at Norwich crown court this afternoon and tomorrow, but DS Williams, here, can help you.'

'Hang on a minute. We want to talk to you about other things. Both me and my dad have received poison pen letters trying to scare us off – to stop us pursuing the investigation.'

But Chloe Cooper was looking at her watch. 'As I say, DS Williams can take down your statement, and I promise I'll look at it as soon as I can.'

'Thanks for bugger all!' I hissed as Dad showed them out of the door.

Dad's ankle was so painful that I went into the police station on my own. DS Williams took my statement, in between huge yawns, for which he apologised. 'My little lad kept us up half the night.' After recapping everything I'd told them about the tripwire, I showed him the two poison pen letters, and he agreed that they appeared to have been written by the same person. He asked if he could hang onto them: I photographed them with my phone and handed them over – glad to be rid of them. 'And you say that other occupants of The Terrace have received poison pen letters?'

'Yes. Geraldine Goodchild got one, though hers arrived before Michael disappeared. And we believe Susan Fredericks got one, too, but won't admit it.'

'Well I'll start up a case file, but I must warn you that it's very hard to prove who sends these things.'

'I know. But in the case of these two, I think they're directly linked to the fact that I'm investigating what happened to Michael Cleverly. I mean, look at them.

Fuck off you sex mad bitch. We don't want you here.

Get rid of that sex mad bitch your daughter or you'll be sorry.

A spark of interest lit up DS Williams' puddingy features. 'Yes. I can see what you mean.'

'And I *know* that someone shoved me in front of that car. I wasn't blotto, by the way. Yes, I'd had three glasses of wine, but that was over the course of a whole evening.'

His baggy eyes looked thoughtful for a moment before he closed his notebook and leant a little closer. 'Off the record, I think someone probably did give you a shove, but it might have been someone who was jealous of you. You're an attractive woman, and that someone might have thought you were flirting with their husband down the pub. They might have followed you down the road. And that same person might have sent the poison pen letters telling you to clear off.'

'They might have, but they didn't.'

Nonetheless, as I walked home, I felt at least someone had paid me some attention. I decided to take any further leads to DS Williams rather than DI Cooper.

After a lunch of ham, crusty white rolls and juicy tomatoes, I retreated to my bedroom to polish up *Sweet Surrender*. At about 3 pm I pressed Send and started assembling my notes for the next commissioned article (working title *Cupboard Love*: theme, having sex in unusual indoor spaces). Normally I found writing Bee Cool's articles as interesting as watching paint dry, but with a bunged-up nose and low energy it was a welcome distraction to research Boris Becker shagging in the broom cupboard at Nobo's. It turned out that *Naughty Wives on Parade* and similar salacious websites gave me plenty of material from which to build a piece. These plump, cheerful women would clearly strip off almost anywhere. School stationery cupboards were popular. My favourite naughty wife was Kath, who specialised in quickies in the pantries of National Trust properties.

After a pleasant hour trawling this sort of twaddle, I

decided to take a walk into town. Napoleon would appreciate a stroll, and surely I'd be safe at 4 o'clock on a June afternoon. Dad was getting ready to watch *The Eagle*, a film about a Roman legion in Britain which he'd watched three times already but thought would take his mind off his sore ankle. 'And it's got that little lad from the ballet film in it, but he's all grown up. Jamie Ball, or something.'

'Jamie Bell.' And Channing Tatum, I thought, as the hunky actor appeared on screen, sparking a vivid memory of Alaric's muscular arms slick with sweat as he leant over me. Napoleon trotted ahead of me into the graveyard and I followed. I liked this place – its sighing yews and crooked headstones. Only those who'd booked a spot were buried here these days: since the 1970s most had been laid to rest in the new graveyard on the edge of town. Napoleon, head alert and tail wagging, made a beeline for the gravestone that read: 'Philip Goodrum, died 1863, aged 77,' and, beneath these words, 'and his relict, Sarah-Jane, died 1891, aged 82'. Would I ever be a relict? Unlikely, though Matt and I had talked about getting hitched, first as a teasing, affectionate joke, during long Sunday mornings in a bed rich with the briny smell of sex, and then with the juniper tinge of too much gin during a boringly chaste fortnight in Corfu ten years into our relationship. We'd discussed marriage in that desperate way couples do when a break-up is hiding over the next hill. Fired up by cheap gin and tonics, I announced that I wouldn't change my name to his (Higginbottom). 'I mean, why would I?' I crowed, as we gulped our drinks looking out at the peach silk sunset. A year later he left me for Felicity, who was only too happy to shell out twenty grand for a wedding in Berkshire and get shot of her own name.

With a shudder at the memory of all that, I headed for my favourite bench close to the little chapel used only to store gardening tools and the ride-on mower these days. Sod it: I'd give Alaric a ring.

'I'm missing you,' he said in a low voice. 'And I wish I could come home, but I can't – not for a few days, in any case. My father's not doing too well; he's still critical, and I can't leave my mother on her own just now.'

'I'm so sorry,' I said, relieved to hear the longing in his voice. 'And I'm missing you, too.' I started to bring him up to date on recent events, but before I could get far he told me that the consultant had just arrived to discuss his father's prospects.

'I'll have to go. Sorry. I'll ring again when I can.'

A watery sun had crept out from the clouds. My heart ached, but in a pleasant way. Yes: this was what it was like when someone got to you, and you wanted them, and they wanted you. But all that would have to wait: right now I had supper to prepare. I'd decided to cook Dad a beef stew – which I knew he loved – so went to the butcher's to buy some juicy stewing steak. At the greengrocer's I picked up crisp carrots and a wine-red onion. Chucked in a few parsnips because they never go amiss, do they? Some new Jersey mids found their way into my basket, too, and a clutch of green beans. I bought a copy of the *Middleham Gazette*, which Dad liked to read. At Asda I sourced some fruity red wine and set off for home, my bones warmed by the conversation with Alaric – by the sexy grain of his voice, and the desire running through it.

As I turned out of Asda's car park, I felt a tap on my shoulder. Gerry, laden with canvas shopping bags, fell into step beside me. 'Hello! How's it all going?'

'Not so bad.'

'Only I thought I heard Napoleon barking early this morning.'

'Dad slipped over, but he's fine now.' I was damned if I was going to say anything more. Experience had taught me that it was best to keep your mouth shut in a small town such as Middleham.

'Oh, I'm sorry to hear he had a fall, but you say he's all right?'

'Yes, but thanks for asking.'

Gerry was staring at me with emerald eyes way too big for her face. Of course! It came to me in a rush: Gerry was a speed freak. She was munching her way through amphetamines. I'd had a boyfriend with a speed habit in my second year of college – a boy who could dance all night and talk all day. A looker, too, with a heavy swatch of black hair pulled back into a ponytail or flowing like ink round his face. It was only when I realised he never stopped grinding his teeth, even when he was asleep, that I started to see the downside. He wasn't much fun when his supplies ran out, either, turning from manic prankster to morose hassler of the few dealers who sold amphetamine sulphate on campus. I'd finished with him after a few weeks. It was all too exhausting. Poor Gerry: an addiction to speed was no fun – no fun at all. It ranked somewhere down there with an addiction to codeine or ibuprofen.

'And how's Iona?' I asked.

Gerry's rigid face relaxed a fraction. 'She's a bit better. Michael's death hit her hard. No one she knew had ever died before.'

'Well I'm glad she's feeling happier.'

Gerry's claw closed on my arm. 'You know she made up all those things she told you in the graveyard. She adds two and two and makes five.'

I gave a non-committal smile, convinced that Iona was the only person I'd spoken to in The Terrace who'd been free of bullshit.

'Oh, and I wanted to give you one of these.' Gerry dug around in one of the bags and pulled out a leaflet. 'Did you know that Hector is running a special pamper event this Saturday?'

'Yes. I dropped into his surgery ...' I began, but she was rushing onwards, not listening. 'He's diversifying into beauty treatments, and from this weekend he's offering facials, Botox, fillers and dermabrasion. You can sample some of them on Saturday. I'll be there, of course, pouring out the chilled glasses of bubbly.'

'Fantastic,' I said, taking the leaflet, though I'd rather have my toes stamped on by a horse than be botoxed, filled or abraded. 'I'll see if I can come along.'

33

Rags

By Saturday Dad was feeling brighter. I'd spent Friday blowing my nose and looking after him. I'd enjoyed shopping, making his meals and helping him hobble into the garden, where he sat on the bench and threw the ball for Napoleon. It reminded me that I like being kind and helpful to others. Over the years of celebrity spotting I'd got into bad habits of Me, Me, Me. A bit like my mother, in fact (I had to admit). Yes, it had been traumatic to lose my job, but it was good to move away from that narcissistic swamp.

Dad was pretty handy with his walking poles, and by now could place some weight on his right leg. Best of all, *Wake up Little Susie* was coming to take him and Napoleon on an outing to Cromer in her car. They were going to potter around then catch a late afternoon showing of *Casablanca* at the cinema. I'd persuaded Dad that I'd be fine on my own, on a glorious Saturday with plenty of people around. 'Go and have fun. You deserve it.' Susie arrived promptly at midday, accompanied by Cocoa, a chocolate Labradoodle daft as a bucket of frogs. I liked what I saw: a shapely woman with a well worn but attractive face and gorgeous auburn hair.

'Lovely to meet you,' said Susie. 'Graham talks about you all the time – how pleased he is to have you here.'

A zing ran through my heart. 'Aw, that's nice. Did he tell you he was working with me?' I said, being economical with the truth, as we'd decided not to tell her about the investigation just yet, so as not to alarm her.

'I know he's been helping you out with your consultancy. I was so sorry to hear about your accident.'

'Thank you. I'm on the mend now.'

'But now he's fallen over, too. You do seem to be in the wars!'

If only you knew, I thought. 'Have a lovely day out, and I'll see you here around seven thirty. Perhaps we could have a drink together?'

'That would be great.'

After they'd left, the day was mine. First I got out my guitar: I'd been neglecting it with all the drama going on. I ran through a few Joni Mitchell songs from *Blue*, then turned to Bob Marley's *Three Little Birds* for light relief. I liked the sentiment of the song: *Don't worry about a thing*. Playing it reminded me of lazy Saturdays at York University, sitting out on the grass near the lake, playing for Carola and other pals, passing a joint round and falling into fits of laughter. After a particularly vigorous strum, the top E string broke. I took the broken string off the guitar, wound it into a near circle and slipped it in my pocket. I'd take it to a music shop and buy a replacement set of the same weight when I had time.

I went down to the kitchen to make myself a coffee and leaf through this week's *Middleham Gazette*, which Dad had left for me on the table. The request for information regarding Michael Cleverly's actions on the night he disappeared was reprinted on page 5, beneath a flattering photograph of Chloe Cooper. I turned to the classified ads at the back, wondering what job opportunities were on offer here in rural North Norfolk. The answer was not many. The only growth areas appeared to be hairdressing and beauty salons. I made a mental note to work on the feature on the marsh harriers, and to research the piece on childcare (or lack of it) I'd promised to write when I talked to Tracey.

At eleven I admitted to myself that I was feeling restless after days cooped up with a cold, and decided to head to the coast on the bus. Now my aches and bruises had faded I'd do a proper, long walk through Holkham Woods to Gun Hill and back. There would be plenty of people around, so I wouldn't be in any danger, and I could jot down some notes for the feature on the marsh harriers. After rustling up a Cheddar cheese and rocket sandwich I set off with a packed lunch, a bottle of water and Dad's binoculars in a small rucksack. The drizzle and leaden skies of the past couple of days had been replaced by thin wisps of high cloud which the sun was busy devouring.

By noon I was striding out through the pine scent of the woods. A coot was sailing across Salts Hole, leaving a widening arc of ripples in its wake. The hide was full of twitchers, so I stood outside on the decking and watched one of the marsh harriers circling as it hunted, then perching on a bush a couple of hundred yards from the hide. When I'd jotted down some notes and taken a couple of pics with my phone, I continued on through the woods until my feet sank into the soft sands of the dunes, where I fed and watered myself. Watching the line of the waves curl into white crests and break onto the pale gold sand, I asked myself whether I could give up London and settle here. I couldn't answer that question. Not yet.

Refuelled, I dusted off my bum, and started the leisurely walk back, this time on the sands, passing the nudist beach that wasn't supposed to be a nudist beach any more, but where a couple of naked families with small children gathered under beach tents and umbrellas.

It was nearly three by the time I got back to the bus stop close to the Victoria Hotel. My water had all been drunk and my throat was crying out for a drink, but my pocket yielded only my return bus ticket and eighty-four pence in shrapnel. That wouldn't buy anything at the bar of the handsome, flint-fronted hotel. Then Gerry's words surfaced in my sun-kissed brain: today was the pamper day at Hector's surgery. I could break my journey, drop in at *A Certain Smile* and get a cool drink (and perhaps a glass of bubbly). I was sure I could persuade the bus driver to let me break my journey and use my ticket again on a later bus home.

Fairham Market welcomed me with its flirty, seductive shop windows and as I strolled towards Hector's dental surgery I was grateful that I'd left my purse with its bank and credit cards at home. Though I'd strimmed my debts to under my credit and overdraft levels, I couldn't afford to spend £1,400 on a beautiful oil painting of the salt marsh, could I? And while that eau-de-nil linen jacket was to die for, I couldn't justify its £199 price tag. After all, I had plenty of jackets folded up in black bags in Carola's basement – which reminded me that I must ring Carola later. We hadn't spoken for a while; I hadn't even told her about Dad's fall. Perhaps I could get her to visit now she was back from Africa: it would be so good to talk to her, to gossip and blob over a few glasses of wine. I had a final nose round the second-hand bookshop then headed to *A Certain Smile*.

The front door was festooned with pastel balloons, and the reception area scented by a huge bunch of arum lilies and ruby-red roses. Half a dozen well-groomed women were lounging on white sofas and armchairs. Gerry, poured into an emerald, sequinned dress, tottered over on a pair of strappy high heels. I had to admit she looked stunning if you ignored her knobbly knees.

'Hello!' she called, batting false eyelashes. 'Come over here and have a glass of bubbly.'

I whizzed over to accept a flute of ice-cold Cava. 'Thank you. I could just do with that.'

'Would you like to have a treatment? I had a makeover this morning, and couldn't believe what they'd done to me.'

'Not right now, thank you, but you look fabulous.'

'Thank you!'

As I took my first delicious sip of Cava, the door marked Beauty Salon opened, and out walked Doll and Freddy. Freddy was glowering, as usual, but Doll had obviously had a makeover which accentuated her grey-blue eyes. Ribbons had been plaited into her hair, which looked pretty but a bit too Bo-Peepish for my taste. Seeing me, she came over, her eyes steely though she was smiling.

'Rags. Good to see you. I do hope we can put our little differences behind us. It's been a difficult time for us all.'

I nodded. 'Of course. Let's make a fresh start.'

'And you'll respect our privacy, won't you? You won't go spreading stories.' This from Freddy, looking anxiously at me.

'I promise,' I said, feeling a little stab of guilt at how I'd threatened to broadcast Freddy's secret. The smell of her cologne crept up my nose. 'Oh, do you mind if I ask you something? I absolutely love your perfume. What is it?'

'It's called Wildwood. Doll got it for me last Christmas.'

'Do you know if you can buy it round here?'

'I got it in Norwich. John Lewis, but I'm sure you could get it over the internet. And now we must get going; we've got a few bits and bobs to buy.'

As they bustled out, Gerry attached herself to me again. 'Would you like to take a look at the beauty salon rooms? No one's in there at present, though we've been bowled over by demands for Botox. I think Hector's booked solid for the next month! I mean, it was a bit of a gamble, diversifying, but it's all going to pay off. You know what they say: "Nothing ventured, nothing gained." And that's always been Hector's philosophy. He's such a go-getter. You wouldn't believe ...'

'Yes, I'd love to,' I said, to shut Gerry up for a moment.

'Come on, then. Unless you'd like a top-up first?'

Never one to refuse icy Cava, I had my glass refilled to the brim before Gerry led me through a door to the two beauty treatment rooms, both painted white and decorated with prints and watercolours of North Norfolk. One contained a massage table, and the second what looked like a posh dentist's chair, into which presumably you were strapped to be sanded down and filled like a piece of Scots pine. Hector was in this second room, tapping something into a computer. When he saw me he hurried over. 'Rags. Thanks for making time to come along.' He took my hands in his and pressed them together. A warm sensation ran through my body.

Gerry was burbling again. 'Don't you just love the decor? I wanted something like pink or pale green, but Hector stuck out for white, because it's clean and classic, and I must say I think he's got it spot-on. He's clever, my husband. Do you know he came first in his year when he was at college? And it wasn't easy. He was at The Royal London Hospital, where they get all sorts of cases. Some of the Asians have terrible teeth from chewing all that – what do they call it? Chat? And then there were all the little East End children who were given too many sweets and had cavities before they were two. In fact, that's where I met Hector. I was training to be a dental nurse, and we met at the Grey Mare, didn't we? Funny old pub, but ...'

'I'm sure Rags doesn't want to hear all about how we met, darling!' Turning to me: 'Do you want to try the couch? I can assure you it's very comfortable.'

'Don't mind if I do,' I said, drowsy from my long walk. Before I knew it I was sinking down on a couch of softest cream leather and being gently tipped back until I was lying flat. A photograph of the dunes and beach at Holkham had been stuck to the ceiling.

'I think I heard the bell ring again,' said Hector. 'Gerry? Would you please go and see if it's another guest?'

'Oh, of course.'

'What do you think?' said Hector, a smile in his voice, as Gerry tap-tapped out of the room.

'The salon's beautiful, and I love that photograph,' I said, pointing at it. 'This is such a gorgeous part of the country: my dad's really glad he moved here.'

'I ran into him this morning and he seemed to be in great spirits. He said he was going to the pictures in Cromer later on.'

'That's right. *Casablanca*.'

'I noticed he was limping. Is he OK?'

'He tripped and fell, but nothing's broken.'

'That's good to hear.' Hector depressed a lever with his foot and I was smoothly lifted back to a sitting position. 'I love that cinema: Gerry and I often head up there.'

With a courteous dip of his head he handed me my glass and flashed a smile as I sipped at the pale straw bubbles: God, his mouth was kissable. And I knew, just looking at him, that he'd be good at it. Good at sex. Abruptly – a bit too abruptly – I stood up and said I must be going. 'I've got a bus to catch. But I'm sure you'll make a huge success of this new venture. It all looks so inviting.'

Hector inclined his head again. 'Thank you.'

I scooted out of the door before he could awaken any

more desires that were A Bad Thing, waving goodbye to Gerry, who was pouring bubbly for two older women who looked as if they'd already benefited from a dose or two of botoxulin. Hector would pick up plenty of trade from women like these; after all, it was so much easier to pop into his surgery than schlep over to Harley Street, and a good deal cheaper. As Gerry held the bottle up to pour out more Cava, I felt a stab of sympathy for her: handsome men were bloody menaces.

Like Michael Cleverly.

Shell rang me while I was on the bus.

'I have studied the coroner's report. It is rubbish: Michael never drank that much alcohol. The *stupide* doctor who examined Michael's body has missed something. But when I have told this to the *officier* of the court, he has treated me like an *imbecile*. I want to see the full post mortem report, which you must arrange *immediatement*.'

'His wife has requested a copy, and it's being sent to my house. I'll let you know as soon as it arrives.'

'When was that arranged?'

'I posted the letter a few days ago, and I'm sure it'll be here soon.'

'Soon? Soon? What is this "soon"? I don't want it soon, I want it now. What are you – a timid *jeune fille*? You must *demand* it now.'

'I've told you, I've ...'

'Pffff! I think we need a serious talk, you and me. In fact I am coming to see you and ...'

'Oh, I'm losing my signal. Sorry.'

And I hung up on Shell and switched my phone to silent. That woman – what was she *like*?

I was yawning by the time I got back to the house to find a message from Dad on the landline's answerphone. 'I hope you don't mind, but Susie and I are going to have a bite to eat after the film. I'll be home around nine. Cheerio.' No, I didn't mind. There was half a bottle of Sauvignon in the fridge. I could listen to *Loose Ends* in the lounge. Bliss.

Humming, I poured myself some wine and opened a pack of Sea Salt Kettle Chips. I took these upstairs to check my emails (nothing urgent) and faff around on Facebook for half an hour. At six I came downstairs to listen to the news on Radio 4. No sooner was I settled on the sofa, than my phone vibrated. Carola.

'Rags! It's me.'

'Hi, darling!'

'Sorry I haven't been in touch. They just keep you so bloody busy at those international symposiums: breakfast meetings, seminars, plenaries, dinners: I'm shattered. But I'm back now, thank heavens.'

I yawned. What had Carola been saying?

'Rags? Are you still there?'

'Yes. Sorry.'

'Have you recovered from your accident? How's your head?'

'My head? Oh, not so bad. As good as can be expected.'

'And the investigation?'

'That bitch Shell has been on my tail for the last couple of days. Oh, and Dad fell over and hurt himself.' I giggled.

Carola gasped. 'Oh my god. Is he OK?'

'He's fine. Indestructible – that's my dad. Solid as a rock. I love him so much, you know. He's totally, totally awesome.'

'I'm glad to hear you're getting on better.'

'And I love you too, babes. I really do, because you've always been there for me, even when I was the most stupid, annoying, whiney, self-centred cow. You're so bloody cool, and clever, and …' My words petered out as my train of thought evaporated.

'Rags? Are you all right? You sound a bit odd.'

A burst of laughter flew out of my mouth. 'Odd? Of course I'm bloody odd. I'm a fruitcake. A fuck-up. Everyone knows that. I lost my job and got thrown out of my flat and had to come running back to Daddy – who's got a girlfriend, by the way, while I sit here all on my lonesome.'

'Come on: don't be so hard on yourself. Things'll look up.'

'Oh, don't listen to me. I've got a nice big glass of wine, and a packet of Kettle Chips. What more could a girl want?'

'I'd love to see you. Do you fancy a trip to town? Or I might be able to drive up to Norfolk to see you.'

I felt my eyelids dipping, and sleep creeping up on me. 'Sorry, babes. Can't talk now. Laters.' And I cut Carola off, letting the phone drop onto the sofa beside me.

As I sank into oblivion a niggle started up at the back of my brain. I shouldn't be this tired, should I? I hadn't drunk much wine – a couple of glasses at the salon, and then half a glass here. I need some coffee, I thought. I need coffee and I need to ring Carola back and tell her something's not right. With a huge effort I forced my eyes open: the walls of the lounge were collapsing towards me. I blinked and started to lever myself up off the sofa. I managed to get to my feet, but felt myself falling backwards before I could take a step. Granted, it was a soft landing, but something was wrong. Seriously wrong.

My phone vibrated again. I fumbled, picked it up: an email from Paddy, with a name I knew in the subject line.

Oh, shit.

Suddenly I felt sick. The phone slipped out of my fingers and between the sofa cushions. Water, I need water, I thought, and tried again to stand up. This time I couldn't get to my feet. Then I heard a key opening the front door, and relief poured through me. Dad must have changed his plans: he'd come home after all, though I didn't know why he was coming round the front. 'Dad!' I cried, but the word got stuck in my throat. 'Dad!'

But it wasn't Dad who came into the lounge.

A moment later a cloth soaked in chloroform was held over my mouth, and I descended into total darkness.

34

Rags

Dust. Dust and plastic and chemicals. A harsh light sticking pins into my eyes. I winced. Shut my eyes again, re-entering the sooty swirl of a headache. Agh! A drenching in cold water forced my eyes open again. As icy drops ran down my face and onto my tee-shirt I tried to focus on the figure in front of me with an empty glass in his hand. A face smiled. A hand put down the glass on a draining board beside a grubby sink. A body sank down in a battered armchair.

'Ah, so the sleeping beauty has woken up. And you looked so peaceful there, snoring and dribbling like an old lush.'

The voice was familiar – melodious and low. A man was sitting opposite me, with one foot resting on the other knee, hands behind his head.

Though his face was swimming before my eyes, I knew who it would be, because I'd managed to read the first few words of the email Paddy had sent: Hector Goodchild, still in the cream shirt and dark jacket he'd been wearing to charm the ladies at the pamper day. 'Fuck you,' I shouted, but only in my head because my mouth wouldn't open and all that came out was the sort of groan old women make when they bend down to pick something up off the floor. My arms hurt. I tried to move them but couldn't. My hands were tied behind my back, and my legs were roped to a dusty old dental couch. I was in a dingy room – a store room, perhaps, with boxes piled round the walls, and a couple of filing cabinets. I managed to focus on the writing on one of the closest cartons: *hypodermic needles.*

'And before you get too scared,' he continued, 'I'm not going to kill you. Not yet. I have to wait for the Rohypnol to work through your system. That should take – oh – 24 hours or so. We'll have another little rendezvous tomorrow. And before I take care of you, I'll fuck you. That'll be something for you to look forward to, won't it?' He laughed again. 'Don't worry, I won't disappoint.'

He glanced at his Rolex watch. 'I'm afraid I haven't got time to see to you right now. My devoted wife is waiting for me at home; we're off for a meal shortly at which she'll eat two carrot sticks and I'll enjoy a fillet steak and some excellent red wine. Can you wait 24 hours before you spread your legs for me, you little whore?' He stood up and came close. 'I want you to be fully awake and alert when I do what I'm going to do to you. It's no fun fucking a corpse.' Leaning forward, he grabbed my chin, yanking my head up so our mouths were a few inches apart. 'You thought you were so clever, but you were no match for me, you stuck-up bitch.'

Arrogant piece of shit. I longed to kick him in the balls, but couldn't move my legs. Forcing my mouth open, I managed to say, 'How did ...?'

'How did I do it?' With a jerk he let go of my head and settled back into the battered armchair. 'After I saw you at the pamper day I arranged for one of my helpers to come into your house and doctor your bottle of wine with a dose of Rohypnol. Wonderful stuff: works a treat. And there'll be no signs of a break in, because your dad gave me and Gerry a key when he moved in, and I've kept it in my pocket for the past few days, in case it came in handy. You know how it is – always good to leave a key with a neighbour. I knew you'd start drinking as soon as you got in the door, and it's worked a treat, hasn't it? Once the Rohypnol has worn off you'll be right as rain – except you'll be drunk. Very drunk. Dead drunk.' Hector's easy laugh rang round the scruffy little room. 'And everyone will believe that your death was a tragic accident. I mean, several of the good ladies of Fairham Market saw you knocking back the Cava at the salon, and everyone in Middleham knows you're a piss-artist. They've seen you necking glasses of wine at the pub, and everyone notices everything in a one-horse town.' He pushed a lock of hair back from his forehead. 'And I'm sure Tiny Tim can be persuaded to swear that he saw you swigging from a bottle of vodka.'

Squirming, I tried to protest.

Hector smiled at my pathetic wriggles and shook his head. 'I've got a treat in store for you, my darling. Tomorrow you're going for a swim in the North Sea. You'll be naked: you're a boho, aren't you? I can just see you taking a skinny dip at the nudist beach after nightfall. Gerry is going to a school reunion and Iona is having a sleepover with a pal, so I'll be a free agent.'

'Dad! Dad'll ...' I slurred, trying to force the syllables out of my paralysed mouth.

'Oh, please! You think your creaky old dad'll raise the alarm? Don't count on that, sunshine. He'll find a note saying you've gone down to Sussex to see Alaric. Everyone knows you've been shagging that miserable eco-fanatic. And I expect your dad'll be pleased to be shot of you for a while so he can get down to some rumpy pumpy with his geriatric girlfriend. Yes, I know about her, too! Gerry has the eyes of a hawk; she's always on the lookout, always alert, and relays everything to me in tedious detail. As I expect you've realised, she has a serious amphetamine habit, though she thinks the pick-me-ups I give her are harmless sedatives.'

He shook his head ruefully. 'Gerry's a bit of an innocent: she's always believed the best of me. Even when I suggested she get Tim to put something into Michael's drink the evening you blew into town, she believed me when I said it was just to give him a dose of the runs – a way of warning him to keep away from Iona, who'd developed a massive crush on him. And Tiny Tim was happy to doctor Michael's wine for fifty quid, no questions asked, because that piece of scum was threatening to tell the world and his wife that Tim had been nicking stuff from the town allotments.

'But you found out Tim was being blackmailed by Michael, didn't you? You got it out of him. And he told Gerry. And Gerry told me. And I figured it wouldn't be long before you realised that Michael had put the screws on me, too. That's when I decided you were getting too close to the truth, and needed to be taken care of. And since it all worked so well with Michael, I thought I'd follow the same *modus operandi* for you – though of course I didn't fuck him! I'm not into men. I'm into women: I love them, even Gerry, who's turned into a bag of bones.

'Where was I? Oh, yes. Michael Cleverly. Did you know that bastard was trying to sting me for £20,000? He wanted it for his ridiculous property company with the naff name. And he reckoned he could get it. He was ruthless. He was ambitious.' He smiled. 'Like me.'

Despite the queasy terror in my belly, I was listening intently to every word. 'Why was he ...?'

'Why was he blackmailing me? Why do you think? He'd found out something interesting.' Standing up, he moved closer and with a clean, warm hand stroked my hair off my face. 'Want to hear a little story? When I was a student

– and I was top of my year, just as my dear wife said – I was involved in an unfortunate incident in which a child died. I messed up the anaesthetic, you see, and gave him too big a dose. The little tyke was having several teeth extracted, and he wouldn't sit still long enough for us to do it under a local. I'd been out drinking the night before then hardly slept because I'd topped off the evening with a few snorts of meth. I misjudged the anaesthetic and the boy snuffed it. He was only five.' His top lip curled into an expression of contempt. 'But none of it would have happened if his bloody silly parents hadn't force-fed him sweets and never taught him to brush his teeth.

'There was an investigation at the college, but I managed to fix it. I paid the lab technician to swear that a valve was faulty. Then *he* went under a 25 bus a couple of days later while he was paralytic.' Hector laughed again, giving me a good view of his perfect teeth. 'Are you seeing a pattern now? Have you finally worked it out with that pretty little head of yours? Oh, it's easier than you think to make a person very drunk. You don't even have to make them drink the stuff. An injection of pure alcohol does the trick without all that nasty business of getting the stuff down someone's gullet. If I say so myself, I'm very skilled at giving injections, and I use a needle so fine that you wouldn't find the puncture hole unless you were looking for it. Plus it's easy to conceal it by grazing or cutting the skin in the surrounding area. Drunks injure themselves all the time, you see. They bang into things. Cut themselves. They're a bloody liability.

'Anyway, where was I? Oh, yes. Michael not-so-Cleverly. I arranged to meet him at the back of the secondary school, so I could hand over an envelope full of cash. I gave him the money and he set off for home, but my little helpers got hold of him and brought him here for a rendezvous with me. I retrieved my money, and the next day did just what

I'm going to do to you. I borrowed their van and dumped him in the river myself – couldn't risk them knowing about that – but it was easy enough. You have to be fit and strong to be a dentist.

'They're never going to shop me. They're casual workers from some godforsaken hole in Lithuania, and, between you and me, they've got criminal records and their papers are not quite in order. They'll never talk, even if they put two and two together.

'So you see, my dear, I'm a sheer, bloody genius. The police have never suspected me. Gerry's never suspected me. You've never suspected me.'

His phone rang. He stuffed a musty dishcloth in my mouth and answered it. 'Hello darling. No, I won't be long. Just finishing up. Love you.' He hung up and wandered over.

'Got to split. I'll leave the rag in your mouth to stop you making a noise – not that anyone would hear you; the other units are empty. Try and get some sleep: you've got a busy day tomorrow.'

Bending over, he planted a soft kiss on my brow and, as a parting gesture, curled a hank of my hair round his finger and yanked so hard a needle of pain pierced my skull.

Then he let himself out, giving me a fleeting glimpse of a dirty van and, beyond it, a field of barley. A moment later he slammed the door shut and turned the key, leaving just a sliver of light stealing beneath the bottom of the door.

Oh, shit. What now?

What now turned out to be hours of dipping in and out of consciousness, as the drug worked its way through my system. Though I had no way of telling the time, I'm pretty sure it was about dawn before I could think more clearly. The musty rag was still stuffed in my mouth, but I managed to shift it around with my tongue so that I could breathe more easily. For a while, as the light at the foot of the door morphed from blue-grey to sparkling gold I struggled frantically to loosen the bonds tying my hands, feeling waves of queasy panic rise up my gullet until I thought I'd throw up.

Then I stopped. I closed my eyes and breathed deeply, forcing myself to think of the yoga sessions I'd been to with Carola for the past couple of years. (She'd paid for them, insisting they'd help me deal with the stress levels of getting further and further in debt.) I remembered the importance of using your breath, of breath being an ally that could help you stretch further, move more freely. As I breathed long and slow I thought of those people I couldn't bear not to see again: Dad, Carola, other close friends. Alaric. Bugger it: Hector Goodchild was *not* going to deprive me of the sexiest, spikiest love affair I'd had in years.

Once I'd composed myself I started again, this time concentrating on my right arm. I don't know exactly how long it took, but after a couple of hours of stretching, releasing and wriggling, I could feel the rope loosening. Eventually I was able to slip my hand, raw and chafed, free. I blew on the stinging red skin then untied the other knots and ropes. Dashing to the sink, I sloshed water into the glass on the draining board, glugged at least a pint and splashed my face. I peed in the glass, chucked the pee down the sink and thoroughly rinsed the sink and the glass.

'Now what?' I muttered, groggy, wobbly. The room was still shifting around me. The door was stout and firmly locked. From my internal body clock I reckoned it was about midday. Hector would be back in six hours.

I needed a plan.

35

Rags

I found a packet of stale digestive biscuits in one of the cupboards and ate my way through them. The carbohydrates perked me up, made me less faint and feeble. As I gained energy a wheel of fury began to turn in my guts: that smug bastard was not going to rape and kill me. No way. What would be the best way to bring him down? I looked around. The ropes he'd used to tie me up. I could wait behind the door and chuck a rope round his neck as he came in. Throttle him. What else? Hypodermic needles. I'd stab the fucker first – distract him so I could get the rope round his neck before he could fight me off. What about something to hit him over the head with? The glass I'd used was too small to do much damage. I started to rip open boxes, but they contained light-weight stuff – nothing that would knock out a man the size of Hector.

I found myself wilting. I sat down in the old armchair, and, though I didn't intend to, I fell asleep, still under the influence of the Rohypnol. I woke with a start to hear the rattle of a clapped-out engine. A tiny flame of hope leapt into my throat. Perhaps someone else had arrived. I crept towards the door.

A key turned in the lock. My body started to tremble. It was him.

As he came in the door I lunged at him with the syringe, but he saw me out of the corner of his eye and jerked away, so the needle caught him on his forearm and not his throat, which I'd been aiming for. At least I had the satisfaction of seeing the panic on his face as he reeled away from me. I went at him with the rope, trying to loop it round his neck. But he got his hands to it and yanked it away from me. He was stronger than me – much stronger – but some primeval rage kept me struggling, thrashing, flailing with my fists.

'You stupid cow! No one gets one over on me. *No one!*' he roared, shoving me back onto the couch. Scarlet with rage, he slapped me round the face once, twice, three times. Pain exploded in my skull. Blood dripped into my eye where his wedding ring had opened up the wound on my forehead. My strength ebbed away. My struggles became weaker.

'That's better,' he puffed, out of breath. 'Are you going to be good girl for me now?'

'Fuck you,' I croaked.

'You thought you were so bloody smart,' he hissed, his handsome features looming over me. 'But you were always a few steps behind me.'

A classy, citric scent crept up my nose. Him! It was him who'd shoved me under that car.

Seeing my reaction, he gave a smug smile. 'Recognise the smell, do you? Wildwood – the same as Freddy wears. That was a stroke of luck! It was fun watching you chase after her after I shoved you into the road. Such a shame that the driver didn't finish you off with his old banger.' He bent down and bit my upper lip so hard I cried out. With a snigger he surveyed me, looking down on my desperate struggles with a self-satisfied smile. I noticed, with a shiver, that today he was dressed in tatty jeans and a paint stained tee-shirt – suitable clothes in which to commit a murder and dump a body.

'And now I think it's time for us to get better acquainted,' he said, straddling my body. 'And don't tell me you don't want it. I could have had you before, if the opportunity had arisen. Perhaps even at the salon with people milling around outside. That would have been fun, wouldn't it? And don't tell me you'd have fought me off!' He gave a bark of triumphant laughter.

I let my eyes close. I was thinking. Hard. His weight was bearing down on me, but as he yanked open my shorts and tugged down my knickers, he left one of my hands free, and I managed to slip it into my back pocket and pull out the guitar string I'd taken off the Epiphone earlier that day. I yanked my arm out from behind my back and went for his face with the sharp end of the guitar string. With a cry of pain he reeled back: by some fluke I'd managed to stab him in the eye. Blood spurted all over me. I managed to get out from under him and, unravelling the guitar string, tried to get it over his head so I could garrotte him. But he caught hold of my wrists and prised the string from my fingers.

He slapped me round the head again so hard that I saw stars – explosions of them – as he dragged me back to the couch. Still kicking and screaming I felt my legs being wrenched apart. A dark tide was rolling over me ...

... when I heard a familiar flurry of barks and felt Hector's body collapse onto mine.

Dad! Dad and Napoleon! Dad was holding half a wooden fence post in his hand. Hector was bleeding from a blow to his temple. Napoleon was doing his best to rip Hector's jeans into shreds.

Between us, Dad and I dragged Hector off me and let

him drop on the floor. Hastily, I pulled up my knickers and shorts.

'Are you all right?'

'I've been better, but no bones broken,' I panted, limping towards the door, with Dad following.

But Hector must have regained consciousness, because he caught hold of Dad's ankle and yanked him backwards so that he stumbled and fell to his knees.

'Leave him alone!' I yelled, trying to hit Hector but still so dizzy and weak that half my blows didn't connect with his body. Through the blood in my eyes I saw Hector reach for a box and pull out a scalpel.

'No!' I cried, as Hector ripped the plastic off the blade.

'Back off or I'll slit his throat.'

'It's all right, Rags,' croaked Dad. 'It'll be all right. You'll see.'

Just as I was thinking Dad had lost leave of his senses, a figure burst through the door and smashed a brick down on the back of Hector's head. He collapsed again. Long fingers sporting glossy purple nails closed round his neck. 'I could kill you, you *morceau de merde.*'

Shell!

As Shell's fingers tightened, Hector started to choke. With a grunt she pulled him up by his hair and tied his wrists behind his back with rope. In one slender, muscular movement, she threw him into the armchair, where she delivered several stinging slaps to his face before tying his ankles together so he couldn't make a run for it.

Then she spat in his face. '*Salaud.*'

She punched 999 into her phone and demanded police and ambulance services, giving the address as a unit on an industrial estate three miles from Middleham.

Dad staggered to his feet and helped me up.

'Are you all right?' I asked. 'Did he hurt you?'

'Just bruises, but I'm glad Shell got here when she did. I knew she was on her way. What about you? Did he ...?

'No.'

We clung together. I wept and he patted me on the back, muttering, 'There, there. It's over now.'

I looked over Dad's shoulder at Shell. 'Thank you,' I squeaked. Shell tossed her head of black curls. '*C'est mon plaisir.*'

As we waited outside in the mellow, late afternoon light for the police, Dad and Shell told me how they'd found me.

'When I got home last night,' said Dad, 'I thought there was something funny about the note you were supposed to have left because it was printed. But there didn't seem to be any signs of a struggle, and I just assumed you'd printed it off at the library, for some reason.

'Then, this afternoon, I found your phone between the sofa cushions and knew something was wrong. You'd never leave your phone behind, would you? I rang Alaric from your phone and he said you weren't with him. That put the willies up me, I can tell you. I called the police, but I couldn't get any help out of that blooming policewoman: she said we had to wait another twelve hours before we could report you missing. I was at my wits' end.'

'And then I arrived,' said Shell, taking up the story. I have come to find you because I am *furieuse*. But while I am talking to your father, I see this man through the window. He waves goodbye to his wife, but when she's gone, he stops smiling and hurries into the house. He comes out a few minutes later in old clothes, looking around him as if he doesn't want to be seen. I have lived in rough places and I know when someone has something to hide. So we decide to follow him.'

'He went round to the garages,' said Dad, 'but instead of getting his Audi out, he climbed into a dirty old van parked round the corner, hidden from the main road. Before we knew it he roared past us. I could have kicked myself: if only I'd had the Mini out of the garage and ready to go, we could have followed him. I figured he wouldn't be going to the surgery in that scruffy old van. But where the heck *was* he going?

'Then we had a stroke of luck. I saw Iona coming up the road. She said she'd got to pick up some things from her house for her sleepover. I asked her if she knew if her dad had a garage or lock-up anywhere, saying I'd arranged to borrow some tools from him, but I'd lost the address. She told us about this place.'

'And I followed your father in my car,' said Shell, 'but some imbecile in a tractor has blocked the road, so I was delayed for a few minutes. But this is good, because now I have saved you both.'

I wasn't sure I agreed with her logic, but I was so grateful I thanked her profusely.

She shrugged. 'It is nothing. That man, he is vain, he is stupid, he thinks he is stronger than everyone else. But he is not stronger than me. I have learned to fight when I am a child. That man is weak. He can only conquer people with drugs and deception.'

Amen to that.

36

Rags

Chloe Cooper looked knackered. Her blonde hair had been hastily pulled back into a ponytail, and her face was bare of make-up. I suspect she'd been dragged away from a happy evening in front of Netflix with a large bag of Doritos. Several hours had passed, and it was now half past ten. I'd been examined by a doctor, had my wounds cleaned up and pronounced fit to be interviewed.

In the stuffy interview room, Chloe Cooper listened carefully to what I had to say, and sent an officer to prepare a written statement. I found myself shivering and sinking deeper into the blue cashmere sweater Dad had brought to the station for me. He and Shell had already been interviewed, and were waiting outside for me. I yawned, so tired I could have fallen asleep on the hard interview chair.

'I suppose you could come in and sign your statement tomorrow,' said Chloe Cooper, showing a smidgen of compassion. Perhaps she wasn't a robot after all.

I thanked her and shuffled out into the reception area.

Seeing us coming, Shell stood up, her eyes boring into Chloe Cooper. A buzz of anticipation ran down my spine:

I had a feeling the DI was going to get it in the neck, and I was going to enjoy every word of it.

'We have done the work of the police force, the work that *you* should have been doing,' said Shell, her voice ringing clear as a church bell. 'Why did you not believe me when I told you Michael had gone missing?'

'I didn't make that decision. That was made by the police station in Diss.'

'Pffff! You are all the same. Rags, here, she has come to you several times to talk about her suspicions and you have sent her away as if she was an idiot, with a pat on her head.'

'Now that's not entirely ...'

'And even when she has been pushed in front of a car, you have said she is drunk and cannot be trusted.'

'Well that's not quite ...'

'You treat her with – what's the word? *Mespris* – and because of this she is nearly raped and killed by that animal. What do you have to say for yourself?'

I kept a straight face, but inside I was grinning like a maniac. Oh, it was fun seeing someone else having strips torn off them by Shell.

Two spots of red appeared on Chloe Cooper's cheeks. 'We were acting on the evidence that was available. And we have to be selective about how we use police resources.'

'Pffff. I have told you Michael was missing. Rags has told you he was not drunk, but you choose to believe men – stupid men – instead.'

'I've already explained that Rags didn't have the evidence to ...'

'Enough! So now you have your evidence are you going to charge Hector Goodchild?'

There was a short pause. 'Yes.'

'*Enfin*. At last my Michael will get justice.'

Shell was subdued once we got out of the police station. I asked her whether she wanted to stay at Dad's house, but she shook her head. 'I have booked a room in a hotel. I wish to be alone with my sorrow.' Holding out her hands, she took both of mine in hers. 'I want to thank you for all you've done.'

I blushed: I'd made so many mistakes, missed so much. 'It's me who should be thanking you. You saved our lives.'

She shrugged. 'I enjoyed beating up that horrible man. I have felt so angry since Michael disappeared – so angry and helpless. I know he wasn't perfect: it wasn't nice to learn that he was a blackmailer. But he hasn't killed anyone, has he? He hasn't raped anyone.'

And with back straight and head held high, Shell got into her midnight blue Porsche. Dad and I watched her roar off up the road.

* * *

Three days later I wriggled into the crook of Alaric's arm, breathing in the salty smells of sweat and sex. With his free hand Alaric stroked my back, where my bruises were fading to inky smudges. 'I'm so glad you're here,' I murmured, drowsy from hours of prolonged, sensual sex. 'I needed that.'

'Always happy to oblige.' He dropped a kiss on the top of my head.

'And I'm so sorry about your dad.'

He gave me a quick squeeze. 'It wasn't entirely unexpected. He'd had a serious heart attack a few months ago which I didn't know about.'

'Why do people do that – conceal the truth from their children?' I made a mental note to quiz Dad later. If he was hiding some serious condition from me, I'd kill him.

'I'm an only child, and they wanted to protect me.' He squeezed me again. 'Are you sure you're happy to come to the funeral? It'll be a bit weird. You won't know anyone.'

'I'll come if you want me to.'

'Thanks. I'd like to have someone with me from this part of the world.'

'Not Jenny?'

'No. We were lovers but not in a relationship, if that makes sense.'

It made perfect sense to me, who'd been in that sort of set-up a number of times myself.

Outside rain was sheeting down, flattening the meadow grass and flowers in Alaric's garden. 'Looks like we might have to stay in bed a bit longer,' said Alaric.

'Mmmm. That sounds good.'

'But I'll make us some coffee and toast. It's nearly eleven and I'm starving.'

As Alaric footled around making breakfast, I ran over in my mind how things were going with the police investigation.

I'd dropped into the station earlier in the day to get an update, and been told that Hector was still denying all the charges, claiming that our encounter in the store room was one of 'consensual sex'. Chloe Cooper, in an unguarded moment, had declared him 'full of bullshit' and said that his testimony would be laughed out of court.

'Your injuries and testimony would be enough to convict him,' she went on, 'and we've also got some forensic evidence – a print on a bottle of Rohypnol we found in the store room. We're still looking for his accomplices, but even if we don't find them, he hasn't a snowball's chance in hell of getting off. Tim Jones has admitted doctoring Michael Cleverly's drink. Gerry Goodchild has admitted giving the drug to Tim, though they both deny knowing it was a 'date rape' drug, insisting it was in an unlabelled bottle, and Hector told them it was just to give him a bad case of diarrhoea. We're still deciding whether to charge them. Between you, me and the gatepost, I don't think they had a clue about Hector's plans, but drugging someone is a serious offence, and I'm not keen to see them walk scot-free. A second autopsy has revealed a faint puncture mark on Michael Cleverly's arm. We're sure that Hector Goodchild injected him with alcohol, as he planned to do to you.'

'So Freddy had nothing to do with it?'

'She may have shoved him over. Nothing more. But he was certainly blackmailing her: she's admitted that.'

'And Katerina? The woman who was drowned on the reserve?'

'Hector Goodchild's denying any involvement, but I think her boyfriend was working for Hector, and that Hector might have killed her, too, to make sure she didn't talk. She's been cremated already, so we can't request an autopsy.'

I was silent, thinking of the young woman Dad and I had met in Holkham woods. The more I thought about it, the more I was sure I'd seen her at the dental surgery. 'I might know of someone who can fill in the gaps. I think she was working as a dental nurse for Hector Goodchild until he gave her the shove.'

Chloe Cooper had taken down the details, and promised to try and trace her.

Just as I was drifting into a doze, Alaric shoved the door open with his bum, and waltzed in with a tray laden with golden toast, marmalade, cherry jam, and a cafetiere of fresh coffee. 'Here we are, Madam. I hope it's to your liking.'

It was. We munched with the keen appetite that comes

from long, languid love-making. After draining the last of his coffee, Alaric turned to me. 'So did you ever find out who was sending the letters?'

'No. My dad is pretty certain they were sent by Tracey but she's refused to admit anything. And since there are no traces of prints or DNA to link her to the letters, the police don't have a shred of evidence. We think she sent the first letters to punish anyone who crossed her. But the letters to me and Dad were designed to get us to back off. Tim must have told her he'd slipped something into Michael's drink on the night he disappeared.' I took a mouthful of coffee. 'Did you ever get a letter?'

'No. I think I was in her good books because I took care of Damon a couple of times after Roddy was born. He's a funky little boy: very bright, and jealous as hell of his baby brother. Since Roddy came along Tracey hasn't had much time for him.' He took a bite of toast and jam. 'Perhaps you and I could take him out now and then. He's good company when he's away from his brother.'

'Yeah. Let's do that,' I said, and meant it. My rescue from rape and murder had prompted renewed resolutions to be more grateful, more kind, less selfish.

'And what about the tripwires?' asked Alaric.

'I'm convinced Hector got one of his helpers to put them up, to give me and my dad a scare, but I can't prove that. The other wires were not as dangerous as the one in Dad's garden, and were obviously put there so the police wouldn't think we were being targeted.'

'And that worked, didn't it?'

'Yes, but I think even DI Cooper is now convinced that I'm right about them – not that she'll admit it.'

We munched for a few minutes then Alaric gently squeezed my hand. 'How's your head? That bastard gave you a terrible beating.'

I lifted a hand to touch my skull gingerly: it was sore but not unbearably so and the cut on my forehead was healing nicely again. 'Getting better,' I said.

We settled into a contented silence. As I was chewing my last, buttery crust my phone buzzed. Shell. Oh heck, I hoped Shell wasn't going to dispute the bill I'd emailed her the day before. In my mind I'd earmarked some of the dosh for a decent haircut and colour at Toni and Guy in Norwich.

With a sigh, I picked up the phone. 'Shell. What can I do for you?'

'I have an idea. A friend who lives in Antibes has asked for help. He owns a bar, and suspects his manager of stealing money from the business. I thought maybe you could investigate. You would have to go to Antibes for a few weeks, but he will pay your usual rate. I said you charge 40 euros an hour.'

I almost choked on the last of my coffee. A few weeks in the South of France, getting paid a nice fat wad? And with any luck I wouldn't have anyone trying to shove me under a car. 'Really?'

'*Mais oui*. So, you will do this?'

And, thinking of Toni and Guy and the Cote d'Azur, I said yes.

Acknowledgements

This book wouldn't have been completed without encouragement and wise advice from Zosia Wand, who's been my writing companion for the last twenty years. Huge thanks are due to her, and to Heather de Lyon, Liz Radley, Karen Evans, Agnieszka Lesiewicz and Marion Brown, who read early drafts and made perceptive comments. I'm also grateful to the members of The Reading Room writers group who provide support and inspiration at our monthly meetings. Jane Dixon-Smith designed the beautiful cover and the interior of the book. Russell Holden at Pixel Tweaks gave excellent technical support.

My friends and neighbours when I lived in North Norfolk were unfailingly kind. Kay Hathway led a wonderful poetry shed group at which I met many Norfolk writers. Heather de Lyon and Richard Crook hosted a launch party at their house and provided excellent company and support when I was flagging. Sarah Yaxley fed and inspired me. Lynn Wykes shared laughter and music.

However, I must stress that all the characters in this novel are fictitious. Though a reader might be able to work out the places on which fictionalised locations are loosely based, the characters inhabiting the book are invented, as are the events. In truth, the inhabitants of Norfolk are much gentler and kinder than some of those walking through the pages of *The Terrace*.

About the Author

Caroline Gilfillan grew up in Sussex, within earshot of the sea. She spent most of her young adult life in London, where she played music in various groups, including The Stepney Sisters, one of the first women-only bands, and joined several inspirational writers' groups. After taking an MA in Creative Writing at Lancaster University, she taught creative writing in universities and communities – work she absolutely loved. She spent a decade in North Norfolk before moving to Cumbria.

She's published four collections of poetry, the two most recent of which are *Pepys* (Hawthorn Press) and *Poet in Boots* (Brewster Press). She received an Arts Council England grant to develop a novel set in the Second World War, which she hopes will soon appear in print. She's a member of the Inprint collective, producing collaborative work between writers and visual artists, and has been involved in creative projects with the Paston Heritage Society, who explore and share the history of the Paston family in North Norfolk. She's a winner of several national short story competitions.

She also writes plays and songs, and performs in the South Lakeland area of Cumbria. She's currently working on *The Theatre*, the second Rags Whistledown novel, which will be published by Cowslip Press in the near future. To find out more about her poetry and fiction, visit www.carolinegilfillan.co.uk